"DAVID..."

She stood unmoving, watching him as she had all evening, as he was watching her. Lord, what a man he was: fair of face, strong of body, graceful and certain. And she was there, gleaming hair unbound, white-limbed, gossamer-gowned, awaiting him.

David held out his hand. He led her out of the room and she went, with a docility that surprised them both. On the second floor, she paused, expecting him to enter his room. But instead, he continued up the narrow flight of steps to her own quarters.

The moonlight was there too. "It is very late..." he murmured. She swayed toward him slightly. He let go of her hand and placed both of his on her shoulders.

"Let me help you," he said gently. At first she didn't understand. Not until his fingers slipped down to undo the lace of her chemise did she realize what he intended. Hardly breathing, she waited as he slowly undid the ties and let the fabric drop...

*

"SENSUAL... vivid descriptions, elegant prose, and dynamic characters."
—*Romantic Times* on *Catherine*

Also by
MAURA SEGER

BEFORE THE WIND

Published by
WARNER BOOKS

MAURA SEGER

INTO THE STORM

WARNER BOOKS

A Time Warner Company

WARNER BOOKS EDITION

Hand lettering by Carl Dellacroce
Cover illustration by Donald Case

Warner Books, Inc.
666 Fifth Avenue
New York, N.Y. 10103

 A Time Warner Company

Printed in the United States of America

First Printing: December, 1990

10 9 8 7 6 5 4 3 2 1

<small>⩲</small> CHAPTER <small>⩲</small>
One

Washington, D.C., Summer 1813

*T*HE man was tall—well over six feet—with a shaggy black beard and hair that reached halfway down his back. His eyes, glaring from beneath thick brows, were red. Standing with his feet apart and his shoulders hunched, his attitude resembled that of a maddened bear. A leather belt was strapped across his massive chest. Attached to it was the curved hilt of a long knife gleaming wickedly in the smoky interior of the tavern.

"Ye brayin' wretch," he shouted at a smaller but no less wild-eyed man who faced him across an upturned table, "Oi'll split ye like a suck-egg rooster!"

Around the pair, gathered at other tables or lounging up against the bar, an avid audience of two dozen or so watched attentively. Those closest to the action had the

1

prudence to step back a pace or two. The rest merely tightened their grips on their mugs and watched.

The angry man's large, hairy hand reached for the knife, only to be knocked away by a quick, hard swat from the end of a broomstick.

"I'll be havin' no such trouble under my roof," the interloper declared. "If ye canna be holdin' yer whiskey any better than that, kindly take yerself off."

The giant looked startled, then abashed as he stared down at the slip of a girl who faced him with steely determination. He towered over her, dwarfing her with his size and rage. Yet she refused to quail before him, refused even to give so much as an inch.

"Ye ain't bein' fair, Annabel," he protested. "Dinna ye hear wha' this no-good piece o' scum called me? Why slittin's too good fer him. Oi outta..."

"Enough! It's my tavern yer standin' in and I'm after tellin' ye that I'll have none of this. The two of ye make yer peace or the two of ye get out."

"But Annabel," the second man whined, "it's only natr'al fer men to fight. Ye can't expect us to be choirboys, ye know."

Nervous laughter greeted this assertion. No one was absolutely certain that Annabel wouldn't turn around and insist they be exactly that. She was known to be outstandingly stubborn when her dander was up.

This time there was a reprieve. "The choir's not been built that could hold ye, Mulrooney, or ye, Johnson. Fight if ye must but do it outside. This is a respectable inn and I'll not have people sayin' otherwise."

The two men glanced at each other, then back to the slender, determined girl confronting them. Both weighed the alternatives. While they could step outside onto the dirt-packed street and settle their differences in the time-honored manner, there was no guarantee that Annabel would let them back in. She just might take it into her head to bar them from the most popular tavern in Washington, the only one where even a stranger could be sure of an honest drink. Above all, it was the only one owned by a russet-haired slip of a nymph with a body men dreamed of and eyes more than a few had drowned in.

"Ah, Annabel . . ." the burly giant muttered.

The other was more direct. "This no-fightin' rule of yers is about as much fun as saddle boils."

His hostess tossed her fire-laced head contemptuously and said, "If ye don't like it, ye're free to take yer commerce elsewhere, Mulrooney. But while ye're under my roof, ye'll behave like a gentleman."

And with that, she departed, not precisely flouncing but leaving no man present in doubt that his sex had been well and truly undone.

Off to one side, beneath the gaudy portrait of a reclining sylph graced only by a smile, two men observed the scene. Both wore soberly cut frock coats and breeches, similar enough to the general attire of Washington gentlemen to let them pass without undue notice. Only the better informed would have noticed the meticulous tailoring and the exceptionally fine quality of the fabric, and would have concluded that the garments—and most likely the gentlemen themselves—were French.

The conclusion would have been correct.

"Magnificent, isn't she?" the older of the two murmured. He spoke with a slight Alsatian accent, whereas his younger companion responded in the pure, unmistakable tones of

Parisian nobility. His leonine head tilted slightly to one side, amusement dancing in his blue eyes, the marquis David Charles Louis de Montfort said, "Indeed, she is. But tell me, is it true what she said?"

"Is what true?"

"That this is a respectable tavern?"

The tone with which the question was asked implied a certain world-weariness, a sophistication that bordered on cynicism, and an assumption that the answer was a foregone conclusion.

But the older man surprised him. Bertrand de Plessis sighed and spread his hands philosophically. "Alas, my friend, I'm afraid that it is. If a man wants an honest drink, good food, and good fellowship, then the Wild Geese is the place to come. If he wants anything else, he goes elsewhere."

The marquis received this revelation with open skepticism. "A young woman—a young and *beautiful* woman—operates a tavern and manages to remain respectable?"

Bertrand shrugged. "To be frank, I can't imagine why she bothers. Washington is an uninhibited town. The people here are too busy looking out for themselves to care very much about what anyone else does. Still, it seems to matter to Miss Annabel."

The marquis glanced again at the subject of their discussion. Annabel was at the far side of the room talking with the barkeep. His eyes wandered over a straight, slim form with high breasts, a narrow waist, and rounded hips. His gaze rose again to linger on the tumult of fiery hair which she had made some effort to contain in a chignon but which was rapidly insisting on its freedom.

For a moment, David allowed himself to imagine what all

that glorious hair would feel like trailing through his fingers as the beautiful Mademoiselle Riordan moved beneath him in an excess of passion. That pleasant image helped to ease the lingering fatigue of his long journey and the faint hint of melancholy that had been hovering over him for too long now.

The shadow that crossed his ruggedly masculine face did not escape the attention of his companion. Bertrand de Plessis was a businessman, one of the bourgeoisie that had risen to prominence under Napoleon. He bore the title of baron though he continued to think of himself as a plain and simple man. Plainly ambitious and simply ruthless.

"I trust," he said as he eyed David across the table, "that you will be staying long enough to enjoy the pleasures of Washington."

David's slanting eyebrows, the same golden-brown shade as his hair, rose questioningly. "The pleasures? Frankly, I wasn't aware that there were any. This is without doubt the least congenial capital city I have ever seen. What on earth possesses the Americans to build it here?"

"I'm not sure of that," Bertrand admitted, "but I suspect it is some sort of compromise. In a democracy, one must always be doing that kind of thing. Must be terribly annoying, don't you think?"

David shrugged. He had sufficient knowledge of the American system of government to be able to deal effectively with its representatives, but he made no pretense of understanding them or their country. Given his background, the notion of a nation ruled by men of all classes and chosen for their abilities alone could only strike him as quaint, not to say bizarre.

Yet he didn't believe that the alternative of dictatorship

was necessarily better. Increasingly, he was aware of the cost a people paid when they trusted one man alone with—as the Americans so eloquently put it—their lives, their fortunes, and their sacred honor.

He lifted his mug and took a long drink of the cool, pleasantly sharp ale Miss Riordan provided. Over the rim of the cup, he observed her talking with a group of men who had just come in. She laughed and joked with them as naturally as if they were her brothers, and they responded in kind, although there was a lingering quality to their smiles and gazes that suggested they would all have liked to be on very different terms with the beautiful mademoiselle.

"I'm not sure how long I will be here," David said at length when he had turned back to the baron. "It depends on how well my meetings with President Madison progress."

"I think you will find Madison agreeable. He is a sensible man with a keen desire to protect his country. He knows this new war with Great Britain can't bring the Americans anything but disaster. An alliance with the emperor is exactly what's needed."

"Not precisely an alliance," David reminded him, keeping his voice down on the off chance that they might be overheard and understood. He paused for a moment, struggling against the sudden chill that swept over him, vanishing almost as soon as it appeared. He had not been feeling completely well recently but had put it down to the rigors of overwork and the stormy voyage. "I am seeking merely an informal agreement to act in concert wherever possible. After all, we have been fighting the British a great deal longer than they have."

The baron nodded. "All the way back to the days of the Bastille and the guillotine." He cast a thoughtful look at the young marquis. "If you don't mind, I cannot help but be curious about something. It was my understanding that you had grown up in England, yet here you are representing the emperor. What explains that?"

David smiled coldly. He was well accustomed to the suspicion his years in England invariably aroused, but that did not mean that he was pleased to have to repeatedly explain them. Nonetheless, Bertrand had so far impressed him as a sensible and fair man. He was glad of the chance encounter with a fellow countryman that had made him feel less of a stranger in the American capital. He was therefore predisposed to give him a fuller answer than he would have offered most.

"I suppose," he said lightly, "that the emperor's own wisdom accounts for it. He knows that despite the fact that I lived in England for several years, my loyalty is to France."

"Interesting," Bertrand murmured. "I had thought that the emperor cared only for one's loyalty to him."

David laughed under his breath. He was liking the baron better and better. Honesty, even when cloaked in caution, was a rare commodity these days. "Are you suggesting that the emperor and France are not one and the same?"

Bertrand shrugged imperturbably. "I am saying that no man is immortal—or infallible."

They were on dangerous ground but that didn't matter overly much because there was no need to go any further. David had received the message loud and clear: Bertrand was one of the growing number of worldly, thoughtful Frenchmen who were increasingly disquieted over the course their emperor chose to follow.

Were he still in France, he undoubtedly would never have

been so frank. But here in America something of the spirit of rebellion that had given birth to the young republic seemed to have been imparted to the baron. David wondered half-seriously if that might not be an occupational hazard of staying too long in the place.

If so, it would hardly be the only drawback to such service. After only two days in Washington, he had already learned that the mosquitos bit with particular viciousness, that it did not—despite what everyone said—get cooler at night, and that it was impossible to find either a bed or a meal that met his admittedly high standards. Freedom the Americans might have achieved—if they could hold onto it—but civilization had so far eluded them.

When he said as much, the baron threw back his balding head and laughed. "Don't rush to judgment, my friend, or you will end by eating your words. Here comes the lovely mademoiselle with our supper."

David glanced up to see Miss Annabel Riordan holding two large, steaming platters. "Good evenin' to ye, gentlemen," she said quietly as she set the plates before them.

At such close quarters, it was impossible to ignore the ivory smoothness of her skin, lightly touched by summer's peach. The curve of her cheek was perfection as was the long, slender line of her throat. Her hazel eyes were large, thickly fringed, and beautifully shaped. She moved with unconscious grace amid the din and smoke of the tavern, a purely feminine presence in an intrinsically masculine domain.

David found himself fascinated. It wasn't merely that she was beautiful, although that was undeniable. He was well accustomed to beautiful women, but there was something more to Annabel Riordan. He sensed a tantalizing spirit in her not unlike that of a strong-willed mare who would recognize only a single master. But even as the comparison occurred to him, he knew it to be lacking. Mademoiselle Riordan was something unique and original, something he had never encountered before.

He wasn't quite sure what that was, but he was absolutely certain of the effect it had on him. He desired her more intensely than he had desired any woman in a very long time—perhaps ever. That being the case, it did not occur to him that he would not ultimately possess her.

His face gave no hint of his thoughts, yet something intangible touched Annabel. She stiffened and looked at him directly.

What she saw disturbed her further. She was riveted by the play of light and shadow over features that were at once hard and unrelenting yet beautiful. Staring into his fathomless blue eyes, she had a sense of looking directly into a timeless space of infinite wisdom and ineffable sorrow. She couldn't help but wonder what possible reason this absurdly handsome, undeniably self-assured man could have for being sad.

Annabel was still puzzling over that when David reached out and without the slightest hesitation, took her hand. Smiling boldly, he said, "I am delighted to make your acquaintance, Mademoiselle Riordan. You are surely Washington's most attractive landmark."

Annabel felt herself flushing but paid it no mind. Deliberately, she withdrew her hand and said coolly, "Tis my pleasure, Monsieur le Marquis. Rare it is for us to be honored by the presence of not one, but two such noble gentlemen."

The baron laughed. He was as delighted by Annabel's quick comeback as by the look of unalloyed surprise on

David's face. It had not occurred to him that she might know who he was.

"I should have warned you, my friend," he said with a chuckle. "Nothing—and I do mean nothing—happens in this city without Mademoiselle Riordan being aware of it. She is better informed than any member of Congress and indeed, many say, than the President himself."

Annabel looked down her nose at this but couldn't completely conceal her pleasure. "Ye exaggerate, Monsieur le Baron," she said mildly. "I'm but a simple tavern keeper."

Bertrand leaned back in his chair and sighed happily. Clearly, he enjoyed the notion that beauty and sensibility could be combined with such success.

"Not so, mademoiselle," he said in an excess of Gallic gallantry. "You are a misplaced princess cast before swine. An inexcusable error on the part of Destiny which no doubt shall be remedied before long."

This time Annabel did more than merely smile. She laughed delightedly. "Really, Monsieur de Plessis, with such a silver tongue as you possess I canna understand why it was thought needful to send the marquis here. Surely you can charm the Americans just fine on yer own."

Abruptly, the easy good humor with which David had been observing their exchange vanished. He looked hard at the baron before turning his full attention to Annabel. Coldly, he said, "There is a difference, mademoiselle, between being well informed and being dangerously so."

The baron inhaled sharply. "*Monsieur . . .*"

"No," Annabel said quickly. She was more than able to defend herself and wanted to make sure that the marquis knew it. Why that was so important at the moment she didn't know, but neither did she question it.

Her head high and her eyes flashing, she said, "'Tis not like the Old World here, monsieur, where a person has to watch her tongue an' fear those who claim to be her betters. We're free in America, praise to God. We can speak our minds and say what we know without lookin' over our shoulders to do it. You'd be smart to remember that."

David was silent for several moments. He was not accustomed to defiance, and certainly not from one of the lower orders. Yet there was again that "something" about this woman that made her refusal to defer to him intensely exciting. So much so that he was willing to overlook her defiance, if only temporarily.

"My apologies, Miss Riordan," he said, inclining his head. "I merely meant to suggest that you might be more circumspect about your country's affairs. These are, after all, difficult times."

"Aye," Annabel said, slightly mollified, "that's true enough what with the Brits almost knockin' at our door."

"Miss Riordan," the baron said, by way of explanation, "is Irish."

David smiled. "I had noticed," he said gently.

For several heartbeats more they stared at one another until Annabel abruptly remembered herself. "Ye best eat before it gets cold," she said as she turned swiftly away. David watched her go thoughtfully. Only when she was out of sight did he turn his attention to what turned out to be a succulent cold beef in jelly accompanied by fresh asparagus and sweet potatoes sprinkled with cinnamon.

The food was hardly what he would have expected in

Paris, but it was excellent nonetheless. He looked at Bertrand in surprise.

"What did I tell you?" the older man said. "Annabel's success is due in no small measure to her culinary skill. Try one of these rolls. She flavors them with dill and something else I haven't been able to identify. She'll tell me, of course, if I ask, but it impresses her if I can guess."

Impressing Annabel seemed to be the prime occupation of a good number of men from all walks of life, David noticed sardonically. She was called over to judge a fierce but good-natured darts game that ended with her awarding a complimentary mug of ale to the blushing winner, a tall, strapping boy who looked as though he had just rolled in from one of the outlying farms.

The capital of the new republic, the city its residents envisioned as a combination of Athens and Rome revisited, was in fact a sparsely settled barrenness surrounded by marshland and fields. Only a few streets were in place and none of them was paved. Of the public buildings, only the President's residence and the Capitol itself were complete, and they had a raw, new look that was not appealing to one accustomed to the architectural splendors of London or Paris.

And yet there was an undeniable excitement about the place, a vigor and enthusiasm David could not help but envy. Hot and bug-ridden it might be, lacking in almost all the basic amenities, and populated by a brand of human who recognized no man as superior to himself. Still, Washington had a brash likability similar to the people it was meant to represent.

"How long have you been here now, Bertrand?" David asked absently.

"A little more than three years," the other man replied.

"Then you've had a chance to get to know these Americans, whoever they may be. Tell me, do you think they have a chance?"

The baron hesitated. Clearly, he was torn between a tendency toward natural optimism and a duty to be truthful. At last, he said, "Twice in the space of less than four decades they have hurled themselves against the mightiest empire on earth. The first time they were very, very lucky. The British made some incredible mistakes which greatly aided the American cause. But this time . . ."

David put his spoon and knife down. He really must have been overly tired. The food, appetizing though it was, had lost its appeal. "This time they can't count on that happening?"

"Alas, no. The British want vengeance. They want to show the world that no upstart people can ultimately get the better of them. The Americans won their independence but ever since then the British have been slowly but surely strangling them. Now they are simply moving in for the kill."

"Perhaps the upstarts will surprise them—and us," David said softly.

Bertrand shrugged. "If the emperor is victorious, if he manages to hold off the British and drain their resources, if the Americans stop arguing among themselves and begin to work together . . . if . . . if . . . if."

David cut a piece of beef with the precise hand of a man accustomed to wielding a sword. He looked at the baron with amusement. "You shouldn't condemn the very imponderables that make life interesting, Bertrand."

The older man snorted. "You are a good deal younger than me, my friend, and I suspect your enthusiasm for the chase colors your liking for uncertainty. But believe me, there comes a time when a man yearns for little more than a warm bed and the certainty that he will still be in it come morning.''

David smiled. He looked up, across the crowded tavern, to where Annabel was filling mugs of ale. A stray lock of red-gold hair fell across the swell of her breasts.

Softly, he said, ''There are times, my friend, when a young man wishes only for the same.''

CHAPTER
Two

ANNABEL moaned and pulled her feather pillow over her head. A donkey braying in the yard beyond her bedroom window had awakened her.

Rays of sunlight falling across the wood-plank floor warmed her slender form. Though it was only an hour or so after sunrise, the day already promised to be hot. Certainly others thought so. Her fellow Washingtonians were already out and about, trying to get their work completed before the worst of the heat struck.

A peddler woman called loudly: "Good sweet shuckers! Get yer good sweet shuckers. Tuppence the dozen."

Hard on her came the deeper, gravelly voice of the Romany man. "Knives, bring out yer knives! Finest sharpenin' done. Knives, bring out yer knives!"

Farther down the lane, high and cracking, was the newsboy's chant: "British plot to blow up Charleston! Dastardly scheme revealed! Ha'penny tells all!"

Barely had he gone on his way when the donkey brayed again, accompanied by the frantic yapping of dogs and, farther off, the steady pounding of a hammer.

Annabel muttered under her breath and sat up abruptly. It was the same every morning but she never got used to it. Hardly did she seem to get to bed than sleep became impossible. Wryly, she acknowledged that she really shouldn't complain. If the Wild Geese hadn't been such a resounding success, she would be far better rested—and far poorer.

Swiftly, she rose from the bed and stretched her arms above her head. She was a tall, slim girl in the first flush of what would one day be mature loveliness. At twenty, the hair that had been copper red in childhood had turned a deeper, more mellow shade, and it was the sure indicator of a sensuous temperament. Her face was heart-shaped with delicately formed features, although her hazel eyes had a hint of steel when they stared out from beneath her arching brows. Her mouth was full but her manner was restrained, deliberate, without the natural impulsiveness of most girls her age.

But then her life had not been like that of most twenty-year-old females, and her behavior faithfully reflected the differences.

Matter-of-factly, she set about dressing. The water in her basin was tepid but she scarcely noticed. With a minimum of motion, she stripped off her thin linen nightgown, washed, and dried herself. Naked, she stood for a moment letting the soft morning air caress her before abruptly recalling the passage of time.

Swiftly, she pulled on a sensible cotton shift with short, puffy sleeves and a drawstring neck. Over it went a skirt of darker cotton that fell to her ankles. With it she wore a vest of matching fabric that laced in the front, leaving the sleeves and neckline of her shift visible. Her hair she braided and secured in a twist at the nape of her neck. Lightweight knitted stockings held up by garters and practical leather boots covered her slender feet. At the last, she secured a wide belt around her narrow waist. To it she attached a braided thong holding a collection of keys. They clanked busily against her side as she walked toward the door.

Annabel's room was on the third and top floor beneath the eaves. To reach the second floor, she descended a steep and narrow staircase. A quick glance assured her that all was in order. Through the door of an unoccupied room, she could see one of the two maids deftly changing bed linen. The other girl gave her a quick smile as she hurried by with an ewer of steaming water for one of the overnight guests.

On the main floor it was much the same. The great room had been swept clean the night before, its litter of empty plates and glasses removed. The long trestle tables were being scrubbed with sand. Behind the bar, a burly man with silver-blond hair stood polishing pewter mugs. He bobbed his head to Annabel as she passed.

She stepped through the kitchen with its wide, polished worktables and shelves of supplies, out into the stable yard where the boy of odd work was feeding the chickens. They clustered round, a motley collection of brown, white, and variegated hens, all clucking and pecking while the boy dug handfuls of golden grain from the wooden pail and sent them scattering on the hard-packed earth.

Annabel smiled. She stood straight and slender, hands resting on her hips, gazing about her with satisfaction. Each morning she made the same rounds, looking for the same signs that everything was as it should be. She was never disappointed. Despite all the predictions to the contrary, the Wild Geese was a resounding success. That was due in no small measure to her determination to make her own way in life without regard for the limitations others might try to put on her, but there was also a dollop of luck involved which she did not hesitate to acknowledge.

Thirty years before, when her late aunt and uncle had first opened the tavern, it had stood on a backwater road used only occasionally by farmers and the odd traveler or two. Times had changed and the world with them. Past the stable yard, beyond the rutted dirt road, rising high against the sky stood the majestic edifice of the United States Congress. The gleaming white-domed building was a bold statement of what the young nation intended for itself; a symbol of what was to be.

The reality was less impressive. Annabel's nose wrinkled as she smelled the familiar effluvia of Washington on a summer morning, a combination of barnyard odors, horse droppings, and the marsh stench that rose from the surrounding wetlands. She should have been used to it but there were times when she yearned for the fresh, clean scents of her Wicklow home. Washington, by contrast, was not a healthy place. Disease abounded, especially in the warmer months. Whereas, Ireland . . .

"There ye go trippin' over yer own blarney," Annabel muttered to herself. She knew full well that Ireland could not possibly be as idyllic as she remembered it, or why would so many of her sons and daughters be fleeing from her as though the very dogs of hell were barking at their heels?

She was far better off in America, vastly so, and yet there were times when she felt the queer pulling at her heart, the pain that had no place or name, and knew that she had only to close her eyes to see again the cottage where she had been reared and the hillside that had given her the first view of the wider world.

And what a world that held such marvels in it as the Frenchman. That was how she thought of him though she knew his name full well. It was easier—and safer—to remain as impersonal as possible when she thought of the man who had made so very personal an impression on her.

"I've bonnyclabber for brains," she murmured again as she stepped back inside the kitchen, only to run smack against a broad chest. The man to whom it belonged cast her a quizzical glance from his one good eye. "Are the pixies upon you again, Miss Annabel, or can anybody join in this conversation?"

"Get away with ye, Cameron," she said, flushing slightly. "Ye know perfectly well I like to have a word with meself every now and again."

Cameron nodded slowly, as he did all things. He was of medium height for his clan—several inches over six feet— with light blond, almost silvery hair. His tough, angular face might once have been handsome until he acquired the long, livid scar that ran from his forehead across the hole where his right eye should have been and down across his cheek.

When he was likely to be around strangers—as when he tended bar of an evening—Cameron wore an eye patch. But during the morning when the tavern was largely empty he preferred to do without. That was fine with Annabel who saw the man beneath the deformed features and knew there was no ugliness in him.

"Has something upset you?" he asked gently as they

both stepped into the kitchen. Annabel could never remember hearing Cameron raise his voice. But then she couldn't imagine him ever having to do so. He had only to look at another man to strike fear into him. That was a useful skill but one which she suspected cost the big, sensitive Scot dearly. Which was why she preferred to intervene herself whenever there was some little dispute such as the previous night's set-to between Mulrooney and Johnson.

"And why would I be upset?" she countered with a quick smile. "Isn't the world chuggin' along just lovely and all of us with it?"

Cameron laughed but continued to look at her thoughtfully. "There's talk about the Frenchman."

Annabel stiffened. She heartily disliked the notion that anyone could look so easily into her mind. Deliberately, she said, "Folk have been rattlin' about de Plessis for years, not that the dear man's ever done anything to deserve it."

Cameron shook his head patiently. "The younger one."

"There's talk about everybody in this town. Besides, I've heard all about him."

The big man's eyebrows rose with amusement. "Including the fact that he may be an English spy?"

"Sweet Lord," Annabel exclaimed. "*That* I hadn't heard."

"Mayhap it isn't true," Cameron conceded. "Still, it's interesting all the same."

With a gently mocking glance he turned to go.

"Wait," Annabel said. "Who told ye that?"

He shrugged vaguely. "Someone in the street . . . you know how it is."

Indeed, Annabel knew. Washington fed on political rumor and gossip, invented and consumed them with insatiable greed. More than anything else, they were the fuel that kept the city going. Some went so far as to say that they were the sole reason for the city to exist.

There was no better place to tap the city's mutterings than at the Pennsylvania Avenue market.

"'Tis all very interestin'," Annabel said with a toss of her head, "but a person canna be standin' around all day. I've things to do."

"We need ice," Cameron said, having no doubt where she was heading, "if you can find it."

"I'll try," Annabel promised. She picked up her straw shopping basket, plucked her bonnet off a hook, and departed with only a single backward glance to let Cameron know that she knew perfectly well what he was thinking about her and the Frenchman and he'd be smart to forget all about it right there, that very instant.

Cameron merely smiled and went on about his work. The kitchen door slammed a little harder behind Annabel than was strictly necessary.

The sound had its echo some distance away in a gracious, two-story house several blocks from the Capitol. A string of perfect expletives—in French—followed the banging of the door. They came from the man stretched out in the large, canopied bed. David lay under a single linen sheet, his powerfully muscled arms folded under his head, his gaze fastened on the ceiling. When he had sufficiently vented his annoyance, he closed his eyes for a moment, took a deep breath, and reopened them.

He really couldn't blame the lady, she had a right to be vexed. Certainly he had given her every reason to expect more than he had found himself able to deliver.

With another explicit curse, he left the bed, trying to ignore the sudden, unsettling dizziness that briefly swept over him, and walked naked into the adjacent smaller room. There a steaming bath awaited him along with several freshly pressed towels, an unused bar of soap, and his newly honed razor.

He took all such amenities perfectly for granted. He never questioned how his valet, Pomfret, knew precisely when to draw his bath. He presumed that it was simply some gift the man had, which was partly what made him good enough to be in David's employ.

Lolling in the tub, the hot water soothing his irate spirits, he set himself to think about the previous night. He was not a boastful man but he couldn't remember the last time he had failed to satisfy a lady. Instinctively, he sought the easiest explanation: his journey had tired him more than he wished to admit, Washington did not agree with him, he was worried and apprehensive about the future, and he kept thinking about that red-haired Irish vixen.

Damn it all. She was at least part of the cause of his unparalleled default. Long after he'd left the Wild Geese and parted from de Plessis, even after he'd met the saucy, blond wench who had appeared so promising, he'd been thinking about Miss Annabel Riordan. He kept remembering the fire in her eyes as she defied him. At the mere thought of her now his body hardened, as it had failed to do the night before when it would have been far more appreciated.

David muttered under his breath again, then abruptly laughed. It was really too absurd. Here he was worrying about his masculinity when the future of his country was being decided thousands of miles away by men whom he increasingly mistrusted, and by one man in particular—Napoleon Bonaparte.

The emperor Napoleon, as he styled himself, and rightfully so for he had been crowned amid more pomp and pageantry than any king had ever dared to muster, had forced David's sister and husband into exile, yet he had also unhesitantly returned David's inheritance and held out the hand of friendship to him. He was a complex, fascinating, ultimately unknowable man upon whom the mark of fate seemed to rest with increasing heaviness.

With a sigh, David hoisted himself out of the bath. He dried off briskly and shaved with equal efficiency despite the unexpected shakiness of his hand. As he did so, he let his thoughts drift. He had a meeting scheduled later in the day with an aide to President Madison. The man would undoubtedly try to feel him out as to the purpose of his mission but David did not intend to oblige him. He would speak directly to the President about the need for joint military strategy or to no one at all.

That still left the bulk of the day to get through. De Plessis was a pleasant enough companion, but David largely preferred to be on his own. He thought this would be a good opportunity to take the pulse of the city in which he found himself.

Exiting his temporary residence on Pennsylvania Avenue not far from the President's house, he stood for a moment looking around him. In contrast to the rest of the disordered, cacophonous city, some effort had been made here to mimic the gracious elegance of Mayfair and the Île de la Cité.

The results had been only partially successful but by Washington standards they were superlative, which was why so many foreign visitors chose to live there. A group of

Prussians occupied the building directly across from him. Next to them was a party of gentlemen from the Confederation of the Rhine States. Down the block was a delegation of Portuguese who, like all the rest, were there to get a look at the young republic and try to make some sense out of what it might, or might not, be able to do.

Not that any of that was considered a very high priority. America was a backwater, far removed from the dramatic events occurring on the European continent. David himself would never have been sent there except that he had a particularly sensitive and important mission, after which he would gladly take himself back to civilization.

But first he needed to get a better idea of how the natives lived.

He started walking idly in the direction most people seemed to be taking and before long found himself on the edge of a sprawling marketplace not unlike those to be seen in London and Paris. Peddlers had set up their pushcarts under little awnings that fluttered in the stingy breeze coming off the Potomac. That was a mixed blessing, providing a little coolness at the cost of considerable odor which mingled with the scents of the market itself.

Around the outskirts of the market were a line of elegant carriages including one he recognized. De Plessis had pointed it out to him earlier, commenting that it belonged to the President's wife. David shook his head wryly. He could think of no other place in the world where the head of government's wife would come to market to do her own shopping.

Not that anyone seemed to think anything of it. They were far too busy haggling for themselves over the chickens hanging from one stand and the ducks from another. Piles of peaches and potatoes, apples and asparagus awaited consideration. One entire stand was given over to pickles of all imaginable sorts, sizes, and smells. Another boasted oysters and clams. People stood about waiting as their shells were opened so that they could suck out the delicate meat directly without the trouble of taking them home.

Regretting not having bothered with his breakfast, David was surprised to discover a stand selling fresh-brewed coffee and popovers that could almost have passed for the brioche of his native Paris. He wished his uncharacteristically contrary stomach would have allowed him to try them but the mere thought made him queasy. The sky was brilliantly clear, and the day, despite its growing warmth, seemed etched in crystal.

He stood to one side taking in the noise, the color, and the bustle. For a few moments, he was transported back to the market near his home of Montfort where his sister had often taken him when he was a child. Back in the earlier, simpler days before they had all gone to court, before the Revolution struck and with it the Reign of Terror. Before the world shattered into a thousand broken pieces which he had never managed, no matter how he tried, to reassemble again.

It was good to remember that there were still places where the search for a plump hen and a ripe piece of cheese was considered genuinely important. Some of the tension that had plagued him for so long eased. He smiled, lifting his golden head beneath the gleaming sun, a strong, tall man much given to struggle but able nonetheless to enjoy a brief moment of peace.

Until his gaze fell on the young woman standing beside a straw-laden wagon. Her laugh had reached him from across the expanse of several yards. He caught a glimpse of her porcelain skin warmed to a pleasing flush, her copper-streaked hair and the gentle swell of her breasts.

Instantly, the ease of his manner fell away. His eyes narrowed and his head lifted, poised, watchful, relentless. He felt at once the hunter, as the rush of blood through his body and the surge of hunger too primitive to be denied flowed through him.

❧ CHAPTER ❧
Three

*A*NNABEL did not appear pleased to see him. Indeed, when she caught sight of him, she frowned and looked away before abruptly changing her mind and staring at him directly.

"Monsieur le Marquis," she said. He had the sense that she used his title deliberately, to remind him and herself of the gulf between them. Also, perhaps, to mock him just a little.

"Mademoiselle," he said with grave solemnity and inclined his head. If the little chit thought she was going to beat him on the niceties, she would find out otherwise. Silence reigned until it became obvious that he wasn't leaving. Annabel heaved a resigned sigh and turned to the man beside her.

"If ye will deliver the ice, this afternoon, I'll pay yer price, otherwise no."

"I've no helper today," the man complained. "Tomorrow will have to do."

Annabel shook her head firmly. "That it won't. I've customers who'll be comin' in with their tongues hangin' down to their shinbones lookin' for a bit of somethin' cool to drink an' what am I supposed to be tellin' them? That Denny Lassiter couldn't be after stirrin' himself to lift a few wee blocks of ice into my cellar?"

"Wee blocks?" the man repeated indignantly. "They weigh a good forty pound each, value for yer money, not like the shavings ye'll get from the others. Lassiter ice is worth waitin' for."

"Not at ha'penny the pound," Annabel said pointedly. "This afternoon or not at all."

The iceman rolled his eyes in David's direction as though asking—one male to another—what a poor fellow was to do. David merely grinned and said nothing.

"Oh, all right," Lassiter said. "If it means that much to ye, ye'll have the bloody ice today. But only this time. I can't guarantee such service regularly."

"Sure an' ye could," Annabel said, all sweetness and smiles now that she had her own way. "Donna be underratin' yerself, Mr. Lassiter. Ye can do anything ye make up yer mind to."

It was amusing, not to say highly instructive, to watch the iceman turn bright red and doff his hat with pleasure. When he was gone David glanced at Annabel assessingly. Looking at her, standing there with her head tossed back, the copper hair flaming in the sun and the light of unholy mischief dancing in her eyes, he felt a thud of warning. Something moved within her, something ancient and powerful, that was absent in other women, or at least so much more deeply buried as to be invisible. He had a sudden jarring sense of standing outside of himself, observing her through a veil of dislocation. The sensation did not ease, though he struggled to deny it.

"You surprise me, mademoiselle," he murmured. "Your English is accented but your French is perfect. How could that be?"

"Very simply," she said, glancing down her nose. "First, my English is most certainly not accented. The Irish speak English exactly as it should be spoken. As for my French, I learned from a gentlewoman who took refuge in our village during your Revolution and ended up staying the remainder of her life. She taught me a great deal."

David was tempted to ask her to elaborate on that but he resisted, if only because he wasn't sure he would like the answer. Miss Annabel Riordan was proving to be too full of surprises. His preconceptions about who and what she was, and how they stood in relation to one another, didn't seem to be holding up too well.

But then neither did he. The day seemed abruptly overbright. He winced against a stab of pain. Moments before he had been uncomfortably hot. Now he felt chilled despite the beading of sweat on his forehead.

He shook himself, trying to clear his thoughts. Annabel's face seemed to sway before him, her lovely features suddenly suffused with concern.

"What's wrong?" she asked softly as she touched his arm.

"Nothing . . . too much sun, perhaps. Or something I ate."

But there had been only the excellent repast, of which he had actually eaten little, at her own tavern the night before. Yet he felt undeniably queasy, to the extent that he thought it prudent to excuse himself.

"Don't be silly," Annabel said brusquely. Still speaking

in French, she said, "Tell me where you're staying. I'll find a carriage."

David wanted to insist that wasn't necessary but his tongue suddenly seemed too thick. It was all he could do to gasp out the number of his residence. After that he was aware of very little—only a whirl of sounds and colors—until blissfully cool darkness received him.

He woke to the braying of a goat.

Gingerly, he opened his eyes. The too bright light was gone. All he saw were pleasant shadows, and he felt a deeply rooted sense of ease. Yet, for the moment, he did not know where he was or what had happened to him.

Slowly he remembered the marketplace . . . Annabel . . . the sudden frightening feeling of disorientation . . .

He was ill. Or at least he had been. His body ached as though he had been beaten from the inside out. His mouth was very dry and when he tried to sit up, he felt unnaturally weak and heavy. Nonetheless, he persisted until he managed to raise himself sufficiently to see around the room. It was small, plainly furnished, and meticulously clean. The slanting roofline indicated that it was placed under the eaves of whatever house he might be in.

He was someplace where there were goats.

Tantalizing aromas wafted through the open window, overriding the barnyard scents that faded before the succulence of roasting chicken. His stomach rumbled. He quickly made up his mind. Whatever had happened to him, wherever he was, he wasn't going to lie around waiting for something to happen. Angling himself off the bed, he managed with some difficulty to stand up, only to discover that he was naked. Wherever he was, it seemed as though he had made himself very much at home. Or else someone had done it for him.

With a shrug, he wrapped the sheet around himself and headed for the door. It proved to be farther away than it looked, or at least that was the effect as David had to lean against the wall to cross the narrow space. At length, he got the door opened and stepped into a hallway at one end of which was a narrow staircase.

He was standing at the top of it, holding on to the bannister and trying to decide whether he could make it down without breaking his neck, when a young girl suddenly appeared. She wore the plain dress of a maid and was carrying a bucket of water which she promptly dropped when she caught sight of David.

"Oh, sir," she exclaimed, turning bright red.

Belatedly, it occurred to David that he ought to have kept a firmer grip on the sheet. The girl turned tail and fled, but could not have gotten far because almost instantly there came the sound of light, running footsteps.

"Blessed Mary," an all-too-familiar voice said, "and all the saints while ye're about it. What are ye doin' out of bed?"

Annabel stood at the foot of the steps. David smiled crookedly. "I thought you spoke French," he said, "or did I dream that?"

"I did and I do," she said, exasperated. Taking the steps quickly, she reached his side. Despite her stern tone, he did not miss the look of relief on her face. "Back to bed with ye then," she said as she slipped an arm around his waist. "No sense pushin' yer luck after what ye've been through."

"And what exactly would that be?" David inquired as he obligingly allowed himself to be helped back into the room. The touch of her body against his sent a sweet ripple of desire through him. He was reassuringly, if inconveniently, alive, a fact which did not escape Annabel's notice.

To his surprise, she blushed. De Plessis's assertions about her respectability suddenly came back to him, and he thought about the tantalizing possibility of her innocence as she determinedly urged him back to bed. Once there, she covered him with the sheet and stood looking down at him cautiously.

"How are ye feelin'?"

David couldn't resist. Without hesitation, he said, "Surely that must be obvious?"

Again, a wave of heated color washed over her. With it her mouth tightened. She clasped her hands in front of her and looked at him narrowly. "Ye've the devil's own luck an' I'm not sure ye shouldn't have to be givin' it back to him."

David stared at her for a moment, then chuckled. "If it's luck that brought me here, wherever here is, I won't quibble with it. But I've the idea that you had more than a little to do with it."

"Ye were sick to faintin' in the market," she said with asperity. "I tried takin' ye back to where ye've been stayin', but yer landlord wouldn't have it. Once he realized you were ill, he barred the door, so I just brought you back here."

David frowned. To begin with, he wasn't at all pleased with being denied access to his lodgings under any circumstances. The gentleman who had done that would regret it. However, he was more interested at the moment in Annabel's willingness to take him in.

"Is this your tavern?" he asked.

She nodded. Annabel guessed that he was bewildered and sympathized with him, but it was just as well that he know the truth. He had been very ill but not so much that she had feared for his life. Given a little time and a bit of patience, he would recover fully.

"It looked at first as though ye might have the sweatin' sickness, although that didn't turn out to be the case," she said matter-of-factly. "It was something milder than that, but folk can get afeared all the same. The sickness spreads fast in these parts, especially this time of year, so most people who get it are shunned, poor souls."

"But not by you . . . ?" he murmured, his eyes alert now and on her.

Annabel shrugged. She refused to let him think she was better or nobler than she was. "Had it meself, I did, five years ago. Nasty it was but I lived to tell the tale and the doctor who took care of me told me I'd never get it again. So it was safe enough to bring ye here so long as the downstairs crowd didn't find out."

"They'd have *shunned* you—and your business—if they'd known." The clear evidence that someone of her standing could behave so *nobly*—there was no other word for it— took him aback. Was nothing sacred in this strange new country, not even his most deeply inborn notions?

Again, the slender shoulders lifted and fell, as though to ask why he should bother belaboring what was both obvious and inconsequential. She'd never lived her life by the standards of others and she wasn't about to start now.

"All's well, as the Bard said. Anyway, ye'll be back on yer feet soon enough. For the moment, ye'd be smart to rest quiet and refrain, if ye can, from startlin' the maids."

David laughed. He was perfectly aware that he was still far from well. Yet that had no effect on the overriding sense of contentment flowing through him.

That couldn't last. There was a world and a reality

beyond the small, sweetly scented room. Sooner than he liked, he would have to deal with it.

Remembering that, he frowned. "How long have I been here?"

"Three days."

That was far worse than he'd expected. Never before had he missed any appreciable quantity of time. More to the point, he had also missed his appointment with Madison's aide.

"I was supposed to meet someone . . ." he murmured distractedly.

"Aye, John Austen. I sent him a message sayin' ye'd been called away suddenly and would be in touch with him when ye got back."

"That must have stirred the pot a bit," David mused, relieved the matter had been attended to.

Annabel smiled. "The thinking is that ye received new orders from the emperor . . . or the king."

"What king?" David asked, confused.

"And isn't there only one, at least that matters?"

"You mean King George? Why would I be . . ." He broke off as understanding dawned. With it came a fine mingling of amusement and fury.

"Are you seriously telling me that there are people who think I'm working for the British?"

Annabel nodded. Her smile was gone. She was watching him intently. "One or two. It makes sense, doesn't it, considerin' that ye're half-British yerself."

"I am hardly to blame for my unfortunate mother's parentage," David said stiffly. For good measure, he added, "I also happen to think that it is not precisely a sin to be British. There are worse things that can befall a man."

"Strange talk for a fellow who's supposed to be workin' for the one the Brits call an archfiend from hell. At least I seem to recall some such phrase being bandied about in the penny press over there."

"And how," David demanded, "would a renegade Irish chit know what the British press was calling Napoleon?"

Annabel shrugged. She refused to take umbrage at his description of her though it stung all the same. He certainly hadn't been any finer than another man when the fever was tearing through him. Then he'd twisted and moaned like anyone else. And she had been so desperately afraid for David that the fear itself had shocked her. Ordinary compassion she had aplenty, but never had she felt so drawn into the life of another, so caught in his own struggle for survival.

Barely had the fear begun to ebb than resentment replaced it. He had no right to make her feel so vulnerable and confused. She had her life well in hand, organized just the way she liked it, and the marquis de Montfort wasn't going to change that.

"I can read, Yer Grace," she said scathingly. "We get the British papers here, a few weeks out o' date but interestin' all the same. They make no secret of what they think of yer Napoleon."

"And what do you think of him?" David asked, relaxing back against the pillows. Now that he thought of it, the charge of working for England wasn't so startling. Indeed, he should have anticipated it. With half his mind, he speculated as to the potential benefits of encouraging the rumors. He might be able to lure the British into exposing their hand to him. The thought put a bad taste in his mouth, and he realized he was more precariously poised between his conflicting loyalties than he'd thought. He wanted France to win but he didn't want England to lose.

"I think," Annabel said softly, "that we can discuss politics some other time if ye've a mind. Right now ye need to rest." She had observed the creeping pallor beneath his burnished skin and was concerned by it. That last thing either of them needed was for him to have a relapse.

David didn't argue but when she made to move away, he did reach out and take hold of her hand. His grip was surprisingly firm for a man who had lately been so ill. Slowly, she sat down on the side of the bed.

"Stay with me," he said. His words were curt, his expression equally so. He disliked having to admit to any need, particularly one which had so taken him by surprise. He had always been a self-sufficient man but suddenly he did not want to be left alone. Especially not when the alternative was to be with Annabel.

Exhaustion crept over him. His eyelids fluttered shut, denying him a glimpse of the unutterable tenderness that suffused her features. At that moment, Annabel was lovelier than she had ever been in her life. All the beauty of her inner self was revealed in her gaze. The carefully stitched armor she wielded against the world was peeled away. Had he looked then, he would have seen straight into her soul.

Instead, he slept and for that Annabel was tremulously grateful.

❧ CHAPTER ❧
Four

WHEN David woke again, it was evening. He lay for a time studying the shadows of the room before hunger drove him to stir himself. His clothes had been pressed and hung neatly away in a small armoire. Beside it was a dresser with a bowl and a pitcher of warm water. Apparently, his revival had been anticipated.

A cool breeze fluttered the plain white curtains as he dressed. From below, he could hear voices raised in laughter and smell the aroma of beef roasting. The sense of well-being that filled him was so strong as to be almost physical. He could not remember when he had last felt so content. He was plainly, humbly glad to be alive. The world looked, sounded, and most decidedly smelled better than it had before. And he himself was far more eager than usual to rejoin it.

A smile curved his mouth as he came down the narrow staircase. This time there was no maid available to startle. A glance through the taproom door confirmed that the Wild Geese was doing its usual brisk custom. The crowd was three deep at the bar and almost every table was taken. Toward the back, the baron de Plessis sat in conversation with another man, a lean-faced fellow in his mid-twenties with a look about him that was at once earnest and calculating.

David did not move immediately to join them. Instead, he went up to the bar, waited until the tall, silver-haired man approached him, and ordered a tankard of ale. With that in hand, he stood sipping leisurely as he observed the scene around him. In fact, he was looking for Annabel but wasn't quite ready to admit that even to himself. He was just relaxing, having a drink before deciding when to join de Plessis and his friend. It felt good to be on his feet again, health restored.

A flash of fire caught his eye. He turned slightly, eyes narrowed, only to confront a thud of disappointment. The fire was merely a kerchief tied around the head of an old peddler woman enjoying her malt with a cluster of like-minded friends.

David sighed inwardly. Matters were getting out of hand when he could let himself believe, even for a moment, that an old woman's kerchief was Annabel's hair. He'd be seeing her in shadows next.

He took a long sip of his ale and set the tankard down. The barkeep looked at him thoughtfully. "Another?"

David shook his head. He'd keep whatever wits he still had firmly about him. He glanced back at the other fellow, noting as he did the eye patch that only partly concealed a livid scar. Instinctively, the warrior in him speculated as to how such an injury could occur.

"Boarding party," the Scotsman said. "Off the Spanish Main. Took a knock from a saber."

"Do you do card tricks, too, as well as read minds?"

The Scotsman laughed. "It's faces I read and there's no trick to yours. She's in the kitchen."

A slashing eyebrow rose. "She?"

Cameron's smile deepened. "Miss Annabel. She's checking up on supper but she won't be long."

David shrugged. "It's all the same to me."

The barkeep's laugh was deep and rich. "Aye, and a man can throw his hat from Edinburgh to Ballykline."

"That would depend on how the wind was blowing, wouldn't you say?" David murmured. He liked the big, solid Scotsman even if the fellow did have the habit of seeing more than he should. But he also caught himself wondering what his relationship was to Annabel.

"From what I hear," Cameron said, "ye've enough on yer plate without dreamin' up problems where there aren't any." He gestured toward the table at the back of the room. "If that fellow has to listen to de Plessis's chatter much longer, his brains will be week-old flummery and precious little good to ye."

"The baron is merely warming him up," David said with a grin. Still, he thought it was time to cross the room and have a word with the pair.

De Plessis was launched on a story involving a shipment of linen from Belgium that had gone awry in Amsterdam, necessitating the intervention of the French consul there who had been found disporting himself with a bevy of Indonesian girls. They were ostensibly intended for training as house maids but in fact bound for the better bordellos of Vienna and Hamburg where their dark beauty and general congeniality placed them in great demand.

The younger man looked glassy-eyed, whether from the effects of de Plessis's conversation or too much hard cider it was impossible to say.

"Ah, de Montfort," the baron broke off without missing a beat. He beamed genially at David though his eyes were cautious. "Nice to see you back. Join us for a spot of something?"

David allowed as to how that would be pleasant. He took a seat, carefully spreading the tails of his frock coat beneath him to avoid crushing them, and smiled at the American. "Mr. Austen, I presume?"

The younger man coughed. "Ah, yes, I am . . . that is to say, you're de Montfort?"

David nodded.

"We expected you three days ago, monsieur. There have been rumors . . . The President is disturbed."

"I'm sorry to hear that," David said smoothly. "But then he must have a great deal on his mind. These are trying times."

Even though he held the position of presidential aide, Austen lacked even the most rudimentary claim to diplomatic skills. Without thinking, he blurted out, "Where have you been? You were reported in Washington, then you weren't. They haven't seen you at your lodgings. Your man—Pomfret, is his name?—is most uncooperative. This really won't do, monsieur. The President is a very busy man. He can't . . ."

"Really," David murmured sardonically as he exchanged a glance with de Plessis, "I had no idea I would arouse such interest. This is, after all, a purely private visit, Mr. Austen. Surely there was no reason for anyone to become agitated."

"Private . . . but, that is, we understood . . . we thought . . ."

David waved a hand, cutting short the babble. "As to that, it is true that I carry certain words for President Madison." For good measure, he added, "And for him alone. Therefore, if you will arrange a meeting at the earliest . . ."

"Impossible," Austen said. Stung by de Montfort's refusal to take him seriously, he took refuge in officiousness. "The President's schedule is very full. We couldn't possibly fit you in before Thursday next, and then only if I approve the purpose of your visit."

He sat back, arms folded over his chest, pleased with himself.

David looked at him silently. Slowly, almost imperceptibly he bared his teeth in what no one over the age of three would mistake for a smile.

"Oh, you'll approve it, Mr. Austen," he said softly. "You'll approve anything that will give this jumped-up excuse of a country even half a chance of surviving. Because if you don't, you and everyone like you will end up swinging from the business end of a British rope. The same one they've been keeping warm ever since Yorktown."

Austen gulped. He struggled against the dawning suspicion that David didn't really give a fiddler's damn what happened between the British and Americans. The man was a bloody aristocrat, bred to the assumption of his own superiority. Briefly, the thought crossed his mind that the French hadn't guillotined enough of them.

"I see," he said slowly. "Then you wish to see the President on a matter of policy."

"I wish," David replied, "to see the President in order to exchange the time of day. Now arrange it."

Austen blanched but managed to retain whatever was left of his dignity. He rose, bowed stiffly, and said, "I'll be in touch. Where can I reach you?"

"Here," David said. At de Plessis's startled look, he added, "I'm changing my lodgings."

The decision had been made on the spur of the moment, almost as he said the words themselves. But having made it, he felt no regrets. The tavern was cleaner and better equipped than any place else he'd seen in Washington. It was far better situated for picking up the local gossip which might well concern him. And then there was the proprietress herself, all icy fire, defiant beauty, and gentle strength, a woman who fit none of his preconceived notions yet strangely suited him. A woman he intended to know a good deal better before he departed.

"I see," the baron murmured when they were alone. "Has the charming Miss Annabel agreed to this?"

David grinned. "She will. I merely haven't mentioned it to her yet."

De Plessis rolled his eyes. He took a prudent swallow of his rather good claret and silently thanked God that life still held such interesting entanglements, even if he was reduced these days more to the role of audience rather than participant.

"Join me for supper," he suggested to the younger man. "Annabel does a marvelous joint of beef and I understand there's also kidney pie."

"Thank you, but no," David said. He forbore mentioning that his appetite wasn't yet up to snuff. "I want to collect Pomfret without further delay."

He smiled as he considered what Pomfret must be thinking. To all appearances, his employer had simply gone off with no notice, no clothes, and no valet. But then Pomfret had always given the impression that he expected the worst.

"Leave here, sir?" the gentleman's gentleman inquired a short while later. "Move to a tavern?"

"The Wild Geese," David confirmed. "It's across from the Capitol. That's the big white building with the dome. You can't miss it. Pack up and I'll meet you there."

"A tavern . . ."

"It's perfectly respectable, Pomfret, not to mention a hell of a lot better than most places I've stayed in. Prisons, public schools, and army camps don't exactly accustom one to luxury. Besides, haven't you heard it's all the fashion these days, staying in taverns?"

"No, sir, that hadn't come to my attention." Pomfret was a small man, barely over five feet tall, but he managed to pack a multitude of suffering into his modest frame. He had endured an unpleasant few days not knowing whether to raise the alarm for his wayward master or remain discreet. With a sigh that would have torn the heart of a Roman galley captain, he went over to the closet to fetch David's valises. "Will we be there long, sir?"

"I shouldn't think so, but it all depends on how things go."

"I shall pray for your speedy success, sir," the valet murmured.

David left him neatly stacking shirts and went to find the landlord. That hearty was ensconced in his parlor in front of a mug of ale. He had just settled down to read the daily flyer when David saw himself in.

"I say . . ." the landlord murmured as he hoisted himself upright. "What's this then . . ." His ruddy color faded perceptibly when he beheld de Montfort. "You... you're alive... I thought..."

"Thought what?" David demanded. "That it was all right to kick me out to lie in the street? Is that how you normally treat people who are ill?"

"I didn't... I couldn't... see here, a man has to take precautions."

"Indeed, he does," David agreed. "If he wants to live a long and healthy life, he has to look to his own well-being, doesn't he? He shouldn't be so foolish as to anger someone who's liable to come back later looking for reparation. That's the sort of short-sighted behavior that can put a man in his grave before he's ready."

The landlord blanched further and ran a hand over his damp upper lip. David spoke perfectly pleasantly, he even smiled. Why then did he feel the chill of deadly rage penetrating down the length of his spine?

"All a misunderstanding..." he murmured.

"But one we can certainly clear up without too much difficulty." Briefly, David outlined what he expected the other man to do. By the time he finished, the landlord was nodding frantically, promising that he'd see to it at once, David could count on it, if only he would leave him in peace.

Ten minutes later, when David saw himself out, he did so with the assurance that Washington's one and only hospital would shortly benefit from the sizeable donation of a concerned citizen anxious to do something for those less fortunate than himself. He carried with him the memory of the pained look behind the landlord's eyes and the amused thought that for such men the loss of money was truly worse than the loss of a pound of flesh.

David's next stop was the French consulate, housed in a modest two-story building several blocks from the President's mansion. At that hour, only servants were about, the rest of the staff being occupied with the Washington social round.

It astounded David how such a provincial backwater boasting only a handful of decent buildings and lacking even paved streets could still manage to generate so complex a society. Yet not an evening went by without a ball, an assembly, a theatrical performance, something to bring together the people who had seen each other only a few hours before but were apparently in dire need of doing so again. What they all found to say to each other he couldn't imagine. It was enough that he himself wasn't obliged to take part.

Having picked up his mail, he lingered for a few minutes reading the latest dispatches from home. Prussia, Austria, and Russia continued to be allied against Napoleon. Though far from defeated, the emperor was clearly on the defensive. Not unexpected, David thought, for a man who had squandered the greatest army ever fielded on an ill-advised attempt to take Moscow.

As a counsel he had argued in private against the Russian adventure, feeling it poorly conceived and unnecessary. Napoleon had heard him out courteously but his decision had already been made. Undoubtedly, David's opposition was part of the reason why he had been sent to America. Prudently, Napoleon wanted him as far from France as possible now that the proverbial chickens were coming home to roost. Yet he had also entrusted him with a genuinely important mission. Contradictory behavior was characteristic of the man who had a genius for such things.

David tucked his letters into the pocket of his frock coat and left the consulate. He walked the short distance to the Wild Geese enjoying the cooler than usual night air. Carriages passed him frequently and from nearby houses he heard the sounds of laughter and conversation. It was difficult to believe that he was in the capital of a nation at war, fighting for its very existence. The Americans simply seemed unable to admit that they were in any danger. He wondered how much longer it would be before they realized differently.

In the meantime, there was the matter of his new lodgings. He pushed open the gate and strolled up the path toward the tavern. A few hens, still foraging despite the hour, squawked at him as they scattered across the front lawn. The tavern door opened. By the light from it, he could make out a man sitting glumly on the outside bench. It was Pomfret, surrounded by all of David's luggage, with a look on his face that suggested life had once again lived down to his expectations.

"What's this then?" David asked.

"She wouldn't let me in," the valet said stiffly. "The proprietress, that is. When I explained what I wanted, she threw me out. Used some rather nasty language in the bargain, I don't mind telling you."

"Did she indeed?" David murmured. He smiled. "Wait here."

With little choice, the servant subsided back onto the bench. David entered the tavern. It was even busier than when he had left. A fierce darts game was in progress and several decks of cards had appeared. At a nearby table, a half-dozen men were playing high-stakes poker. An audience had gathered around them.

David made his way through the crowd until he caught sight of Annabel. She was at the bar, talking with the Scotsman. When she caught sight of him in the mirror, she turned, her head high. Not for anything would she let him know how she had felt to discover suddenly that he was gone without so much as a farewell. "And what would ye be wanting?"

"I think you know perfectly well." He put a hand on her arm to draw her away. Instantly, she stiffened. Cameron put down his towel and glanced at them both. Almost imperceptibly, Annabel shook her head.

"Thank you," David said dryly when they had reached a private corner. "I appreciate your calling off your guard."

"Donna ye be speaking of Cameron in that way. He's worth two of you."

"Is that all? I'd have thought you'd say ten, at least."

She opened her mouth to reply, but decided against it. Instead, she merely glared at him.

"Now what's this about no room at the inn?" David asked.

Annabel's green-gold eyes widened. "Have ye no respect for anything?"

"I'm not a hypocrite, if that's what you want to know. The Testaments are filled with humor as well as wisdom, not to mention having more than a bit to say about the duty of hospitality."

"That's all well and good," Annabel said, "but I canna be havin' ye here now that ye're well again."

"I fail to see why not. I'm a visitor to Washington and I need accommodation. So why shouldn't I stay here?"

Annabel flushed, torn by her own conflicting feelings. She'd been willing enough to care for him when he was ill, but healthy he was far too disturbing to her peace of mind. Besides, she feared she was being mocked. "Because you're an aristocrat, that's why. You're used to far better than this."

"Maybe it's time I got a dose of democracy," David suggested with a smile. He sensed she was weakening and didn't hesitate to press his advantage. Deliberately provocative, he added, "Of course, if there's some reason you don't trust yourself around me . . ."

"*Ooooh*," Annabel exclaimed. Her face turned red, and she shot him a look that should have nailed him to the wall.

"Full of yerself, ye are. I'll have ye know ye're no more to me than . . . than the old billy goat out in the yard. And he's a damn sight better behaved, let me tell you."

"If I promise to try to live up to his standards, may I stay?" David asked. His eyes held a teasing gleam and the hard curve of his mouth was well nigh irresistible. Annabel felt herself weakening.

"Besides," he added quickly, "there's poor old Pomfret to think of. He's really too sensitive for this kind of treatment."

Annabel thought of the woebegone little man sitting outside her door and felt a twinge of guilt. Kindness to others had been drilled into her from earliest childhood. Though her parents had hardly been wealthy, neither had they ever thought of themselves as poor. So long as they could share with others, they were rich in the only ways that counted.

She sighed and refused to look at David lest she see too great satisfaction in his eyes. Damn the man. He had the devil's own nerve coming into her life, setting it on end, and without a by-your-leave sending all her hard-won security flying out the door. She was sure he knew nothing about being afraid and alone, with no place to call home and no prospect of ever having one. No shadow of violence and cruelty could have ever darkened his door. It was easy enough for him in his fine silks and hand-tooled leather boots, smiling like God's own gift, and tempting her to thoughts she had firmly exorcised from her mind the day she'd decided she wasn't going to be any man's property. Not, she thought wryly, that he showed any sign of wanting to own her the way a husband would. His fine lordship wouldn't be interested in more than the temporary run of the premises, whether by loan or rental.

Her cheeks flushed. Damn him and all his kind with him. If blessed Saint Patrick were still around, he'd be running off the high muckety-mucks and leaving the snakes in peace.

But in the absence of such holy intervention, it appeared that she'd have to find her own way of dealing with his lordship. Running him off might be the easiest solution, except that he didn't appear inclined to go. That being the case, the only thing to do seemed to be to ignore him.

She smiled. Now there was a solution that was positively inspired. On the one hand, she'd take him down a peg or two—to the inevitable benefit of his immortal soul. And on the other, she'd do herself a bit of good as well. Put a bit more starch in her spine, it would. Not to mention strengthening her resolve to let men and their blandishments go a-tangling.

"All right," she said grudgingly, "ye can stay and that poor old Pomfret with ye. But only if ye abide by the rules."

"And what might those be?" David inquired. He stood,

towering over her. Cameron was taller but he didn't seem so to Annabel.

She held up her right hand and unfurled three fingers. Firmly, she counted off. "One: no fighting on the premises. Two: no wenching on the premises. Three: all bills paid on time. Break the rules once, ye get a warning. Break them twice, ye get booted out. Understood?"

The broadness of David's smile suggested that he was doing his level best not to laugh. "Absolutely," he assured her. "I shall warn Pomfret immediately. He will simply have to ameliorate his behavior for the time we are here. Of course, it won't be easy for the poor fellow. Habits die hard and all that. But still . . ."

Annabel tossed her fiery head and gave him a quelling glance. "Get on with ye. There's some of us have work to do. Just don't be forgetting what I said."

Without waiting for a reply, she turned on her heel and headed back into the main room. The speculative glances and sly smiles she encountered there did nothing to improve her temper.

Nor did David's failure to put in an appearance through the remainder of the evening. Once his man was settled unpacking in their rooms, he vanished into the swirling mist of the hot Washington night.

Not, of course, that she cared tuppence about what he did.

Not at all.

❧ CHAPTER ❧
Five

*I*T was a standing joke in the young capital that the politicians outnumbered even the mosquitos. They outnumbered everything in fact except the whores, although that was debatable, since the difference between the two couldn't always be determined.

What Washington lacked in civilizing amenities, it made up for in the variety and vigor of its fancy houses. They ranged up one side of Pennsylvania Avenue and down the other, overflowing into the adjacent streets and leading the outward reach of the city's boundaries.

For the sailors running cargo up the Potomac, there were modest establishments along the river's Watergate. For the more prosperous, there were elegant premises maintained by discreetly amiable ladies whose looks and manner rivaled those of the European demimondaine. Of these, the unquestioned best was Madame Colette's. Conveniently situated less than a half-dozen blocks from the Capitol, it catered to what passed as Washington's elite.

David took note of the spittoon placed squarely in the front hall, next to the stand for walking sticks and the hatrack. It looked as though Madame Colette's was doing a brisk custom that evening. The rack was jammed with everything from elegant top hats to coonskin caps, authentic down to the small life forms at home on them.

After the briefest hesitation, he entered. He was there for one reason only, to prove to himself that the occurrence of several nights before had been no more than a sidebar to his brush with illness. It didn't do for a man to leave such things unresolved. They tended to distract from more serious business. And to give cheeky little spitfires like Miss Annabel Riordan too much of an upper hand.

Madame Colette herself came hurrying forward to meet him. She was an elegantly dressed blonde on the far side of forty with a well-preserved figure and a genteelly business-like manner. Exactly what was called for in such an establishment.

Having accepted the offer of a brandy, David sat down on a nearby settee and surveyed the night's amusement. A half-dozen young women stood or sat in languorous poses around the parlor.

They were in various stages of undress from the almost fully clothed to the almost not at all, but all were indisputably lovely. Pleasantly surprised by the caliber of the house—an impression backed up by the really quite good brandy—his eye settled on a curvaceous brunette. The merest inclination of his burnished head was sufficient to bring her swiftly to his side. She smiled engagingly as she settled onto his lap.

They were just beginning the enjoyable process of getting

better acquainted when David's composure received a rude and unexpected jolt. Emerging from a door at the top of the nearby stairs was a tall, handsome man impeccably dressed in a dark frock coat and trousers. His dark-blond hair was streaked with silver and his aquiline features were weathered, but otherwise he looked little different from when David had last seen him eight years before in London.

Paul Delamare. The man who had engineered David's own escape during the Reign of Terror. The man who had helped to bring about the overthrow of the mad Jacobins and restore France to sanity. Only to be exiled by the one man who most understood the danger he represented—Napoleon Bonaparte.

Paul Delamare. David's brother-in-law. Yet he was not in Boston where he had lived for many years but here, in Washington, in a brothel. It was not precisely the ideal setting for a reunion.

David rose, unsettling the friendly little brunette. She landed on her butt with a squeal of surprise. He stepped over her absently, his eyes staring at the other man.

Paul was in heated discussion with Madame Colette. That is to say, the madam was heated. Paul himself appeared disdainfully calm.

"Please, *monsieur,* I thought you understood . . . your presence here requires discretion." She waved a hand agitatedly. "The back stairs . . ."

"Enough," Paul cut her off coldly. "I have just come from the side of a young woman who almost died from an abortion. That hasn't put me in the mood to hear about discretion, madam. A little common sense would go a good deal farther."

"Bah, that Felicia is a bad egg," Madame Colette said

dismissively. "She should be glad I troubled myself so far as to send for you."

Paul's topaz eyes narrowed to dangerous slits as he surveyed the woman. "And you should be glad she is still alive, madam. Pray that she remains so. Even the Washington authorities, lax though they are, have been known to ask questions when young women die under such circumstances."

Madame Colette blanched. Though she paid the usual skim, she wasn't so deluded as to think that afforded her blanket protection. Worse yet, if she got a reputation for running an establishment where unfortunate events occurred, she could say goodbye to the most profitable trade. Wealthy men tended to be fastidious about such things; they could afford to be.

Abruptly changing her mood, she said, "I really can't thank you enough, Doctor, for coming as you did. It was most kind."

"Not at all," Paul replied. He meant exactly that. Simple human decency prevented him from ever turning his back on anyone in need.

Madame smiled. "As to your fee..." She waved a hand toward the assorted young women. "You seem to find yourself alone tonight..."

A look of distaste flitted across Paul's handsome features. Clearly, nothing could be of less appeal. He was about to tell her so when he stopped abruptly. His gaze fell on the tall young man studying him from a few yards away.

He took a step forward, a tentative smile curving his mouth. "David...?"

His answer was a broad grin and the flashing laughter that reminded him so much of his beloved Dominique.

"By God," David murmured as the two embraced, "I

would never have thought to find you here. I thought you were still in Boston with my sister."

"I was until three days ago," Paul said. "Sweet Lord, it really is you. You've . . . changed." The gangly, slightly awkward youth he had known on his last visit to England was gone. This was a man, solid as the rock-hard muscles beneath his elegant frock coat and confident in a way that spoke volumes about what he had experienced in the last few years.

"You've stayed just the same," David said with a smile. "I knew there would be no time for me to come see you and Dominique in Boston before I returned to France, but now we can at least spend a little time together. Unless . . . Dominique isn't here, is she?"

Paul shook his head. "Not yet, though she will be joining me soon. And why didn't you let us know you were coming? We would have made plans to join you here."

"It's all rather on the quiet," David said, still grinning. "Government business, you know. But enough of that. By God, it's good to see you!"

Paul heartily agreed. They stood eying each other with unalloyed delight until Madame Colette intervened. Clearly, the sight of two men so enjoying each other set her nerves on edge. Perhaps that was only to be expected given her profession.

"Ah, gentlemen . . ." she began, "since you know each other, perhaps you would like to take a late supper in one of our private rooms. I could arrange for several young ladies to join you." If, her manner implied, they wouldn't be entirely superfluous.

Paul and David exchanged a look as both men broke out laughing. Paul recovered first. "Thank you, madame, but no. I have another place in mind." More sternly, he added, "Remember what I told you. Should Felicia take a turn for the worse, send for me at once."

Glumly, Madame Colette nodded. She saw them off with a mixture of relief and regret. That the two most attractive men to ever visit her establishment should prefer each other's company to that of her girls was enough to make her shake her head over the foibles of human nature.

"How long have you been in town?" Paul asked as they proceeded down the cobblestone street. It was by now very late. Most of Washington was at home in bed, or at least considering going there. Even the peddlers had retired for the night.

"A few days," David replied. He forbore mentioning any details of the reason for his visit. Paul's present feelings about the French emperor were unknown, but David doubted they were overly charitable. "What about you?"

"I arrived this afternoon to confer with members of the government about the conditions our soldiers are living under. They're appalling, as I've tried to convince people of for several years now. No matter how many times I come here, I don't seem to make much headway. But enough of that. I was called to Madame Colette's almost immediately. Fortunately, the friends I'm staying with are very understanding."

"Why you?" David asked. "Surely there are doctors here in Washington whom Madame could call on."

Paul grimaced. "Indeed there are, but they aren't anxious to take care of so-called fallen women. Not that they necessarily deny themselves their services. By the way," he added, "I hate to lecture you when we've only just met after so long, but you know you really would be well advised to be more prudent in your amusements. Even the best-run brothel can be a breeding place for disease."

Always the doctor, David thought with a faint smile. Paul could no more stop trying to keep people healthy than he could stop breathing. The irresistible desire to heal had shaped his entire life. That and his love for Dominique.

"Actually," David said. "I don't frequent such places. It was only that..." He broke off, discovering himself less than anxious to explain his difficulty even to one so understanding as his brother-in-law.

"Good, good," Paul was saying. "Then I needn't apologize for dragging you off. The mention of a late supper reminded me, I haven't eaten all day. Would you care to join me?"

"Certainly," David agreed. "Where would you suggest?"

"The best place in Washington," Paul said. "Indeed, the only place for good food and a decent bottle of wine. The Wild Geese."

"Ah, yes..." David murmured, "the Wild Geese."

"You've discovered it then?"

"Actually, I'm staying there."

"Excellent choice," Paul assured him. "You couldn't do better. Annabel Riordan—I presume you've met her—is a true marvel."

"She certainly is that," David said under his breath, wondering what the "marvel" would make of it when he arrived in such respected company. Perhaps she would at least be a bit less anxious to throw him out again.

In fact, Annabel didn't even notice him at first. It was late, she was tired, and for a moment all she saw was the face of her old friend, Paul Delamare.

"Paul," she exclaimed, her weariness fading in a rush of

genuine pleasure. "It's so good to see ye again, but where is Dominique? Donna say ye're here without her."

"Only briefly," he assured her.

David's eyes narrowed as his brother-in-law caught Annabel in a quick, unmistakably affectionate hug. It was absurd to be jealous of what was so clearly no more than a demonstration of friendship, and yet that was undeniably how he felt. Jealous of a tavern-keeping hoyden with an adder's tongue. What would the world dream up next?

"David . . . ?"

Realizing that Paul was waiting for him, David shook himself from his reverie and managed a smile.

"This is my brother-in-law," the good doctor was saying, "David de Montfort. But I presume you've met already. He tells me he's staying here."

"Hmmm," Annabel murmured. She took a quick step back and glared at David narrowly from beneath her thick lashes. "I had no idea you had family in America, *monsieur*."

Or anywhere else, David added for himself. By the look she was giving him, he might have hatched from a large and not very attractive egg.

"Dominique is my sister," he explained sweetly. "As is Nicole, for that matter. I take it you've met her?"

Annabel shook her head. She was clearly still grappling with the notion of him being related to people she not only knew but truly liked.

"Nicole has stayed in Boston," Paul explained, "when Dominique and I made our trips here. But she'll be joining us this time."

David grinned. He'd last seen the younger of his sisters three years before when she visited him in France. Being responsible for an irrepressible young woman who also happened to be stunningly beautiful had proven enlightening. When she left, he'd been torn between missing her and being grateful for simply having survived the experience.

"And how is Nicole?" he asked.

"Much the same," Paul replied with an understanding smile. "But come, let's see what we can persuade Annabel to provide for us. It's not too late for supper, I hope?"

She shook her head absently, her russet hair dancing in the firelight. "There's a haunch of beef with dumplings and cold beans. The pork roast is gone but we've still the chicken. Oh, and there's shad in jelly."

Before they could comment, she murmured, "I'll bring it all, you can pick what you like." She hurried off toward the kitchen.

"Let's sit then," Paul said after a moment. A smile danced in his eyes as he took a chair opposite his brother-in-law. David had a peculiar look about him, almost like a man about to put his foot into a wolf trap and curiously looking forward to the experience.

When they were seated with a bottle of wine and two glasses in front of them, Paul said, "A great deal has happened since we last saw each other. Where shall we begin?"

"With you," David said promptly. "Tell me more about what's been bringing you to Washington."

Taking note of his brother-in-law's reluctance to talk about himself, Paul answered succinctly. "Typhoid, that and several other types of fever that tend to run wild down here. It seems the government has woken up belatedly to the fact that they're building their capital on one of the unhealthiest spots in the country."

"Seems they should have thought of that sooner," David murmured, thinking of his own recent brush with ill health.

Paul shrugged. "They should have thought of a whole lot of things. But as you'll learn soon enough, nothing ever happens here until its too late. Or almost."

That was hardly encouraging news, though it didn't surprise David. There was a languor about Washington that extended far beyond its fancy houses. Perhaps it had to do with the steamy temperatures or the overbrilliance of the sun or the frequent mists that rose from the river. Whatever the cause, the place seemed to engender a "wait-and-see" attitude of immense proportions.

"You've done this kind of work before, haven't you?" David asked.

Paul nodded. "I became interested in the seasonal spread of disease while I was still in France. Cholera was wiping out a good part of the army and I thought that . . ."

He broke off, a shadow passing over his handsome face as he remembered the circumstances that had put a stop to his research. Bad though cholera was, the Reign of Terror had been worse. They had all been lucky to escape with their lives. David and Nicole had been children, but that wouldn't have saved them from the guillotine.

"Well, it doesn't matter what I thought. At any rate, I've made several trips down here while trying to get matters in Boston settled enough so that I could leave them for awhile. That's finally worked out."

David nodded. He knew that Paul managed a large medical practice while also teaching at Harvard University's School of Medicine. His talents were constantly in demand and he never refused to share them.

"You said you're staying with friends?" David asked. He

was aware that he was making small talk, at least to some extent. He needed to while he worked out what he was going to tell Paul about his own reasons for being in the capital.

The older man nodded. "They have a house not too far out of town but rather more comfortable than most. They'll be leaving shortly themselves for business in the South. Dominique will miss seeing them."

Casually, David asked, "I got the impression that you and Dominique are both friends of our hostess." He hesitated a moment. "Is that . . . sort of thing common over here?"

Paul sat back in his chair and regarded him over the wine. "I'm not quite sure what you mean."

David frowned. He'd be willing to bet that his brother-in-law knew perfectly well what lay behind the question. He merely found it amusing to pretend otherwise. So be it.

"I mean," David said succinctly, "that I find it odd enough for a young woman to be running a tavern while also claiming to retain her respectability, apparently strictly by her own definition. When you add to it that all sorts of people, including some from the best walks of life, seem happy to claim her acquaintance, I admit to being a little surprised."

With a gesture that was almost apologetic, he added, "Things like that simply don't happen in France . . . or in England for that matter."

"England I can understand," Paul said quietly. "They're still steeped in aristocracy over there. But French had a chance to throw off all the nonsense."

"Aristocracy isn't nonsense," David refuted quietly. "It's the natural order of things."

Paul muttered a word that was short and to the point, if

also obscene. "There's nothing natural about any man—or woman, for that matter—believing themselves superior to another simply by virtue of birth. It's what you do with your life that counts."

"I agree, but those born into a certain level of society naturally contribute more. Oh, I grant you there are exceptions but for the most part it's the circumstances of a man's birth that determine his character. And character *is* all."

"At least we can agree on that," Paul said with a faint smile, "if nothing else. At any rate, Miss Riordan is . . . unusual. I met her when she went to the aid of a man who had been struck by a wagon. He was trapped under one of the wheels. She happened to get to him first and was trying to lift it off."

David's eyebrows rose at the thought of the small, fine-boned woman attempting any such thing. "Surely she knew she wouldn't be able to?"

"I have no idea if she knew it or not. In fact, I'd rather doubt it. Annabel is one of those rare individuals who simply presumes she can do anything she sets her mind to. The odd thing is that more often than not, she turns out to be right."

David took a sip of his wine and stared down into the glass. Softly, he said, "She may have saved my life. I became suddenly ill a few days ago. My landlord thought it advisable to leave me in the street. Annabel brought me here and nursed me back to health, at not inconsiderable risk to herself."

"I can't say that surprises me," Paul said. "It's the sort of thing she would do. And it proves my point: people from all walks of life are capable of acting nobly—or ignobly—depending on their individual character."

David was about to reply but stopped as he glimpsed Annabel approaching their table. Her cheeks were flushed and stray tendrils of her hair wafted gently around her slender throat. She did not look at him as she set down several platters. Delectable aromas rose to tantalize them.

"If there's anything else . . . ?" she said.

Paul gave her a kindly smile. "I don't think there possibly could be."

She nodded quickly and turned away, but not before her eyes met David's. For a moment, they stared at one another. In that single glance was a world of meaning—and doubt. Then she was gone, leaving only the memory of her scent and the soft murmur of fabric against her body.

He picked up his knife and fork, and prepared to eat. But though the food was excellent and the company superb, he found he had no appetite.

Or at least not any that could be satisfied.

DESPITE all that he had on his mind, David slept soundly that night. His body, vigorous though it was, was still in the process of recovering. Even had he wished to stay awake, nature would not have permitted him to do so, which was fortunate since it prevented him from hearing Annabel tossing and turning in the room above. She tried every device she knew to court sleep, but failed.

Each time she closed her eyes, she saw the Frenchman, his high-and-mighty lordship, he of the flashing smile and oddly sorrowful shadows. She saw and moreover felt the racing attraction between them whenever they were in the same room. When she did slip into a half-conscious doze, she dreamt, encounters from which she awoke with a pounding heart and her breath rushing, her body yearning.

Finally she gave up. Long before the goat brayed, she left her bed, dressed, and slipped downstairs. In the gray half-light before dawn, the air was actually cool. She stood at the open door, savoring it.

Her skin remembered the touch of such air even if her mind barely did. The air of Ireland was cool like this, slightly moist and fragrant with nature's scents. As a child, she had lived enveloped in it, cushioned for a time from the harshness of the world beyond. Not until her parents died and she was sent away did she understand how precious her childhood idyll had been.

Her hand slipped down lightly to the flatness beneath her waist. She would have liked to give a child of her own the same love and security she had once known, but for a much longer time. Sometimes her arms ached as though for something they had never held, yet still remembered.

"Ye're addled, Annabel Riordan," she murmured to herself. "Just what ye need, a tribe of wee ones clinging to yer skirts. Ye've seen what childbearing does to a woman—wears her down, puts her in thrall to a man, robs her of any chance for a better life. Or else she has to turn her back on her bairns an' go off after her star, never minding what happens to them."

Remorse darted through her for having such a thought. It was true that her mother had left her to go with her father on the ill-fated journey that cost both their lives. But Constance Riordan believed in what she was doing, she had acted out of the desire to make a better life for her child and all others. And surely she hadn't foreseen the deaths that would rob a small girl of the only safety she had ever known. If she had known her fate, she wouldn't have gone.

She told herself there was no merit in turning over things best left still. Worse yet, the small hours were no time to be doing it. If she was up, then she should be working. Nothing was better for banishing ill thoughts.

Minutes later, she was settled in the kitchen, busily chopping carrots and potatoes for the stew she'd decided to make. Cameron found her there when he popped in his head.

" 'Mornin'," he rumbled deeply. "You're up early."

"And ye're up late," she said with a smile. "Just getting in?"

He nodded without explanation. Lately, the big Scotsman had taken to coming and going at odd hours. Annabel suspected he'd acquired a mistress, but never asked. His privacy was his own.

He settled at the big oak worktable with a cup of tea he made for himself. Cameron was a self-sufficient man; it didn't seem to occur to him that women should wait on him. Not for the first time, Annabel found herself wishing that she might have reacted to him as she did to the damn Frenchman. Nature was oddly perverse sometimes.

"There's news," Cameron said after a bit. "Two more merchant ships have been sunk, the *Carlisle* out of New York and the *Princess McGee* from Charleston. It looks like the survivors will go to the press gangs. Meanwhile, the Brits are still saying there'll be no terms. They're in to the end this time."

Annabel cursed softly under her breath. Since its beginning the year before, the war had been largely a bloody stalemate, at least on land. On the seas, it was different. There the British Navy ruled, running down American merchant ships seemingly at will, sending them to the deep and making virtual slaves of any crew members who survived. And all the while, the government of President James

Madison seemed able to do nothing except argue among themselves.

"The Brits can't win, Cam," Annabel said, praying she was right. "I know they aren't the worst people on the face of the earth, but they've got some damn strange ideas about how things ought to be. This place...this America...is different. It deserves a chance."

"It'll have to fight to get it," the big man said. "And do a hell of a better job than it has so far." He was silent for a moment before he said, "Annabel, do you ever think, if you had to leave here, where you'd go?"

She shot him a startled glance. "Leave? Why would I do that?"

He smiled gently. "If these 'Brits' you're not too fond of should happen to come calling, you might want to be somewhere else."

Her eyes widened. "Ye don't really think it could come to that...?"

"I think it doesn't do any harm to be prepared. The government sure isn't doing it, neither is the Army, and the Navy's a joke. So it might not be a bad idea to give it some thought ourselves."

"I don't know..." she murmured, thoroughly confused. Leave the Wild Geese when she had worked so hard to make it a success? Where would she go? What would she do?

"It might only be temporary," Cameron said soothingly. "If the Brits do win, they'll want the taverns open for sure. You'll just have to grit your teeth as you take their money. All I'm saying is that if they come and if it's the way I think it might be, you could be wanting to be away for awhile."

"Aye, and *if* ye're right, so will every man jack in this town. How do ye imagine I'll fare against them?"

Cameron didn't answer directly but his expression suggested that he had been considering exactly that point. Gently, he said, "I've a friend who keeps a skiff on the river, down at the bottom of Red Wharf. We've had a talk and it's agreed, if you need the boat, it'll be there for you. Just keep it in mind, is all I ask."

Annabel was taken aback. She'd had no idea that Cameron saw the situation in such serious terms, much less that he'd given such thought to her own well-being. For a moment, she couldn't respond. Then she reached over and squeezed his hand gently.

"Thank ye, my friend," she said. "I'll remember yer kindness."

"Remember the boat, too," he advised, flushing slightly.

She laughed and leaned over, brushing her lips against his shadowed cheek. "That I'll do, Cameron, but first I'll remember this fine stew. If I don't put it on now, it'll not be fit . . ."

Halfway out of her seat, she stopped. Standing in the door of the kitchen, his white shirt half undone down his broad chest and a jacket slung carelessly over his shoulder, stood David.

His hair was disheveled, but his breeches were perfectly fitted and his boots shone. Clearly, such sartorial splendor, even casually acquired, did nothing to guarantee his mood. The look on his face suggested he could cheerfully have throttled both of them.

"What sweet domesticity," the marquis drawled. "Pray, don't let me interrupt."

"Pray, don't make an ass out of yerself," Cameron said.

He stood up, stared hard at them both, and took his teacup over to the wash basin. "Miss Annabel and I have been discussing the situation here in Washington. I've been trying to convince her to consider leaving, should the need arise."

"Do you think it will?" David asked. He took a seat at the table, ignoring Annabel's frown, and looked matter-of-factly at the Scotsman.

"It could," Cameron said. "It depends on what your Napoleon does. If he keeps the British busy on the Continent, they won't have the men to wage a full war over here. On the other hand, if he loses . . ."

"Don't even mention the possibility," David said with a slight smile. "The emperor is infallible."

"And the Russian snows were damn deep," Cameron said. He dried off his cup, put it back on the shelf, and prepared to leave.

At the door, he turned. "Your emperor ignored a fundamental fact of nature. He marched two hundred thousand men into Russia and he lost almost every one of them. The Greeks called that *hubris*, pride so great it begs for destruction. Unless your man's changed more than most humans can, he'll pay the piper 'fore long."

Silence followed in the wake of his leaving. Finally, David said, "He's an interesting man, your friend."

"That's right," Annabel said, still eying him furiously. "My friend, and don't ye be goin' around suggestin' anything else."

The marquis had the grace to look contrite, or at least try to. "I'm sorry. It's a terrible habit I have, jumping to conclusions."

Annabel guessed that looking so heart-stoppingly desirable at such an ungodly hour was also a terrible habit of his.

"Never mind," Annabel said. "I suppose ye'll be wantin' breakfast."

"If it isn't too much trouble."

Humility didn't suit him, Annabel thought as she took bread from a large tin box and began slicing it. That done, she set a skillet over a trivet on the hearth and broke eggs into it. As they cooked, she cut off generous portions from a side of bacon and fried them separately. Meanwhile, she started tea steeping in the water always kept hot in a kettle hung over the fire.

All this she did automatically, having done the same tasks almost every morning of her life. David watched her graceful movements appreciatively. It startled him to realize that with all the meals he must have consumed in his twenty-two years, he had almost never seen one prepared. The process was more involved than he would have expected.

When the food was ready, Annabel hesitated. "If ye'll be wantin' to eat in the main room . . ."

"I'd rather stay here, if you don't mind."

She shrugged to show that it meant nothing to her one way or the other, but in fact his continued presence made her acutely uncomfortable. She refused to meet his eyes as she set the plate before him.

"Aren't you going to join me?" he asked.

"I'm not hungry." When he still hesitated, she added, "Go on then, before it gets cold."

He fell to obediently and quickly demolished the food. Meanwhile, she kept her back turned, stirring the stew far more than was needed and tending to various other tasks that could easily have waited.

When he was done, he surprised her by bringing his plate

over to the sink. "Here," he said as he took the pump handle from her, "I'll do that."

"Looks like whatever Cam's got, it must be catchin'," she murmured.

At the mention of the Scotsman, David's eyes narrowed. "What's that?"

"No matter. You don't have to do that. I'm sure you'd rather be on your way." Which was about as loud a hint as she could drop. Not that he seemed inclined to take it.

"I'm in no hurry," David told her with a smile. "The fish will wait."

"The fish . . . ?"

"Oh, didn't I mention I'm going fishing this morning? Perhaps you'd care to join me."

Fishing. The grand marquis in his fancy clothes and his lordly manner mucking about with fish hooks and bait. The image was incongruous, to say the least.

"Don't you believe me?" he asked, his smile deepening. "I happen to be quite good at it. Come along and you'll see."

"I can't . . . that is, I've things to do here."

"And people to do them for you. Besides, we won't be back late."

"But . . . aren't there things you're supposed to be doing? Seeing people and the like?"

He had the most intriguing lines around his eyes when he smiled, Annabel thought. And the corners of his mouth turned up in the most enticing way, making it look not hard at all.

"There's only one person I'm interested in seeing," David explained, "and that's President Madison, who happened to pick today to go off inspecting his troops, such as they are. He won't be back until tomorrow, leaving me at sadly loose ends.''

"An' your solution is to go fishin'?''

He appeared wounded by her skepticism. "Fishing is a noble endeavor. It offers the opportunity of communion with nature while providing obvious practical benefits. Some of the greatest scientists and philosophers have been fishermen. Did you know there's a school of thought that Sir Isaac Newton discovered gravity not when an apple dropped on his head but when he dropped his fish hook into a trout pond on his estate? Makes a good deal more sense if you ask me. What would you get from an apple dropping on your head besides a headache?''

Annabel laughed. This whimsical side of the marquis was most unexpected and appealing. She was almost tempted . . .

"I canna remember the last time I was fishin','' she admitted.

"What? Why that's terrible. One should always know precisely the last time one was fishing. I don't see how you've managed. Still, we can fix it simply enough.''

No, Annabel thought, not simply. There was nothing at all simple about going off to spend the day with him. Still, the bright morning beckoned. It had been so long since she'd broken with routine, done something daring and impetuous, something . . . romantic.

"All right," she said suddenly before her wiser self could stop her. "I'll go.''

"Splendid,'' he murmured, looking down at her from his great height. "The fish and I will be eternally grateful.''

He opened the door with a flourish and waved her through. As she passed, her arm brushed his, and warmth pooled in a knot near her midsection. For a moment, it was very hard to breathe. She clenched her fists to keep them from trembling and stuck her chin in the air. Not for anything would she let him see how he affected her.

So busy was she at concealing her own reactions that she didn't notice his. At the merest touch of her skin against his, David's body had hardened to a startling degree. His eyes narrowed to mere slits. The infinitely masculine gaze that followed Annabel would not have reassured her in the least.

She might have wondered what exactly he was after that fine morning. The fish darting like silver ghosts among the shoals and eddies of the river? Or the girl wrapped in a fiery veil of pride and dreams through which no man had ever reached.

Yet.

❧ CHAPTER ❧
Seven

"**Y**OU know," David said as he leaned back against the trunk of an old oak tree growing beside the Potomac, "Cameron had a good point when he said you should think about how you'd get out."

"Not ye, too," Annabel said. She was loath to break the peaceful mood between them, if only because it was so unexpected.

The river flowed slowly near their feet, birds chirped in the laurel bushes, the fish were cooperative without being overly demanding. All in all, it was turning out to be a perfect morning.

Until David suddenly raised the specter of the war that seemed so far from the hazy capital . . . but wasn't.

"I only meant," he went on, ignoring her resistance, "that sometimes it pays to think ahead. You Americans aren't terribly well organized. 'Ragtag' is the term that comes to mind. The British could prevail this time despite themselves.''

"What do ye mean, 'despite'?'' Annabel asked. ''I thought they were doing everything they possibly could to win?''

"Oh, they are . . . for them. But they're great bumblers. It comes from having too many people in charge and not enough people actually doing the work. That and the fact that they tend to be very inflexible in their attitudes. What worked in 1066 is still good enough today. That sort of thing.''

"It sounds," Annabel said, "as though ye donna think much of them.''

"On the contrary, I have the greatest respect for the British. Why not, since I'm half British myself?''

He flashed her a sudden smile before he added more seriously, ''They do have a great tradition of plugging away long enough and hard enough until they eventually crack whatever it is that they're after. The price they pay may be absolutely appalling, but they never seem to mind that.''

"I know," Annabel said softly. Her face, flushed by the sun, suddenly had gone pale. The slender hands holding the fishing rod shone white at the knuckles. ''But ye've got it a little wrong. It isn't the price to them that's so horrible, it's what they force others to pay.''

David was silent for a moment, looking at her. His eyes were gentler than she had yet seen them. ''It sounds as though you're speaking from personal experience.''

So long a time passed without her responding that David wondered if she had decided to ignore the comment. But at length, she said, "My parents were at Vinegar Hill in '98. Does that mean anything to ye?"

It was his turn to be silent. Finally, he replied, "I was at school in England at the time. I remember the ... incident quite well."

A faint, sad smile curved her mouth. " 'Incident.' Yes, I can imagine that's what the British called it. Good Irishmen— Catholic and Protestant both—rose in rebellion because they could no longer stand being killed and brutalized. Fifty thousand of them died like cattle at the slaughter, my parents among them. And the British call it an 'incident,' like something that happened between a lorry and a dog on the road."

"I'm sorry," David murmured. It was utterly inadequate and he knew it, but he had no idea what else to say. That this beautiful, proud woman should have borne such anguish hurt him deeply. That she should hold him and his kind responsible was almost more than he could bear.

Thickly, he asked, "What happened to you afterward?"

She shrugged. "My aunt and uncle were already in the New World and they sent word that they'd take me. I didn't want to leave, but young as I was, I knew there was nothin' left for me in Ireland. America offered a better chance, maybe the only one."

David sighed deeply. He was no stranger to the achingly personal effects of violence, but each time he confronted them, his hurt and anger were born anew. How long would it be before people stopped inflicting such pain on one another? A hundred years ... a thousand? Or would time simply run out and the dream die unrealized?

Refusing to dwell on such thoughts, he lifted his fishing

hook from the water and set the rod down beside the tree. "Let's see what we've got for lunch," he said.

Annabel followed suit. The simple pleasure of fishing had paled beneath the onslaught of her memories. She was glad enough to turn her attention to other things, however mundane.

They had stopped on their way to the river to buy a loaf of bread, some cheese, and a bottle of wine. Annabel had protested the extravagance, saying they could have brought all those things with them. But David had brushed her objections aside. If a day to be spent fishing wasn't also a day to throw frugality to the wind, what was it?

Privately doubting that he had ever been frugal a day in his life, Annabel had complied. Now she was glad that she had. The wine had been set to chill in the river, secured by a length of the same cord David used for their fishing lines. It was now pleasantly crisp when poured into the exquisite crystal goblets he nonchalantly removed from the pack he'd been carrying.

"Do ye always travel in such style?" Annabel asked bemusedly. She gazed down at the sunlight fracturing within the crystal into radiant colors.

"A man has to have some standards," he replied. Delicate, hand-painted plates followed, accompanied by fine damask napkins. There was even a silver setting for each of them, the knives, forks, and spoons perfectly polished, undoubtedly by the long-suffering Pomfret.

He filled both their glasses before matter-of-factly rolling up his sleeves and setting about the business of making a fire while Annabel watched him. The wine was sweet on her tongue, the sun was warm on her skin. She felt dangerously relaxed, yet at the same time tensely expectant. This man of contradictions seemed able to fill her with the same.

"Ye do that very well," she murmured.

"Thank you. Turn your head if you don't like seeing fish cleaned."

Annabel, who had scraped more than her share of scales in the past, continued to watch him. He worked smoothly and efficiently, without wasted motions. The razor-sharp knife fit his big, burnished hand perfectly. She had a sudden conviction that he had used the knife in other ways under different circumstances, but did not pursue that.

Instead, she said, "Is it the fashion these days for the French nobility to play at being peasants?"

Far from being offended, as he might have been, he laughed softly. "It's the fashion to be useful. We found out the hard way that being superfluous carried too high a price."

"Yer title . . ." Annabel said slowly, "does it date from before the Revolution?"

His attention still on the fish, David nodded. "By several hundred years."

He glanced up in time to see her frown and knew what she was thinking. So many thousands had died during the Reign of Terror that it was hard to believe that a few remnants of the old aristocracy still remained.

"I survived," David said softly, "by the grace of God, and the help of Paul Delamare. Didn't he or Dominique ever tell you that story?"

Annabel shook her head slowly. "I've never heard either of them speak of anything except their life here in America."

"I suppose that's understandable. They left painful memories behind when they were exiled from France."

Annabel's eyes widened to reflect the cloudless sky. "Exiled? I had no idea of that. What happened?"

Briefly, he explained. "Paul inherited the title of Marquis de Rochford from his father, but he believed that France should be a republic and he helped to lead the fight to that end. Unfortunately, everything went terribly wrong. Paul got my sisters and myself safely to England but then he went back to France to work for the overthrow of those who had launched the Reign of Terror. He still hoped that France would become a republic. Instead, Napoleon came to power and Paul eventually realized that he had to leave. He and Dominique came here, or more properly, to Boston."

David paused, frowning slightly. "I have to admit, I thought they would settle in England. As an exile from Napoleon, Paul was perfectly welcomed there. But all he was willing to do was visit occasionally. After the current unpleasantness began, even that had to stop."

"I can't imagine him living in England," Annabel said firmly. "Not when he still has enough faith in people to believe that they should be free."

"Yes," David said softly, "I suppose that is exactly what he thinks."

The fact that David didn't think so lay between them, unspoken and undenied. She sensed that his curiously dispassionate recital of what had happened concealed a great deal more.

He could only have been a child during the Reign of Terror. How many had he seen die? How close had he come to death himself at the hands of the mob? No wonder he so distrusted people who wanted to change the old, ordered way of society. People like her parents . . . like herself.

The gulf separating them had never seemed wider. Staring into its depths, Annabel said the only thing she could think of, "I'll cook the fish."

He let her, after he had made sure that the fire was right. Sitting back against the tree, wine glass in hand, he closed his eyes and tried not to listen to the soft sound of her movements.

It had been a mistake to ask her to come with him. Why had he done so? Had he really imagined that they could share a simple, pleasurable day together as though they were—what? Friends? Lovers? Equals?

None of the three was true, although they all had an odd sense of rightness to him. Women and men were never friends, except possibly in very rare cases such as his sister and brother-in-law. Similarly, men and women were virtually never equals. The natural order decreed that men ruled and women obeyed.

His mouth quirked in a smile. Somehow, he didn't think Annabel was capable of much obedience. Fiery independence and prickly pride, yes. Obedience, no. But then, it was a long time since he'd found compliant women anything other than boring.

Which brought him to the third possibility: Lovers.

He had wanted her from the first moment he saw her in the crowded tavern, through a mob of hungry, sweating men. Each moment he spent with her increased his desire. She was more than merely beautiful. She was knowledge and innocence, purity and sensuality brought together so enticingly that his loins ached when merely looking at her.

And yet—she was also a person who could laugh and frown, undoubtedly even cry. She was a woman who could take him into her home at risk to herself and her business simply because it was the right thing to do. Although she had lost her parents in a devastating act of violence, she had found the courage to rebuild her life in a far land.

In short, she was a tempting, bedeviling, fascinating problem.

A flash of sunlight touched her fire-tempered hair. She raised a hand to push back a tumbled curl and their eyes met. The last sip of wine he had taken slipped coolly and invitingly down his throat. It was suddenly very still.

"Annabel . . ." Her name was a whisper on the air, soft, enticing, soothing.

"The fish are ready," she said. Her voice sounded strange even to herself, thin and somehow breathless. Quickly, she slid the golden-edged trout onto the plates and reached for her wine glass too quickly. Her hand struck at an awkward angle. For a moment, the goblet teetered as she grabbed for it. Too late. The crystal shattered against a nearby rock even as her hand closed around it.

"*Ohhh . . .*" Her scream was one of surprise more than pain. Blood oozed from her palm, falling in droplets onto the soft grass.

Instantly, David was at her side. He took hold of her hand, pressing firmly on the wrist, and gently pried her fingers loose.

"Let me see," he murmured.

Wordlessly, she obeyed. His touch was unexpectedly comforting. She could feel the pain now but it was as though it came from a distance. Another, more demanding, sensation crowded in on her.

His skin was very warm. She could feel the heat of it through his fine linen shirt and the cotton chemise she wore. He smelled of crisp soap, sun, and polished leather. His hair gleamed in the sun like the pelt of a mighty animal. It was slightly long, curling at the nape of his neck. She wondered how he had escaped Pomfret's ministrations.

He looked up suddenly, catching her gaze. The look in his blue eyes was so grim that she blinked.

"It's all right," she said. Somehow it didn't seem strange that she should be reassuring him instead of the other way around.

"Come over to the stream," he said huskily. With his arm around her, she did as he said. They knelt together beside the clear, rushing water. He removed a finely made linen handkerchief from his pocket and wet it thoroughly, then pressed it to her palm.

"Paul should see to this," he said, staring down at the slow seepage of blood through the cloth.

Annabel shook her head. "Don't be daft. It's nothing but a little cut. Oh, I'm sorry about the glass."

"Do you think I care anything about that?" he demanded. Anger flared in him. Her hand was so small and slight yet he could feel the calluses where incessant work had worn the skin rough.

That wasn't right. She should be pampered and cared for, not struggling and alone. She should be surrounded by luxury, bejeweled, lying on silk, aroused and waiting . . . for him.

His head dropped, blotting out the sun. Kneeling beside the river, alone in the high summer day, her blood warm and sticky on his skin, he kissed her. His mouth was hard but the force behind it was held in iron control. Instinctively, he did not want to frighten her, for her innocence was still an open question, although he sensed that she had very little, if any experience. The thought of doing anything that would shock or disgust her made him wince. He had never given any particular thought to a woman's feelings before, since he had always been blithely certain that the way they threw themselves at him made such thought unnecessary.

Annabel was different. How, exactly, he didn't know, but the sight of her hurt and bleeding had struck him to a depth he had never before known. Surely, he would not have reacted so strongly had he been the one injured. But her pain and her fear were something else.

A tremor ran through him. She was stiff in his arms but she did not try to pull away. Her lips were soft, her breath fragrant. He could feel the gentle swell of her breasts against his chest. Slowly, tentatively, she began to relax. A faint sound came from her.

He deepened the kiss, still gentle, still holding himself in check. Such restraint cost him dearly. He was on fire with need for her, every muscle in his body clenched. The throbbing pressure of his loins was almost unbearable. He could not remember when he had so desired a woman, or when he had been so close to losing control.

That, more than anything, stopped him.

Self-control, the certain knowledge that he would never betray himself, had more than once been his salvation. To throw it away now, over a woman no less, was unthinkable.

Annabel dimly felt the change in him. She was afloat on a dream of pleasure. Her own responsiveness stunned her. Never had she imagined that she could feel this way. The touch of his mouth on hers, the closeness of his body, the strength of his arms all enraptured her. She might have gone on forever, lost to the world and all concern, had not she realized that something was wrong.

David raised his head. His eyes were hooded; she could

catch only a glimpse of whatever was passing through his mind but that was enough to make her shiver. He seemed to be withdrawing behind a shield she could not penetrate. Although he still held her, he might as well have pushed her away.

Quickly, she jumped up. Her hand brushed her mouth, now swollen and tender. She saw the wound on her palm, the bleeding stopped, and her trembling increased.

"Annabel..." he murmured, close behind her.

"No," she said, warding him off. "I'm fine but that... that was a mistake."

He couldn't disagree. The desperate, burning need he had glimpsed in himself was almost terrifying. He wanted to bury it deep where he would never again have to admit that such yearning existed. And yet...

Oh, lord, but she was sweet standing there in the sunlight and the soft breeze, her hair tumbling around her and her clothes slightly disarranged. She looked wanton in the most enchanting sense, a sylvan nymph glimpsed in the depths of a faery wood, gone before a man could be sure that his mind—or his heart—hadn't tricked him.

What nonsense was this, faery wood? He was a rational product of his century, a clear-thinking man with no time or interest for the fey side of life. Leave that to the women and children, and to the dreamers. Give him the straightforward, the knowable and the no-nonsense. He wanted nothing else.

"The fish are getting cold," he said, trying to break the spell he felt drawing them together.

Annabel sat down again on the ground, hoping he couldn't read the confusion she felt inside. She took the handkerchief he had given her and deftly tied it around her palm, using her teeth to secure the knot. Then she picked up her plate and began to eat.

The trout tasted like sand, which she knew could not be. Undoubtedly, it was as sweet and succulent as always. But she was shut away from such enjoyment. Her body felt numb, as though a deep, icy coldness had suddenly sprung up within her.

Slowly, his eyes on her, David sat down and followed suit. They did not speak as the meal was finished. Nor did they exchange many words on the walk back to the inn. Both were deep in their thoughts, and both were experiencing an unfamiliar self-consciousness as startling as it was inhibiting.

Finally, at the door to the tavern, David said softly, "I meant what I said, Paul should look at your hand."

"I'll stop by and see him later," Annabel murmured.

Her ready acquiescence surprised them both but she was simply too weary to argue. Though the day was still young and she had many hours of work to get through, she felt tired enough to seek her bed. Instead, she lifted her chin and glared at him.

"Let there be no misunderstanding between us, *Monsieur le Marquis*. Tis respectable I am and respectable I'll remain. Nothing else interests me."

He did not respond at once but merely looked at her with fathomless eyes deep as the sea and as impenetrable. Slowly, he smiled.

His breath brushed her cheek as he bent nearer, his voice the merest whisper.

"Liar."

It took a moment for his meaning to sink in. When it did,

fury gripped her. Her fists clenched and her cheeks flushed. Another instant and she would have struck him.

Except that he was gone, striding away as though he hadn't a care in the world. Nothing was left except the soft, elusive sound drifting behind him.

The blackhearted spawn of the devil's own was whistling.

The stableboy coming round the corner stopped cold and stared. He'd had no idea that his beautiful young mistress knew such words nor that she could employ them so effectively.

But then Annabel was full of surprises. As, she vowed, the insufferable marquis would learn to his most profound regret.

❧ CHAPTER ❧
Eight

*T*HE woman who stepped from the carriage was in her late thirties, slender and elegant from the top of her carefully coiffed ebony hair to the bottom of her silk-shod feet. Possessed of sea-green eyes, a perfectly formed nose, and a mouth that was at once sensual and self-possessed, she was startlingly beautiful.

Indeed, so lovely was she that she might have seemed almost inhuman were it not for the air of irrepressible gentleness and femininity that clung to her. She was a woman who cared nothing for appearances and even less for pretenses, as evidenced by her aplomb when confronted with the grubby hand of the small child clinging to her skirt.

"Charles," she murmured, gently reproving, "whatever have you gotten into?"

"Taffy, *maman*," the little boy replied, giving her a grin

that lacked nothing for the absence of two front teeth. "Nicole gave it to me."

"She should know better," Dominique said, catching the eye of the younger woman who was getting out of the carriage behind them. Nicole shrugged philosophically.

"He wanted it."

Dominique suppressed a sigh. She loved her younger sister dearly but she had to admit that Nicole spoiled the children. From the eldest—Jean-Paul who was now thirteen and in boarding school near Boston—to the youngest—baby Charlotte snug in her nurse's arms—Nicole indulged them all.

In between came Elizabeth, at eleven already very much the young lady; Philip, eight; and Charles, six. Charles had supposedly completed their family, Paul and Dominique both agreeing that four children were enough. Baby Charlotte had been a surprise, but one her doting parents were delighted to receive.

The journey from Boston had tired them all. Dominique was glad of Nicole's help as they shepherded the younger children into the house. Discreetly, Nicole withdrew with them to give Dominique and her husband a few minutes alone. They had been parted barely a week but their reunion was still as tenderly passionate as though months had passed.

Her head lying against Paul's broad shoulder, Dominique murmured, "I've missed you, my love."

"And I you," he said gently, his hand stroking her slim back. He never ceased to marvel at how deeply she affected him. Once a solitary man, proud of his independence and self-sufficiency, he had become—as he himself put it—

disgracefully domesticated. Even a few days away from his wife and family were enough to pain him.

"You are well?" he asked, stepping back a pace to look at her. What he saw reassured him. Despite the passage of years and the births of their children, she was little changed from the lovely young girl he had saved from the guillotine twenty years before. Then as now she had invariably looked far more fragile than she really was.

"And the children?" he added when she had assured him that she was perfectly fine.

Dominique smiled. "Apart from being able to wheedle anything they want from Nicole, they're perfect."

Paul laughed. He looked forward to seeing his sister-in-law again although there were times when the two of them did not precisely agree.

Paul loved Nicole as a brother and worried about her. Her refusal to marry despite having reached the age of thirty and her insistence on living apart from the rest of the family concerned him. While he was broad-minded enough to acknowledge that her life was her own, he feared she would ultimately regret the choices she had made.

Not that there was any sign of regret in Nicole when she joined them a few minutes later. As tall as her sister and as slender, she was also beautiful, but in a very different way. Whereas Dominique was all gentle loveliness, Nicole was bolder, more challenging, and more inclined to speak her mind.

Invariably, she frightened some men while others were drawn to her irresistibly only to be turned away by the discovery that she was far stronger and more intelligent than they would ever be.

"I will have you know," Nicole said with a smile, "that I

was very firm with the children. They all agreed that the trip had tired them and they are having a little rest before supper.''

"What did you use to bribe them?'' Paul asked.

Nicole shot him a chiding glance. "Nothing at all. I merely mentioned that I might be available to take them to the market tomorrow, provided that they were all very good.''

"You're too generous to them,'' Dominique said. The gentleness of her tone robbed the words of any reproof. She was about to suggest that they find some other excursion for the children the following day when the drawing-room door opened and a tall young man entered.

"*David*,'' Dominique exclaimed joyfully as she rushed to embrace the brother she had not seen in several years. Although he now towered over her, she still remembered the child he had been, the proud young boy she had struggled so hard to save.

Watching them, Nicole hung back. She had not seen David in an even longer time, having been only twenty-two when she visited him in France. Though he had been kindness itself, he had also made it clear that he thought she should be safely married and having children instead of gallivanting around on her own. She resented his disapproval at the same time that she ached for the closeness they had once known.

When he at last stepped back from Dominique, Nicole smiled tentatively. "Hello, David.''

He hesitated only a moment before embracing her with such tenderness that her gaze blurred. Softly, he said, "You're lovelier than ever, Nickie. I'm so glad to see you.''

"What a surprise," Dominique said. "I had no idea you were here. Paul, why didn't you tell me?"

"I only found out two days ago myself," he explained, "and by that time you were on your way. Apparently," he added with a grin, "David is on some sort of secret mission."

"Are you really?" Nicole demanded. "For Napoleon?" She frowned thoughtfully. "It must have to do with bottling the British up here so that they can't make full use of their resources in Europe. That's his only chance, of course. The business in Russia was really quite absurd."

David agreed but he wasn't about to say so. Instead, he frowned at his sister. "Since you seem to know all about it, I won't bore you . . . except to say that I would appreciate a certain amount of discretion. If," he added censoriously, "you can manage it."

Nicole stiffened. Despite the warmth of their reunion, she felt herself at odds with him almost at once. "I'll do my best," she said before she turned away.

Paul and Dominique exchanged a glance. Words were unnecessary, they understood each other perfectly.

"Come now," Dominique said swiftly, "while the children are asleep, we must catch up on all the news."

"I believe there is chilled wine," Paul said as he rang the bell for a servant. The house their absent friends had provided was very well equipped; he had complete faith in the butler's ability to produce virtually anything on request.

Short minutes later they were seated outside on the veranda catching a precious breeze and sipping their drinks.

"Is it always so hot here?" Nicole asked. She was still chafing at her brother's behavior but she wasn't about to show it. From childhood, her greatest refuge had been her ability to bury her emotions and appear unmoved by events around her, no matter how upsetting.

"It may seem that way," Paul replied. "Actually, most of the year is perfectly pleasant."

"You'd never know it now," Dominique said, fanning herself. "I'll never understand why they put the capital here. Boston would have been a far better choice."

David laughed. Despite her lingering accent and the decidedly European grace of her dress and manner, his sister had become an unabashed New Englander. So far as she was concerned, anyone who lived elsewhere was a fool.

They chatted on, or at least Paul, Dominique, and David did. Nicole was largely silent. Observing her brother, she couldn't help but feel that there was some source of tension in him other than what could reasonably be assigned to his mission. Her memory of him was of a determinedly self-confident, almost arrogant man certain of his position in life and his absolute right to it. Now he seemed not so much diminished as shaken, as though possibilities had occurred to him which he had never before considered.

Nicole chided herself not to read too much into what might be perfectly innocuous behavior. She had a tendency to overanalyze, yet it was also true that she was generally right about people's needs and motivations. That being the case, she was not altogether surprised when her brother suddenly broke off in the midst of a sentence and stared at the woman alighting from the front seat of a cart. She was simply dressed in clothes that, while hardly elegant, were meticulously clean and well cut. Her fiery hair was swept back in a knot at the nape of her neck. Free of powder or other artifice, her porcelain skin glowed with health. For the briefest instant, her gaze flicked to David before being resolutely averted.

"Excuse me," Annabel said softly, "I didn't realize that you were engaged."

"Not at all," Paul assured her as he came halfway down the steps. "Please join us."

"By all means," Dominique added. "It's been too long since we saw you." She frowned slightly, surprised by the uncharacteristic stiffness of the young woman she thought of as a friend.

"Thank you," Annabel said. Unbending somewhat, she said sincerely, "It's good to see you again, Dominique. Are the children all well?"

"Excessively. I don't believe you've met my sister, Nicole, and this is David, my brother."

Nicole inclined her head automatically, her attention fixed on David and this surprising young woman. No, she had not been mistaken. There was definitely some connection between them which, at the very least, made them both uncomfortable.

"Monsieur le Marquis de Montfort and I are already acquainted," Annabel said. "But it is a pleasure to meet you, mademoiselle."

Even as she was offering the conventional response, Nicole realized that pleasure didn't quite describe whatever was happening between Annabel and her brother.

She broke off as David rose to his feet. Curtly, he said, "I'm glad to see you had the sense to take my advice." Before Annabel could reply, he went on, "Miss Riordan hurt her hand today, Paul. I told her to come and see you. It needs looking at."

"Of course," Paul said. "Why don't you come inside, Annabel? We'll see what we're dealing with."

"It's nothing really," she said, eyeing David coldly. "The marquis is being presumptuous—as usual."

Nicole had all she could do to stifle a laugh. Dominique looked faintly shocked. She had never heard Annabel speak critically of anyone; the younger woman seemed to have an endless tolerance for the foibles of human nature. But not, it seemed, where David was concerned.

The two sisters stared at each other over the head of their brother. He had slumped back into one of the wicker chairs and was scowling darkly. They could only guess at the thoughts going through his head.

"Well, then . . ." Dominique said tentatively. "How long do you think you'll be staying, David?"

No answer. He continued to stare off into space as though hoping to find there the solution to a mystery which otherwise eluded him.

"David . . . ?" Dominique repeated gently. When he still did not reply, she laid a hand on his arm. He started, as though finding it painful to be yanked from his private reverie.

"Are you all right?" Dominique asked. Her face was suffused with concern that did not lack an underlying touch of humor. She could not quite believe what she was seeing, yet it appeared there was little doubt. David was, at the very least, taken with Annabel.

"I'm fine," he murmured. Abruptly, he stood up and walked over to the porch railing. Braced against one of the pillars, his eyes narrowed against the bright sunlight, he said, "Sometimes a man can be a fool."

Again the two sisters glanced at one another. David

seemed to be speaking almost to himself, yet they could hardly pretend not to have heard.

After a moment, Nicole took it upon herself to do what was needed. Arching a finely shaped eyebrow, she said, "Sometimes? I'd say most of the time, wouldn't you, Dominique? Men have the most extraordinary ability to complicate the simplest matters, to their own and everyone else's detriment."

She held her breath, waiting for David to reply. When he did, she was not disappointed.

"What exactly is that supposed to mean, Nicole?" he demanded. "You are always more than willing to speak your mind, yet I wonder if it is ever possessed of anything more than snap judgments and ill-formed opinions."

"At least I'm willing to say what is in my mind, Brother," she shot back. "And more importantly, to deal with it. There is clearly something between you and Miss Riordan."

When he would have interrupted, she plunged on. "That is your business, not mine or Dominique's. But you are our brother and we care for you. We dislike seeing you so obviously concerned."

Her voice gentled even as she went on. Time and experience had forged a unique bond between her and David. They had shared imprisonment, terror, the ever-present shadow of death, and the more than ample demonstration of humanity's capacity for evil.

Through it all, they had managed to snatch some fragment of a happy childhood. Perhaps that was the greatest triumph either of them would ever know. Certainly, it gave them both rights and obligations toward one another that no one else could have.

Nicole smiled gently. She reached out a hand and touched

her brother's lean cheek. Beneath her fingers, she could feel the slight roughness of a day's growth of beard. He was a child no longer. Yet that made it all the more imperative for her to speak.

"I want to say only this: Dominique and I each have a particular experience with love. She possesses it, I do not. But our different paths have led us to the same conclusion. Only a fool refuses to follow his heart simply because the world has made doing so awkward or inconvenient."

Despite himself, David smiled. It was outrageous that Nicole should be lecturing him in this manner—a virgin advising a man of the world on the overriding importance of pursuing his desires. And yet that was precisely what she was doing with all sincerity and honesty. He could not help but be touched by it.

"Although I doubt Miss Riordan would see things as you do," he said softly, "I'll keep your advice in mind."

His tenderness caused Nicole to blink. Briskly, she said, "Good."

Dominique smiled, relieved that they were friends again. Conflict of any sort made her intensely nervous. She understood well enough that not all disagreement led to sorrowful ends, but she also had great difficulty dealing with it.

Speaking lightly, about nothing in particular, she led them back into easier straits. They were chatting about Washington social life when Paul returned to the porch with Annabel. Her hand was neatly bandaged. She was still pale but she also seemed more in command of her emotions. Enough so to address David directly.

"It appears you were right, this did need looking after."

"I put in several stitches," Paul said. "Annabel was very

brave, but I imagine a restorative wouldn't go amiss." He smiled as he handed her a glass of chilled wine. "Can you stay awhile?"

"I'm afraid not," she replied with a shake of her head. "The tavern is very busy. I must get back." As an after-thought, she said, "By the way, yer man Pomfret asked me to give this to ye." She withdrew a sealed envelope which she handed to David.

He opened it and scanned the contents briefly. They were not surprising. Austen, the President's aide, had grudgingly arranged a meeting the following day between David and James Madison. He was to come to the side entrance of the President's house off Pennsylvania Avenue at 8:00 A.M. "precisely." The emphasis on punctuality made him smile.

"Something amusing?" Paul asked.

David shook his head. Slipping the note into his pocket, he said, "Merely the realization that bureaucrats are the same all over the world. They hate having their pretensions exposed, particularly when there's nothing they can do about it."

As it was evident that he intended no further explanation, the others sipped their wine in silence. Annabel drank enough of hers to be polite.

Much as she hated to admit it, Paul's swift and expert surgery had left her weaker than she would have liked. Her legs felt reluctant to support her and the distance back to the tavern, ordinarily inconsequential, suddenly appeared immense.

Nonetheless, she rose to go. "Thank you, Paul, Dominique. Nicole, it was a pleasure to meet you. Monsieur." She inclined her head to David without looking at him.

For the moment, all she wanted was to regain the safety

of her own home, the one place where she felt that she knew exactly who she was and what she should be doing.

But David was having none of it. He was at her side before she could take a step from the porch. "Don't be a damned idiot," he muttered. "You're going nowhere on your own."

"Perhaps you could see Annabel back to the inn," Paul suggested benignly. For good measure, he added, "After all, you are staying there."

Shooting his brother-in-law a look that suggested he needed no such reminders, David took Annabel's arm. "Let's go."

Acting as if by reflex, she tried to pull away, only to quickly discover two things: he wouldn't let her and she didn't really want him to anyway. The touch of his fingers against her skin was oddly reassuring, unlike the way she had felt by the river when she had been shaken to the core of her being. He was more tender than she had known.

That realization shook her. She knew instinctively that tenderness was the one emotion with which she had almost no experience, and as such was the one to which she was most likely to fall victim.

Her green-gold eyes were wide and dark as he lifted her onto the back of the horse he had left tethered in front of the house. Although the animal was one of those rented out for the day or week by local stables, he was a cut above the usual breed. Annabel could not help but take note of that as David settled behind her. He was accustomed to the best, he took it as his due. And when he was done with it, he moved on.

His chest was wide and warm beneath her back. She closed her eyes, turning her face to the sun. Behind her lids, she saw a blueness so piercing as to be almost painful. She did not move, remaining still within his arms, feeling the beat of his heart and the rhythm of his breath as though they were her own.

Sensation crowded out thought. She felt the cautionary voices of her mind becoming silent. A far older imperative was gaining within her, suspending reason, safety, even survival.

Quietly, she let it come.

❧ CHAPTER ❧
Nine

THE President's house—or as a few were beginning to call it, the White House—stood on a bare, unlandscaped knoll adjacent to Pennsylvania Avenue. The house itself was unexpectedly pleasing to the eye. Apparently, the architect had absorbed at least the basics of the Greek Revival style. The portico of Ionic columns which formed the main entrance provided a sense of balance and light which the infant nation could only hope to emulate.

Or so David thought as he entered the center hall and stood looking about him. Various reception rooms led off on either side, their windows opened to admit the smells of the marshy estuary that lay not far removed. A little stream, called Goose Creek, could be glimpsed in the distance. Closer at hand, a tangle of elder bushes, swamp grasses, and tree stumps marked what would one day presumably be a lawn.

But for the moment, the simplest amenities of day-to-day life seemed all that the Americans could manage. Although the President's wife was reputed to keep a fine saloon, David saw no evidence of it as he followed the wizened old footman who had admitted him. Neither, however, did he glimpse the lines of hanging wash or the foraging chickens which gossip had it were both habitual presences.

Upstairs, in the third-floor rooms which served as a residence for the President's family, David was shown into a private study. The room was small and filled to overcrowding with books, maps, and an assortment of curious objects whose purpose could not be readily discerned. It appeared to be the retreat of a man with many interests unfettered by any desire for tidiness.

And yet when James Madison entered the room, he was impeccably dressed in a silk frock coat and breeches that would have gone over well at Versailles. Despite his small size and seeming frailness, his keen eyes, proud carriage, and direct manner made it evident why the Americans had chosen him as their leader, even if in doing so they had chosen to ignore everything he told them.

"Monsieur le Marquis," he said pleasantly as he extended a hand to David, "do sit down."

Having done so, David surveyed the other man frankly. Madison appeared perfectly calm, yet he had spent the previous day inspecting his troops and must be vividly aware of the danger in which he stood. The Americans could hardly have been less prepared to confront the British. Washington itself lay virtually undefended while the Congress and the administration argued and postured, wasting precious time with no apparent concern for their own survival.

"The emperor has charged me to extend his greetings, sir," David said, "and to express his hope for the continued well-being of your nation."

"His Excellency is most kind," Madison said dryly. He touched a handkerchief to his upper lip before continuing. It was very warm in the study yet neither man would have considered moving elsewhere. At least here they could be assured of privacy from the hordes of office seekers, hangers-on, and the just plain curious who habitually crowded into the President's house.

Continuing, Madison said, "I trust he is in good health."

"So I understand, sir," David replied.

"Indeed?" Madison said. He made no attempt to hide his skepticism. Abruptly, he said, "Your emperor would have done far better to confine his attentions to what he had already seized rather than go seeking adventure. Russia has absorbed more would-be conquerors than anyone will ever know. Shattered hopes and destroyed reputations litter every route into her. Napoleon has proved no different. Now it remains to be seen if he can rescue anything from the debacle."

David was silent for a moment, weighing his options. Finally, he said, "You must know, sir, that I cannot comment on that."

Madison looked at him squarely. "When loyalty demands dishonesty, young man, grave consequences follow. However, I appreciate your position. Let us cut to the heart of this matter. Tell me what Napoleon proposes."

It took David almost an hour to do so. The strategy he outlined called upon the American Navy to work secretly in tandem with French warships in a series of feints and retreats. The goal was to draw off the British forces and spread them so thinly that they would lose effectiveness on both sides of the Atlantic. The plan was imaginative and audacious—typical Napoleonic thinking—but in fact it was David's own creation. More correctly, he had dredged it up in response to his own assessment of the increasingly desperate military situation. The emperor liked it because it was reassuringly grandiose. Madison liked it because it actually had some chance of success.

When David was done, the President was silent for what seemed like a long time. At last, he said, "Two things occur to me immediately. If the British understand our position— both its strengths and weaknesses—as well as you do, we are in an even worse position than I had thought. The second is that you have obviously not always been a diplomat. I would enjoy knowing where and when you gained your military expertise."

Quietly, David said, "I was with the emperor in Russia."

Madison got up and went to a sideboard where he poured them two glasses of brandy. Returning with them, he offered one to David before taking a long swallow of his own.

"How are you managing our Washington summer?" he asked.

David smiled slightly. "As you may suspect, I find the heat a welcome change."

That did not surprise Madison. He was a pragmatic man little given to flights of fancy, yet he was not lacking in imagination. The winter in Valley Forge had been torture enough but compared to the French retreat from Moscow, it would have seemed a holiday outing.

Two hundred thousand had died in the frozen wastes of

that vast land. Men were buried alive in snow drifts, frozen to death as they stood sentry duty, and saw their limbs waste and fall away before the unremitting onslaught of cold so intense there could be no protection from it. And no escape.

Yet David de Montfort had survived, and now even joked about having developed a preference for hot weather?

"You are half-British," Madison said, "and as I understand it, heir to considerable properties in England. Yet you fight for Napoleon. Why?"

Very few people would have dared to ask such a question. Fewer still would have had any hope of receiving an answer. Yet to this small, unassuming man, David somehow felt that he owed the truth.

"In England I was a refugee," he said slowly. "I never felt as though I belonged. I do belong in France, despite the efforts of madmen during the Revolution to destroy people such as myself. If I abandon my heritage there, the madmen finally win."

"Then I would think you would support a restoration of the Bourbon dynasty," Madison said, "as the British do."

"The only reason Britain favors that," David replied, "is because any attempt to bring back the Bourbons will weaken France. The plain fact of the matter is that the Bourbons were never very good kings and there's no reason to think that would be different now. What they would do is cause dissension and conflict throughout France. We would be less able to challenge Britain anywhere in the world which, of course, is exactly what the British want to accomplish."

Madison nodded slowly yet he still appeared perplexed. "But why Napoleon? A man of ordinary birth distinguished only by his extraordinary ambition. He's committed neither to the aristocrats or the republicans. Indeed, I don't think he believes in anything other than himself.''

"But he does have a vision," David said softly. "He sees a strong, united France secure from its enemies and at peace within. He believes in the rule of law, the suppression of anarchy, the protection of life and property.''

And that, Madison thought, would appeal mightily to a young man who had seen the entire fabric of his world rent asunder by—as he said—madmen.

"I hope you are right, my friend," Madison said softly. He finished the last of his brandy and stood up. Once again, he held out his hand. "I will think over the joint military strategy you propose, then we will meet again.''

David nodded. He had not expected this first meeting to be their last, but he also had to admit that he did not mind having a reason to remain in Washington, if only a little while longer.

After leaving the President, he did not return immediately to the Wild Geese but went instead to the French consulate. De Plessis was there. The baron looked unusually grim when he spotted David.

"New dispatches," he murmured after they had greeted one another. "It is not going well.''

"How so?" David asked.

"Austria has declared war.''

David was surprised although realistically he knew that he shouldn't be. Napoleon's marriage to the Austrian princess Marie Louise had included no guarantee of her country's friendship. Indeed, it might have been said that her wily father was merely biding his time, waiting for the opportune moment to strike. For this the emperor had given up his Josephine, the only woman David suspected he had ever truly cared for. David did not dwell on the irony of it. He had other, more immediate concerns.

"I may have to return sooner than I thought," he said.

De Plessis hesitated a moment. He glanced around to be sure he would not be overheard. Softly, he said, "Perhaps you would do better to remain here."

David smiled faintly. He understood well enough what the older man meant, he was merely surprised by his reasoning.

"If Napoleon falls, there will still be a France—at least in some form. But let the British do as they wish with these Americans, and this place will be unrecognizable."

"A pity," de Plessis murmured. "I'm growing rather fond of it."

"Still, you should make your plans. It isn't wise to remain much longer." Despite Madison's willingness to listen to his proposals, David had very little confidence in the Americans' ability to defeat the British a second time. They were a disorganized, contentious lot who seemed unable to come to terms with the reality of their situation. Further proof, if any was needed, that the absence of a true ruling class doomed a nation.

"As it happens," de Plessis said, "I'm considering staying."

David was genuinely surprised. Whatever the baron's fondness for this strange, new land, it had never occurred to him that he might be so taken with it as to stay. Particularly given the present dangers.

"Frankly," the older man said, "the choice of France under either the Bourbons or the Bonapartists doesn't appeal to me very much. I rather like the way they do things here."

"I hadn't noticed that they *do* anything," David said bluntly, "other than argue among themselves and waste precious time. Do you truly wish to trust your life to men who cannot even put aside their differences temporarily when their nation's survival hangs in the balance?''

"It's difficult to explain," de Plessis admitted. His dark, slightly protruding eyes surveyed David. "Somehow I believe that when it really comes down to it, they will surprise us all."

David shook his head. He did not wish to disagree with the baron but neither could he share his apparently fathomless optimism. The Englishmen he had known at school possessed little in the way of cleverness, but they more than made up for it with iron determination and selfless courage that had to be admired. As for the Americans, they were far harder to discern, being little more than a motley collection of dreamers, ne'er-do-wells, and fools. Men calling themselves Americans spoke different languages, worshipped in different ways, saw the world from different perspectives. Given that, how could they truly expect to function together as a nation? It was impossible.

And yet, if he were to ask him, his brother-in-law would surely say that he was an American. So undoubtedly would the overly large Scotsman Annabel employed. And now de Plessis, who whatever else he was, possessed a survivor's instincts. Could such disparate men possibly work together? Could they possibly endure?

"I wish you luck, my friend," David said at length. "But as for myself, I'll take my chances with the emperor."

"May you not regret it," the baron said gently. "So you will be leaving soon?"

David nodded reluctantly. "Whether my business is concluded or not, it appears I will have to."

"Would it be possible for you to carry letters back for me? I would deem it a great favor."

After assuring the baron that he would be happy to do so and making arrangements to have them delivered to him, David took his leave.

He returned to the Wild Geese where he went directly to his room. Having dismissed Pomfret, he settled down at the small desk and spent the next several hours writing out a detailed account of his visit to date, particularly his meeting with Madison.

He did so in order to set the facts clearly in his own mind, but their effect was to give him pause. The more he wrote, and the more he thought, the less he was certain of his conclusions.

The Americans were weak, undirected, and ill equipped to withstand the coming crisis, and yet he had written of the great size and variety of the marketplace he had visited, of the crowds of people there, their apparent affluence, the confidence and energy with which they struck their bargains. The more he stared at the words, the more significant they appeared. Despite all that it lacked, Washington fairly burst with vitality. He thought of the men and women he had seen on the streets, going cheerfully and eagerly about their business as though they knew nothing on earth could stop them.

And he thought of Annabel. Surely, if anyone was an American, it was she, although her attachment to Ireland was still such that she might not acknowledge it. He smiled to himself as he imagined her reaction to being told that she could not do something. Even if it hadn't occurred to her to try, she would immediately set forth and keep at the thing until it was accomplished.

She had not been disposed to remain in his company when they had returned to the tavern the previous afternoon, but had hurried off with hardly a word. Later, when he had come down to supper, she had sent one of the maids to serve him and kept herself well away from his table.

That wasn't surprising given how he had challenged her by the river and afterward. He remembered the touch of her mouth against his and smiled. For a moment, he could almost forget who he was, who she was, and the tangle of circumstances surrounding them. His body stirred. He put down his quill pen, regarded his ink-stained fingers, and decided that he had done enough. As though to confirm his decision, his stomach growled.

In the soft light of early evening, the tavern was already crowded. The doors were open, admitting a steady stream of men and a smaller number of women who had finished their labors for the day and were in the mood for camaraderie.

Talk abounded, as did laughter. After the quiet of his room, the noise struck David like a hard, bracing wave. It roused him from his introspection which he was glad enough to leave.

Cameron was behind the bar. The Scotsman looked up as David entered and nodded to him cordially. Without having to be asked, he slid a glass of brandy across the expanse of gleaming oak. It was the same vintage Madison had served in his study. David doubted it was a coincidence since there seemed nothing the Scotsman didn't know.

"How is it," David asked, "that despite the British blockade, there seems to be more cognac here than there is in Paris?"

Cameron shrugged. "It was all laid down years ago," he explained. "People remembered the problems they had gettin' decent drink during the first Revolution, so they planned accordingly."

"Are you saying they knew they'd have to fight the British a second time?" David asked.

"They knew they were in for trouble sure as they knew anything."

"It doesn't seem to worry them."

"Wait," Cameron said. "There's only so much cognac to go around, also only so much patience. When we begin to run out of both, we'll act."

"By that time you could be bowing to old George again and singing 'God Save the King.' "

The Scotsman laughed. He put his towel down on the bar and added a further measure to David's glass. "I doubt that."

"Why not?"

Cameron flashed his teeth in a predatory smile. "It seems like none of us can remember the words."

David laughed appreciatively. He liked the man's irreverence, so refreshing after the years he had spent in a court where humor was always closely guarded lest it be taken amiss.

"I almost regret that I have to leave soon," David said.

"Tis a shame you do," Cameron agreed. "Ye've had little enough chance to get to know us."

David agreed. He was surprised by his own reluctance to leave. America—and Americans—were growing on him, whether he wanted to admit it or not.

The brandy had enlivened his spirits but done nothing for his hunger. He left Cameron a few minutes later and took a table in a corner. Seated with his chair rocked back against the wall, completely at ease, he waited for Annabel to appear.

She did not disappoint him. When she emerged from the

kitchen a short time later, David smiled appreciatively. As always, she was simply dressed but in a departure from the usual she had left her hair down. It flowed over her shoulders, secured only by a single strand of ribbon.

He felt as well as heard the murmur that ran among the other men as they, too, noticed the change. Annabel ignored them. She exchanged a few words with Cameron before coming directly to David's table.

Apparently, she had decided not to ignore him that evening.

"I understand," she said quietly, "that ye'll be leaving soon."

Cameron must have mentioned it to her. David wasn't displeased although he was reluctant to confront the matter himself. His silence, however, was confirmation enough to Annabel.

Her chin tilted. Proudly, she met his gaze. "Before ye go, is there anything else ye'd like?"

*B*LESSED *Mary and all the saints, she'd actually said it.*

A wave of heat washed over Annabel. She curled her hands into her apron to hide their trembling. Not for anything would she let him see the tumult of emotions at war within her.

Long hours of soul-searching had left her weary but resolute. She might never in her life feel for another man what she did for David. With him everything was brighter, more exciting, more meaningful. He banished the darkness of the past, if only for a little while.

When he was gone everything would be as it had been. She would have the tavern, her work, the life she had made for herself. But she was also determined that she would have the memory of him.

David was looking at her oddly. The slight smile that had hovered around his mouth was gone. The flicker of surprise she was sure she had seen in his eyes had also vanished. He looked wary.

He also looked determined. Yes, that was it. She was looking at something she had never seen before, or never allowed herself to see: male determination. Yet he made no move. Slowly, she understood what he was telling her. If she had spoken carelessly or on impulse, if she regretted what she had said and wanted to withdraw it, now was the time.

Another moment, another breath, and the chance would be gone.

Her throat was dry. She swallowed and met his gaze. "I said: is there anything else ye'd like?"

"Yes," David said softly. The smile returned slowly, lighting the shadows behind his eyes. "I understand there's to be a fair tomorrow over in Georgetown. Come with me?"

A fair? She was at once relieved and disappointed. The longing to be alone with him again as they had been by the river was almost overwhelming. But fear of the unknown made her want to postpone her confrontation with it. Her own lack of courage dismayed her.

"All right," she said slowly. "I'll come."

He nodded, seemingly satisfied.

Annabel went back to work. She did the things she had done every night since taking over the Wild Geese—seeing to it that the food coming from the kitchen was exactly as it should be, that everyone had plenty to drink, that the tables were cleaned between customers, and that the floor was kept tidy. Where she saw tempers flaring too brightly, she intervened to smooth over trouble. Where she saw loneliness, she had a kind word and a smile.

Let a man come twice to her tavern and she remembered

his name. Come a third time and she'd know the name of his wife and children, if he had any. At the least she'd know what he called his horse and his favorite dog.

Because she was a businesswoman, she knew who had money and who was in debt. Men confided their schemes to her, along with their triumphs and their failures. She knew the pasts of most of the people who came through the door, and she knew what they hoped would be their futures.

And all the while she kept the food coming and the drink flowing.

David watched her at first merely because she was the most pleasant thing he could think of to look at. She was beautiful, feminine, sensual. Why wouldn't he look at her? But as the hours wore on, his perception grew. Despite the press of demands weighing down on her, she was unfailingly cheerful and patient. Would that she would be the same with him!

But then he thought of that again and decided he preferred things the way they were. With him, she had weaknesses. With her, he had the same. It made them equal.

He paused in the midst of lifting his cup to his lips. Equal they could never be. They were male and female in a world that decreed women must submit to men. But even more than that, he was an aristocrat and she a commoner. Americans pretended such things didn't matter. Wiser men knew better.

There was a sudden burst of laughter. He looked across the sultry room through the dim summer light. Annabel was smiling. He fancied he could smell the perfume of her skin across the distance separating them.

The evening proved long. He knew he should leave, go to his rooms, complete his report. He would see her tomorrow and all else would follow. He would have her, he would be satisfied, and he would leave. Why then should he feel so anxious? So oddly sad?

He remained as though held by a power he could not deny. He watched her unabashedly, not caring if she or anyone else was made uncomfortable by his scrutiny. Nor did he concern himself with what he was revealing about himself. Alone at his table, his chair leaned casually against the wall and his long legs stretched out in front of him, he watched. From time to time, he caught a nervous stare from some other quarter of the room and smiled inwardly.

He knew the picture he must make. He was clad all in black save for a snow-white linen shirt. His skin was burnished, his hair streaked with gold. In the hard, tensile strength of his body there was a hint of purely male recklessness, as though he would welcome an outlet for the forces barely restrained within him.

Yet no man even thought of challenging him. Put simply, they were not fools. Fighters they might be, even brawlers when the mood was upon them. But the marquis David de Montfort was a warrior. Honed to battle in the harshest school, he could be merciless in a way they would never comprehend or duplicate.

They gave him a wide berth even as they wondered what the outcome would be when the warrior clashed, as he clearly would, with the woman as indomitable as she was enticing.

It was well beyond midnight before the tavern emptied. Cameron dried the last of the glasses and put them away. The serving girls said their good nights and went off tiredly to bed.

Annabel moved silently about the long, quiet room,

extinguishing one by one the lanterns hung from the smoke-darkened beams. Each time she raised herself on tiptoe and lifted her right arm to snuff out the flame, the movement emphasized her breasts and accentuated the narrow grace of her waist.

Outside the moon reigned. In the absence of the lanterns, silvery light filled the room. It fell across the man still seated, watchful and silent in his chair, suddenly revealing him.

"David . . ."

Her voice was a whisper, borne on the moonlight. Slowly, he straightened himself. Across the empty room, he came to her.

She stood unmoving, watching him as she had all evening in the midst of everything else, as he was watching her.

Lord, what a man he was. Fair of face, strong of body, graceful and certain, he was a man for the bards' ancient legends, the kind of prince they sang of in the long timber halls around the fires. And she was there, gleaming hair unbound, white-limbed, gossamer-gowned, awaiting him. In the silent room, bathed in moonlight, time and place had no meaning.

David held out his hand. It was hard, the palm calloused from years of swordplay and riding. By contrast, her own felt small and fragile.

He led her out of the room and she went, with a docility that surprised them both. On the second floor, she paused, expecting him to enter his room. But instead, he continued up the narrow flight of steps to her own quarters.

There the radiance of the moonlight transformed the simple furnishings, making them appear as though cast in silver. Transparent curtains blew at the windows. The scents of lavender and thyme filled the air. They were in a far land, divorced from reality, the realm of magic in which all things were possible. Slowly, David raised the small hand he held. He stared at it, as though he had never seen such a hand before. And indeed, he had not. The women he knew were pampered, cosseted. They did no manual work. Annabel was different.

She worked hard and long, yet her nails were buffed, her skin smooth and soft except for those places where it had toughened to protect her from harm. Was her soul the same? Why on earth would he think of such a thing? He had never had such thoughts about any woman, but particularly not about one he desired.

"It is very late . . ." he murmured.

Panic flared in her. Surely he did not mean to leave? She could not bear it if he did, not having come so far. Yet she had no idea what to do. That was the worst of it. Having resolutely kept herself from men, she knew nothing of how to give herself to one.

Or she thought that she didn't. David knew better. Her eyes were softly beguiling, her mouth shaped for promises. She swayed toward him slightly. Her perfume enveloped them both. He let go of her hand and placed both of his on her shoulders.

"Let me help you," he said gently.

At first she didn't understand. Not until his fingers slipped down to undo the laces of her chemise did she realize what he intended. Her body tightened but she forced herself to stand still. Hardly breathing, she waited as he slowly undid the ties and let the fabric drop open.

Her breasts gleamed white and full. They were unexpectedly large for so slender a girl. He swallowed with difficulty and forced himself to continue. He unbuttoned her skirt and let it drop around her feet. Beneath she wore a thin petticoat through which he could glimpse elegantly rounded legs. He went down on his knees, ignoring her soft gasp, and grasped the petticoat between his hands. Slowly, he lowered it until it, too, lay crumpled on the floor. Small clothes were not the fashion for women. Aside from the unbound chemise, she was naked.

He stood again and ran his hands along her arms. He could feel her quivering, knew the effect he was having on her, and wondered if she realized how much greater was her own power. Consumed by the need to make her desire him as much as he did her, he slid his hands beneath the chemise and raised it over her head.

Sultry night air touched her bare body. She stood, torn between terror and elation. No man had ever seen her like this. Her upbringing dictated that she should be outraged, yet the light in his eyes filled her with joy. Unconsciously, she straightened her shoulders and looked at him proudly.

He turned away and went over to a low table by the wall. From it, he took a towel which he unfolded and spread on the floor. Taking her hand, he led her to stand on it.

A basin on the table held cool water. He dropped a cloth into it, wrung it almost dry, and began slowly, meticulously to run it over her body. Annabel bit down hard on her lower lip to stifle a gasp. She could not believe he would perform such a service for her.

He did it as naturally and as simply as he would care for a weary child. And that surprised her even more. She hadn't thought of him as a man who would be good with children, yet she had seen him with his family and sensed the deep current of love binding them, despite the obvious tension that existed between him and Nicole. They were too much alike, those two. Both strong and proud, firm in their convictions and determined to live by them. Yet they loved each other.

She trembled beneath his touch. This was a far different kind of love. There was carnality in it as well as tenderness. He slid the cloth down her flat belly and she came close once again to crying out. Her hands went to his shoulders, attempting to push him away.

"Be still," he said. The sound moved through her, deep and stirring. She felt the strength go from her arms and let them drop.

He turned away to wet the cloth again. Water trickled between her breasts. Her heart was beating so tumultuously that she thought it must surely show through the pale skin. She closed her eyes for a moment and let her head fall back. The weight of her hair arched her neck even farther. She stood, a finely pulled bow, vibrating to his touch.

Beads of sweat shone on David's forehead. The rigid control required to do as he did and nothing more almost overwhelmed him. Far in the back of his mind, he wondered why he had begun this. His plans had been made. Tomorrow, after the Georgetown fair, he would take her to an inn where she was not known where they could have the privacy they needed. It would all be very sensible, exactly what would be expected of a man who had enjoyed his share of assignations in the past.

But this was a sweetly mad, insanely tempting intimacy he had not anticipated.

Between her legs, nestled at the juncture of creamy thighs, was a soft down of curls as fiery as the hair upon her head. He touched the cloth there and saw her knees buckle.

Quickly, he caught her, holding her against the iron strength of his arm. Her eyes opened, reflecting the moonlight. She made no sound as he laid her on the bed and stepped back a pace. Unflinching, she watched as he undressed.

It was only fair, he thought. He had stripped her bare and touched almost every inch of her. She should have as great a familiarity with him. Why then did he feel so unaccustomedly self-conscious?

Other women had always found him attractive. In truth, they had often expressed a desire for his body that left him quite startled. Surely, Annabel would be no exception. He would believe so if only she weren't so still. If only she smiled or said something instead of lying white and quiet, watching him with the huge, unwavering eyes of a child.

He stopped, his hands at the waistband of his breeches. His chest was bare, the hard breadth of his muscles gleaming darkly. His discarded frock coat and shirt lay on the floor, forgotten. Beneath the remaining garments, his manhood sprang alive and urgently demanding.

How afraid would she be? How . . . disgusted? he wondered. She was most likely a virgin, and it belatedly occurred to him that he knew nothing of such creatures. For good reason, he had always scrupulously avoided them. Doubt filled him, feeling perilously close to fear.

And then she moved. With perfect naturalness, she knelt on the mattress before him. Her small hands brushed his aside. Matter-of-factly, she began to undo the buttons. Her eyes danced as she looked up at him. "You are too slow," she said.

Relief flooded him. She was not so very different from the other women he had known. His confidence regained, he smiled down at her.

Annabel took that smile for what it was, a reward for her own courage. Seeing his fear, she had hid her own. It was that simple, or so it seemed. It did not occur to her then to wonder why she put his needs so far above her own.

He sat down on the edge of the bed to remove his boots. The task proved more difficult than he'd expected. The gleaming black Hessians were meant to be removed by the wearer's valet, not by the wearer himself.

David tugged. Nothing happened. He tugged again and this time the right boot did ease a bit. A further pull and he thought he felt it give. Resolved to end the matter, he yanked hard, too much so. The effort unbalanced him, he tumbled over onto his back even as the boot slipped loose and went bouncing from his hands across the floor.

Annabel laughed. She put fingers to her lips in an effort to stifle the sound but did not succeed. David glared up at her balefully. "This sort of thing isn't supposed to happen."

"I imagine not," she agreed when she had regained sufficient control of herself. "Just out of curiosity, do ye usually have such problems?"

"No," he answered curtly lest she think any further along those lines. Pointedly, he added, "I usually have assistance."

A slow flush spread over her cheeks as understanding dawned. "Oh, I see . . . the lady . . ."

His bedmates knew what needed to be done while she was woefully ignorant. And not just about the matter of boots. How much more didn't she know? How much greater would be his disappointment . . . and his disdain?

"Oh, no," he said suddenly as she tried to draw away. His lean, brown fingers curled around her wrist. Lightly, he pressed a kiss to the pulse point hidden there.

"It's only a boot, sweetling," he murmured, "not the world."

"I'll help . . ." she said quickly.

"No." He stopped her before she could scramble off the bed. Oddly, the thought of her bending to remove the boot disturbed him. A service numerous other women had provided laughingly, seductively, bawdily, he did not want to receive from her at all.

Was it because the barriers between them were already too clearly written and needed no stressing? Or was it because he felt some deep-seated scruple against thinking of her as a servant, an inferior, someone to give him pleasure and be forgotten? Such niceties were unlike him, for life had left him little time or inclination to puzzle over such things. And yet he wondered about them now.

The second boot gave more easily than the first. He stood again and stripped off his breeches. Quickly, not meeting her eyes, he slipped onto the bed beside her.

She did not look so very afraid after all, although he was sure she had at least glimpsed him. The sudden, overwhelming need to banish whatever lingering doubts she felt drove him to gather her close. Murmuring to her, he stroked the slim line of her back soothingly.

Her breasts pressed against him, enticing him with their soft fullness. Her head dropped, finding its place on his shoulder. It all felt right and perfectly ordained.

A deep, shuddering breath escaped him. Tenderness was all very well but he was on fire with need. Carefully, he turned, guiding her beneath him. Her lips were slightly parted, her eyes wide and luminous.

He touched his mouth to hers, first gently, then with increasing intensity. The taste of her was indescribably sweet. She was all velvet warmth and honeyed moistness. His tongue plunged more deeply, coaxing hers. When she responded, a bolt of pure ecstasy shot through him. Abruptly, his control snapped. His mouth and hands, his body and his will all engulfed her insatiably. She became not Annabel, a separate individual, but a vessel of his desperate need and his overwhelming determination.

Dimly, he heard her soft cries but they were meaningless to him. Mindlessly, he bent her to submission. Her body was his, every soft, silken curve, every secret, beckoning place. Never had he been driven to know a woman so completely.

His passion threatened to burst all bounds, yet still he held back, driving them both higher and higher until finally he could bear no more. At the moment that he entered her, their eyes met. Every muscle in his body tightened in surprise.

Her innocence was confirmed, yet in her gaze he saw not a virgin's fear but a woman's power shining lambent and triumphant. She moved, her hips rising, and he knew that he had lost. He was not the possessor but the possessed; not the conquering male but a supplicant face-to-face with the very source of life, both humbled and exalted by it.

And then it was over. They lay in a tangle of limbs, their breathing labored as consciousness slowly returned. For Annabel, that return was especially difficult. She was caught in a tumult of contradictory emotions.

His lovemaking had been almost savage. She knew she would bear the marks of it. Yet he had not hurt her, not even at the moment he took her virginity. She had been far too engulfed in pleasure to feel even the slightest sensation of pain. Only now, in the aftermath, did she feel misused.

He had, it seemed, put no value on her innocence.

Certainly, he had paid it no heed. But then why should he? It wasn't as though she was his bride.

Tears stung her eyes. She turned away before he could see them, not wanting to betray herself. She had known the choice she was making and had accepted it freely. Life was too short and too precarious to weep over what could never be.

Beside her, David stirred. He raised himself up on his elbow and gazed down at her. "Annabel . . . ?"

She blinked hard and took a deep, fortifying breath. When she turned to face him, the tears were gone. She even managed a brave smile.

Still, he wasn't entirely fooled. Gently, he drew her to him. Already, his passion was building but he firmly restrained it. There would be time for that later. For the moment, he was content to simply hold her as she slipped softly into sleep.

❧ CHAPTER ❧
Eleven

A FOUR-HORSE Conestoga wagon had overturned in the midst of Georgetown's main street. Small boys swarmed around it as angry, sweating men attempted to free the horses and recover the bales of tobacco before they could vanish into the nearby warren of alleys. Their shouts and grunts mingled with the cacophony of sounds rising up from the busy seaport.

Annabel and David took a detour around the wagon and continued on their way. Both were simply dressed—Annabel in her usual garb with her hair left loose over her shoulders and David in the plainest of his shirts and breeches.

They strolled hand in hand, no different from dozens of other couples who had come for the fair. Yet despite this they drew more than the usual number of glances. They were young, beautiful, and so obviously happy with one another that a special glow seemed to emanate from them.

Older eyes, watching them, remembered long-vanished summers and smiled.

Sunlight glinted off the nearby river as a warm breeze stiffened the pennants of sailing ships. Seagulls circled overhead, their raucous cries joining the din. David looked around bemusedly.

"I hadn't expected this," he said. "It's as busy here as any port in France, or Europe for that matter."

"Did ye imagine the fine merchants of Georgetown would stop their trading just because the British told them to?" Annabel teased. "Not likely. Many of the people here came from Scotland originally. Next to the Irish, ye won't find a stubborner bunch."

"Apparently not," David said. He was frankly astounded to see so much activity. The American coast was under blockade by the British Navy, ostensibly the most powerful in the world. Yet to all appearances, it had no effect.

The wharves were thronged with high-masted frigates and cutters. Horses, wagons, and carriages jostled one another along the cobblestone streets. Patrons spilled out of the nearby shops and taverns. When a troop of seamen off one of the military vessels came ambling along, people stopped to cheer them. But otherwise there was no sign of a nation at war, much less one on the brink of destruction.

"What accounts for this?" David asked. Though he spoke out loud, he really didn't expect Annabel to answer. The question was posed more to himself than anyone else. He was surprised then when she touched his arm and pointed.

"Look, over there."

Ahead of them stretched an immense red-brick building that straddled several of the wharves and dwarfed everything else around it. Smoke rose from its twin chimneys. A steady stream of wagons could be seen moving within the fenced courtyard.

"They make guns there," Annabel explained. "They have since before the Revolution. Tis the largest gun factory on the continent and it's right here in the middle of Georgetown."

She paused for a moment before adding, "When the Brits started actin' up again, the factory went to double shifts. No one's sayin' exactly how many guns are comin' out of there now, but I'd wager it's a lot."

David stared at the building for a long moment. It was impressive, all right, but not convincing. Moreover, it touched him with the cold hand of dread. The British might—just might—be tempted to attack Washington as a symbolic gesture. Or they could just as easily pass it by. But a gun factory—the largest on the continent—would be a strategic target they could not possibly ignore. For himself, it did not matter, he would be long gone. But for Annabel . . .

He turned and was about to speak when she suddenly danced away. "Come on," she called over her shoulder. "The pipers are here."

He followed, catching up with her swiftly. Around a corner came the swirling lilt of a Highland fling blasted heavenward with raucous grace. David winced. He had never found it in himself to appreciate the pipes. The clans had invented them to terrify their enemies, a use to which he thought they should be restricted. To claim them as instruments of musical pleasure was to defy the senses.

Yet Annabel was clearly elated. Her small feet tapped in time with each measure. Her cheeks glowed and her eyes danced. She appeared almost unbearably young and innocent, utterly unlike the passionate, tantalizing woman of only a few hours before.

David could not look away. He, who had possessed some of the most beautiful and seductive women in Europe, was fascinated by a fey Irish tavern keeper whose prickly pride, sharp tongue, and fierce love of freedom surely made her the most unlikely of bedmates. Moreover, he could not wait to take her to bed again. All around them were inns possessed of discreet upstairs rooms which even on a busy fair day could undoubtedly be had for appropriate sums. Yet he found the notion of asking her to join him in such a place suddenly distasteful.

He didn't want to make love to her in a bed others had used for similar purposes. Through her he had touched something special, unique, and infinitely satisfying. That experience deserved to be protected, for both their sakes. He restrained himself while the seemingly endless day ran its course. Not that it was without amusement. Following the pipers came clog dancers gaily dressed in bright red-and-blue costumes. What their cavortings lacked in grace they more than made up for in energy.

Barely had they moved on when a bevy of trained dogs took their place, jumping through metal hoops and flipping over backwards at the command of the gaunt, flashing-eyed Gypsies who led them. With the dogs came peddlers swarming through the crowd, offering honey cakes and candied apples. David and Annabel bought some of each, eating them there on the street as they followed the cheerful mob to the fairgrounds.

A major attraction of the fair was the cattle show. Farmers came from a hundred miles around to inspect the prize-winning bulls and cows, and to bid for the strongest teams of oxen. In addition, there were horses, donkeys, sheep, and the usual snorting, rooting pigs who appeared at home wherever they went. All this animal life had an inevitable result.

"Mind where ye go," Annabel warned, just in time to prevent David from setting his foot down on a still-warm cow pat. His discomfiture made her laugh. "Have ye never been to something like this before?"

He shook his head. "We have fairs in France, of course, but I haven't had the opportunity to attend."

Or the desire, Annabel thought. She wondered what had prompted him to suggest such an outing. Was it genuine interest or merely the search for some amusement that would not make her feel out of place? The thought that he could treat her with such condescension stung.

"We don't have to do this, ye know," she said.

He frowned. She was upset and he had no idea what had caused it. After all, he was the one who had almost stepped in the cow pat. "Why not?" he asked.

"Because this isn't yer sort of place. Because ye'll be bored or worse. And because I'll be damned if I'll trail after ye while you pretend to have a good time, all the while looking down your nose at the poor simple peasants."

David stared at her disbelievingly. Had this exquisite, enticing woman who had purred so contentedly in his arms actually said that? Where was her gratitude, her respect, her proper deference to the man who had taken her as his own? He was about to upbraid her when he paused. Deep within the flickering shadows of her eyes he saw something he recognized all too easily. As a boy torn from his homeland and given over to strangers, he had fought to survive against others bigger, stronger, and crueler than himself. He had learned to face them down with steely pride, to conceal the fear he felt and to never, ever let them see how much he cared.

She was doing exactly the same thing. Except in her case there was no crowd of baiting bullies. There was only him.

Slowly, the tension flowed from him. He reached out, his hands closing around her upper arms.

"Let me tell you something, Miss Riordan," he said quietly. "I've never been to a fair before not because I didn't want to go but for exactly the reason I stated, because I've never had the chance. When I was a boy, people were too busy killing each other to go to fairs. Later when I escaped to England, I was too alone and afraid to bother with such things. And when I became a man and returned to France to claim what was mine, I walked straight into a war. A stupid, brutal, endless war that I sometimes think has been going on all my life and will never end. There's been no time for fairs . . . or picnics by a river . . . or long hours spent in bed with a girl I still can't quite believe is real but who seems determined to hate me."

"No." She stared up at him, appalled by what he was saying. "I donna hate ye. That's not at all the way it is. How could it be when I . . ."

"When you what?" he demanded fiercely.

Her lips trembled. Desperately, she wanted to look away from him but he would not permit it. His gaze held hers as she murmured, "When I . . . like ye."

" . . . *Like me*?" he repeated incredulously. A slow, wry smile mocked her. "Ah, Annabel," he said, "before I'm done, there won't be such a tepid little emotion left in you."

She opened her mouth to reply but had no idea what to say. All the rules she knew, the patterns of living that she understood were useless where he was concerned. She felt like a rudderless boat, swept inexorably along by the current that seized it.

A moment ago she had been afraid and hurt. Now suddenly she felt as though the sun had exploded within her. The swift rise and fall of her emotions jolted her, for it was utterly foreign to her temperament. All her life she had striven for security and stability, and to a large degree she had attained it. Until now.

Yet whatever else might lie ahead, at least they had the next few hours.

Wandering among the cattle pens, they laughed over the antics of the livestock who seemed determined not to cooperate with their masters in any way. One particularly recalcitrant bull required the efforts of five men to lead him into the show pens. When he sold for a record sum, they breathed sighs of relief.

Children darted everywhere, running among the crowds, perching on the rail fences, rolling barrel hoops through the mire. The pipers had struck up another tune and people were dancing. Joints of beef roasted over an open fire while ears of corn soaked in salt water and potatoes coated with mud were set down among the embers. David bought them cups of cider and they took their food and sat under a spreading oak tree. They ate in silence for a time, until the worst of their hunger was satisfied.

Afterward, they dozed or at least Annabel did. She was still feeling the effects of the long, tempestuous night. David gathered her close and stroked her hair as her breathing became steadily slower and deeper. Gazing down at her, he felt a tug of emotion that was almost physically painful. He wished life could always be as simple, direct, and safe as this.

And yet it was all an illusion: The sun-drenched day framed a country at war. The people moving so gaily around them might not even exist in a few months. Macabre though that thought was, he forced himself to face it.

All his life people he knew and cared about kept vanishing into death. Behind his shuttered lids, he saw the small, frail dauphin of France who had been his boyhood friend and playmate. So many others had died with him, boys he had gone to school with, men he had come of age with, some whose names he could remember, others he could not.

Annabel stirred in his arms. He tightened his hold on her, breathing in the scent of her hair and drawing solace from her soft, yielding warmth. Asleep, she seemed the gentlest and most compliant of women. Awake, she was anything but.

A purely male smile lit the somberness of his eyes. It had taken him far too long to find a woman who enchanted him as she did. It was absurd to think that he would let her go, or that she would leave him of her own accord. She was young, innocent, and despite the success of the Wild Geese, relatively poor. He was rich, powerful, and attractive and should therefore keep her with him.

He thought of Annabel in France. Properly dressed, she would dazzle Napoleon's court. Moreover, she would be welcome there. Whatever else one could say about the emperor, he was no hypocrite. Mistresses were as welcome under his roof as wives, perhaps even more so.

David presumed, of course, that Napoleon would survive. But even if he did not, Annabel could be kept safely at Montfort, David's ancestral home. There he was *seigneur*, ruler and master. His will was absolute law; no one would attempt to gainsay him.

The problem solved, he smiled. At the same moment, Annabel awoke. The first sight she saw was David, looking down at her, his face alight with tenderness and approval. Instinctively, she reached for him, twining her arm around his powerful neck. Their lips met. They kissed deeply, unhesitantly. The passion kindled in the night and early morning surged again. Swiftly, without the need for words, they left the fair and made their way back to the Wild Geese and the quiet room hidden beneath the eaves. There they remained through the rest of the day, lost in the dream of each other.

At twilight, David and Annabel lay snuggled together in the bed, the sheet smoothed over their damp bodies. In the aftermath of their tumultuous lovemaking, all was peace between them. It seemed as good a moment as any for David to disclose the decision he had reached earlier in the day.

"Come with me to France," he said. "I have an apartment in Paris that you'll enjoy and afterward we'll go to Montfort. Once the present trouble quiets down, we could even visit Ireland. I'm sure you'd like that."

Annabel went very still. She couldn't believe what she was hearing.

He mistook her silence for shyness and was touched by it.

She was such an endearing combination of daring and innocence, how had he ever managed to get along without her? "Don't be concerned," he said soothingly, "everyone will welcome you. Napoleon is quite tolerant." He chuckled. "Of course, with his past, he has to be."

Fiery hair nearly covered Annabel's face, hiding her expression. Only her eyes could be seen gleaming darkly, indicative of the storm brewing within.

"Ye want me to leave here and go to France with you?"

He shrugged as though the idea was obvious—and obviously acceptable. "It makes sense, don't you think? We'll be together and you'll be away from the situation here."

"The situation in France isn't much better," she reminded him. "But besides that, I've a business to run."

"Cameron can take over for you. Or better yet, you could just sell the place."

"Sell it? In the middle of a war when I'd be lucky to get ten cents on the dollar?" Her practical soul was deeply offended. He might not know the value of money, having never had to struggle for it, but she most surely did. Moreover, she knew the value of independence, something she would most surely lose if she did as he wished.

David was taken aback. It had never occurred to him that she would consider his suggestion in so mercenary a light. A touch of hardness entered his voice as he said, "You needn't worry about that. I assure you, I can be very generous."

Annabel straightened. Sitting upright on the bed, she glared at him. "I'll be no one's mistress but my own. I fought hard for that all my life and I'm not about to give it up, not for ye or any man."

"What do you think happened between us these last two

days?'' he demanded angrily. ''We've lain together, touched, shared ourselves. You can't simply pretend none of that was real.''

''Oh, it was real enough,'' she said softly. How hateful the past tense sounded, how terrifying. ''And precious. But it didn't change me.''

''The hell it didn't!'' He reached for her only to find himself grasping empty air.

Annabel had left the bed. Wrapped in the sheet, she stalked to the other side of the room and seized her clothes. As David watched, she dressed hastily, not turning to face him again until she was fully dressed.

He remained stretched out on the bed, unabashedly nude. Soft evening light illuminated the powerful muscles and lean hardness of his body. Her throat tightened. Shorn of the trappings of civilization, he was magnificently, primitively male. Everything female in her could not help but respond. The need to return to the bed was almost irresistible. Yet how could she? To do so would be to lose herself, perhaps forever.

David saw the struggle going on within her. He did not relent entirely but his expression did soften. Gently, he asked, ''Is it so terrible that I want to take care of you?''

''No,'' she said, ''if that was all ye wanted. But we both know yer motives aren't so pure.'' He started to protest but she went on. ''For that matter, neither are mine. If there was a way to keep ye here in Washington, I'd take it and the consequences be damned.''

He frowned. ''You know that isn't possible.''

''I do, and I've never been one for moonin' over what can't be.''

''But it can and I've told you how.''

She tilted her head, meeting his gaze. "And I've told ye the price is too high." Wistfully, she added, "How I wish it weren't."

Then she was gone, her footsteps swift and sure on the narrow steps. Of her silent tears, he knew nothing. But of his own shock and the growing certainty of pain he was only too aware.

❧ CHAPTER ❧
Twelve

"**I** PRESENTED your recommendations for coordinating our military activities to the Cabinet," President Madison said. "As I'm sure you will understand, I didn't reveal their origins. The result is that I am thought to have been hiding my light under a bushel, as it were."

David tried to respond to the older man's dry humor but the best he could manage was a somber nod. They were meeting again in Madison's private study. Outside a summer storm was brewing. Heavy thunder clouds were moving up from the south. Already he could see thin fingers of lightning in the distant sky. The air seemed to crackle with electricity.

"Perhaps this will break the heat," Madison said. He glanced out the window at the hard-packed earth rutted by wagon wheels and dotted by a few yellowing clumps of grass. "And then we can get on to other things."

"I wish you luck with them," David said coldly. "But to be frank, the odds appear formidable."

The President shrugged. He didn't appear so much disinterested as fatalistic. "We live or die according to the will of one far greater than ourselves. But I cannot believe that having allowed us to come so far, He will abandon us."

David fought against his annoyance. His temper was short, his patience strained. Annabel's refusal of the day before still ate at him. He was in no mood to deal gently with her stubborn, opinionated, infuriating countrymen.

"I will relay your intentions to the emperor," David said. He rose to leave. "Is there anything else you wish me to tell him?"

Madison eyed the grim-faced young man tolerantly. He knew more than David realized, having bid Austen to investigate their French visitor before agreeing to receive him. He knew, for instance, of his dalliance with Annabel and he suspected the affair had somehow gone awry.

A pity, for he liked the marquis. Even given his aristocratic bent, the fellow had potential. "When this is over," he said quietly, "you may wish to return. There is a great deal of our country still for you to see."

David inclined his head courteously, but said nothing. He could not envision circumstances that would return him to America. Europe was the world and there he intended to remain.

Madison saw him out a short time later. The sky had continued to darken. A damp, threatening wind gusted down Pennsylvania Avenue. Although the rain had not yet started, people were already scurrying inside.

David felt no such need. He walked slowly, hands thrust deep into his pockets. Earlier that day, he had sent Pomfret to the offices of the shipping companies to inquire about upcoming departures. Prudence dictated a roundabout route down to Mexico and across the south Atlantic, although that would add months to the passage. On the voyage from France, he had opted for a quick, daring dash through the British blockade. This time he would do the same, provided he could find a captain willing to risk it.

Before then he would need to see his sisters and brother-in-law again. He would miss them, but that could not be avoided. His mission was too delicate to risk involving them, and he was well aware that they saw things differently from him. He clung to his faith in Napoleon, believing that while the emperor was far from perfect, he remained France's best hope. Paul and Dominique disagreed, believing as they did in the democratic ideal of freedom. For that ideal they had accepted exile. For his own convictions, David had also paid although he was only beginning to suspect the price.

A fat, cold drop of rain struck his bared head. He ignored it and went on, forcing himself to concentrate on the details of what had to be done before his departure. Anything was better than thinking about Annabel.

It began to rain in earnest. He kept on walking, heedless of the discomfort. His golden hair darkened into damp curls. Rain coursed down his lean face, clinging in droplets to his thick lashes. He stopped and threw his head back. The sky was a thick, sullen yellow. As he watched, a finger of lightning tore across it, followed hard by a clap of thunder that made the air shake all around him.

David laughed. All his life he had enjoyed the wildness of nature. It reassured him to know that something vast and unimaginable lay beyond humanity's reach. Kings and peasants, soldiers and priests, poets and executioners were all equally helpless in the face of such power. In France when he was a boy, even the guillotine stopped for a heavy enough rain.

He continued walking again until finally he was wet through. With his frock coat and breeches clinging soddenly, his hair trailing water, and his boots stained with mud, he reached the Wild Geese. Only a handful of incorrigibles sat at scattered tables. As usual, Cameron was behind the bar. He saw David coming and reached underneath for a bottle of the choice brandy.

David drained the snifter, then nodded appreciatively. "Thanks. It's a bit damp out there."

"Aye, tis that. A man could be forgiven for callin' a carriage or maybe even stayin' where he was till this blows over."

"I needed the walk," David said. He did not offer any further explanation and Cameron did not ask for any. Instead, the Scotsman gestured toward the door leading to the kitchen. "There's a lady waitin' for ye."

"A lady... ?"

"Came awhile ago. She couldn't sit in here by herself so Miss Annabel took her in hand. Says she's yer sister, by the way." A faintly disapproving frown furled Cameron's brow.

"Dominique? But why would she... ?"

"Not her, the other."

David sighed. He wasn't sure he was up to confronting Nicole just then. Trust her to come out in the midst of a storm, to a place no lady went alone, and end up in a tête-à-tête with her brother's mistress. He remembered that Annabel had made it clear that she declined the title. He grimaced, wondering what the two of them were discussing.

"I believe I'll have another," he murmured, gesturing to the brandy.

Cameron obliged. He went so far as to take a draught himself.

When the fiery liquid had been downed, the Scotsman said, "Yer sister . . . she's not from around here, is she?"

David shook his head. "Nicole is from Boston. She runs a school for young ladies up there."

Cameron frowned again. "A teacher . . . and her own school . . ."

If David had not been so preoccupied with his own concerns, he would have wondered at the Scotsman's interest. But as it was, he took no notice. Instead, he stared fixedly at the kitchen door. Finally, he took a deep breath, rose, and went toward it.

Barely had he pushed open the door when he was assailed by the scents of cinnamon and cloves. Annabel stood beside the big worktable. Her sleeves were rolled up and she had a large white apron tied around her narrow waist. There was a streak of flour on her nose and another on her chin. She had bound up her hair but it was beginning to work loose, spilling in a fiery cascade down her back. Her cheeks were flushed with the heat from the oven. Their color deepened when she looked up suddenly and saw David.

By contrast, Nicole appeared far cooler and collected. She was seated at the table in front of a large bowl of red apples. A knife flashed deftly as she carved the peel from one and sliced it into crescents. Annabel's sudden stillness interrupted her. Nicole glanced up, her eyes widening.

"Good Lord, what happened to you?" she asked her brother.

"I got wet." He continued to stare at Annabel. He had

not seen her since the previous day, although he had thought of her almost constantly. A flicker of satisfaction darted through him when he saw that she, too, showed evidence of a difficult night. There were violet shadows beneath her eyes and her neck bent sightly as though unable to bear the weight of her thoughts.

Remorse filled him. It came so suddenly and unexpectedly that he was taken unawares. He was on the verge of going to her when he remembered what had passed between them. Getting a grip on himself, he turned to Nicole.

"What brings you here?"

His sister hesitated momentarily. "I thought you might be leaving soon and I wanted to talk with you before then."

He didn't point out what she must surely have known, that he wouldn't have left without seeing her as well as Dominique and Paul. "All right . . . perhaps we can . . ."

He broke off, not sure where to take her. If the weather had been better, they could have walked. But as it was, he could hardly bring her into the tavern any more than he could ask Annabel to break off her work so that he and his sister could have the kitchen to themselves.

Annabel understood his quandary. Quickly, she said, "There's a small parlor in the back. It's not used much but . . ."

"That would be fine," Nicole said. She stood up, smoothing her skirt, and smiled at Annabel. "You're very kind."

Annabel turned away hastily. "I'll send ye in some tea," she said.

The parlor was small and had the shut-in feeling of a room where people rarely go. Yet it was meticulously clean and once the window was opened, the air freshened quickly.

Nicole sat down on the horsehair sofa as David took the

chair across from her. Outside the rain fell in straight, heavy curtains. Each waited for the other to speak. Finally, they both spoke at once.

"I know it must seem odd my doing this..." Nicole began.

"I'm glad you came," David said at the same time.

They broke off, looked at each other, and laughed. Softly, her voice muted by the rainfall, Nicole said, "Seeing you like this reminds me of the way we were as children." She was silent for a moment, staring down at her hands, before she went on. "Do you ever think of how it was then?"

David sighed. He leaned his head back against the chair but did not close his eyes. Above him he could see the rough-hewn ceiling with its carved beams. A tiny brown spider moved among them, industriously spinning her web.

"Sometimes," he admitted. "More than I would like."

"It's the same for me," Nicole said quietly. "Try though I do, I cannot forget it. Perhaps that's why I wanted to see you, just the two of us, before you left. Dominique understands much and so does Paul. After all, they both lived through it, too. But they weren't children as we were."

In the strange yellow light of the storm, her face was hauntingly pale. Looking at her, David realized with a brother's surprise that she was truly beautiful. But it was beauty tinged by sorrow so deep and profound that it seemed insurmountable.

He wondered if the same impediment wasn't in him.

"You are a woman," he said quietly. "You were meant for better things than men can know."

She looked up, startled. "What a strange thing to say. The world is dominated by men."

"To our detriment. Which do you think is the greater accomplishment—to fight a war or to give birth to a child?"

"It depends. Sometimes wars are fought to protect children and everyone else."

David wasn't moved. Harshly, he said, "More often than not they are fought solely because there is a terrible need in us to destroy. Women do not seem subject to that."

Nicole looked at him for a long moment before she said, "You are an idealist . . . and a romantic. I would not have thought it possible."

"Don't fool yourself. I have killed and in all likelihood I will kill again. After the first time, it becomes much easier. But as for love—beyond caring for you and Dominique, I don't believe I am capable of it."

Nicole rose from the couch. She came and knelt before him, clasping his hands in hers. Her face, turned up to him, was filled with gentle sympathy and entreaty.

A soft smile curved her mouth. "It is fear that stops you, David, not inability. I know because the same fear is in me. Dominique and Paul believe I have never married because I cherish my independence too highly. In fact, it is simple terror that stops me, the fear that if I love, that person will be torn from me or I from him. Reason says this doesn't have to be but the nightmares of our childhood undermine reason. They still control us."

Was she correct? Was he not merely a man content to satisfy the needs of the body and immune to those of the heart? Was he still also a child, dazed and terrified, running endlessly from death? It was a dismal thought and yet beneath it hovered the glittering light of truth.

He touched her cheek softly, cupping her face in his hand.

Their difficult last encounter in France no longer seemed to matter. What counted was the closeness of their lost childhood when they had clung together against all the world's turmoil and brutality. "Ah, Nicole," David murmured, "you were always wiser than the rest of us."

Nicole laughed and shook her head. Life had made her independent and straightforward, unwilling to let old hurts lie. This one in particular needed healing.

Gently, she touched his hand in turn, then rose. "Not wiser, merely more talkative. I have a tendency to blurt out what other people sensibly keep hidden." Smiling, she looked at him. "Or at least I do with you. Perhaps it's just as well you return to France . . ."

Neither of them believed that; they would miss each other now more than ever. But there was no help for it. Life called them in different directions.

The door to the parlor opened. One of the little maids stepped in, eyed them shyly, then scurried over to deposit a tea tray on a nearby table. David was not surprised that Annabel had sent someone instead of coming herself, but he was disappointed.

When the maid was gone, Nicole walked over to the table and began pouring their tea. Quietly, she said, "Miss Riordan told me she grew up in Ireland."

David nodded. He accepted a cup. "Her parents died there, killed by the British."

There was a clink of spoon against porcelain. When Nicole was done with her stirring, she said, "I find her a remarkable young woman."

David did not disagree but neither did he comment. He merely sipped his tea and stared out the window at the dark, rain-swept day.

* * *

The rain continued into evening. After seeing Nicole off in a carriage, David went back upstairs to finish his report. He was there when Pomfret returned. The valet knocked respectfully and entered when bidden. But at the first sight of his master, he stopped cold and stared.

"Sir . . ."

David had removed his sodden frock coat and tossed it carelessly over the back of a chair where it dangled forlornly. He wore only a white linen shirt minus cravat, his breeches, and his boots. Both the garments were badly wrinkled and still damp.

As for the boots . . . those proud objects of endless hours of polishing, Pomfret's pride and joy, looked as though they belonged on the feet of a carriage driver or a jockey. Mud-splattered, dull, and scratched, they clearly had no business anywhere near a gentleman of fashion.

"Really, sir . . ." The valet could not prevent a note of censure from creeping into his voice. There were limits after all. Being spirited away to America was bad enough, but the sullied boots were, in Pomfret's mind, most reprehensible.

Seeing his man's concern, David glanced down at himself. He didn't notice anything amiss but then he was much less sensitive to these things than Pomfret.

"If you wouldn't mind removing those, sir," the valet said stiffly, "I will endeavor to restore them."

Consideration for servants was bred into David's bones. He couldn't subject Pomfret to such a task and be at ease with himself. Drawing a coin from his pocket, he said, "Get the stableboy to do it. But first tell me what you learned at the shippers."

Pomfret's already mournful face took on the aspect of a man standing helpless and awe-struck before a cataclysm of nature. "I visited three offices and was told the same at each. They all have vessels leaving soon for France by the shortest route."

David felt a surge of relief. The sooner he could put Washington behind him, the better. "Excellent. When is the nearest sailing?"

"Tomorrow, the S.S. *Galena*, but, sir, don't you think..."

"Start packing, Pomfret. I'll send a message round to the ship to tell them we'll be boarding."

He penned the note quickly, then added another informing Paul and Dominique that he would call the following day to say his farewells. A sense of haste compelled him. He wanted to be gone, away from this strange new country, away from the questions Nicole had raised in his mind, away from the ache he felt whenever he thought of Annabel. If that was cowardice, so be it.

Pomfret went off glumly with the boots after assisting his master into a clean pair. He tried to convince David to also don a fresh shirt and breeches but did not succeed. The marquis waved him away with an impatient flick of his hand.

With his notes ready, he went back downstairs. Although it was getting dark, there was the usual gaggle of street urchins loitering about in hopes of catching a stray penny or two. David picked out the likeliest looking of the bunch, told him where to take the notes, and flipped him a shilling. The boy caught it on the fly and grinned.

"There's another for you tomorrow if I find you did as you were bid," David said.

"Right-o, sir," the boy said as he trotted off. His comrades looked after him enviously before clustering around

David in the hope that he might have other errands for them to do. He tossed out a handful of coppers before going back inside.

The tavern smelled of ale and sawdust, rain and old wood. It was beginning to fill up as people straggled in, shaking themselves like wet dogs and calling out their orders. There was no sign of Cameron. Instead, Annabel was in his place.

David approached her warily. Simple decency demanded that he tell her he was leaving. But pride also required that he conceal his true feelings and appear as unaffected as possible.

As it turned out, he had no chance to tell her anything. The tavern filled up quickly and Annabel was kept busy drawing pints of ale and pouring drams of whiskey. In between, she darted back and forth to the kitchen, making sure the food was being properly prepared. Once or twice her gaze met David's. Finally, she came over to him.

She stood a little stiffly beside his table, her hands clasped and her eyes averted. Softly, she said, "I enjoyed meetin' yer sister again. Did she get off all right?"

David nodded. He put down his knife and fork, and endeavored to appear equally matter-of-fact. "I sent her home in a carriage. Thank you for keeping her entertained, by the way."

"I was glad to do it. After all, she couldn't very well sit in here, could she?"

"No," David said quietly, "she couldn't." Their eyes met again as unspoken thoughts moved between them. Nicole couldn't sit in the tavern because she was a lady, but Annabel could sit, stand, talk, shout, do whatever was needed there. She was freer in certain respects than Nicole but she was also far less protected. Simply put, society thought her less valuable and less deserving. She had to depend on her own wits to survive.

"Where's Cameron?" David demanded suddenly. "He shouldn't have gone off and left you to all this. Especially with your hand not healed."

"It's fine," Annabel insisted. "He needed some time off, that's all."

"Doesn't he care that he's got responsibilities here?"

"Of course he cares. He's a damn sight more reliable than most men, I'll tell ye that."

David's face darkened. He liked the Scotsman well enough but he didn't enjoy hearing Annabel praise him. Nor did he care for the suggestion that she preferred the other man's character to his.

"Is that so?" he shot back. "Maybe you think so highly of him because he's never done anything to upset your tidy little notions of what's right and wrong."

"That's a bit of the pot callin' the kettle black, if you ask me."

David took a deep breath, schooling himself to patience. He was not going to lose his temper with this fiery-haired Irish termagant. She might get under his skin in a way no other woman had ever done, but he wasn't about to let her see it.

"Think what you like but we both know that you're only angry at me because I had the temerity to suggest you trade all this"—he gestured disdainfully around the tavern—"for a life of pampered luxury. How could I have been so inconsiderate?"

"By all the saints," Annabel muttered. Her hands were on her hips, her chin thrust out. She glared at him ominously.

"Ye're the most pompous man I've ever met. Ye think ye should be able to snap yer fingers and have me come running. Well, no thank ye, *Monsieur le Marquis*. I've better things to do any day of the week."

"That's fine with me. I don't know what I was thinking of when I made you that offer. No man deserves to be saddled with such a virago."

"Why ye . . ."

"Hey," a drunken voice interrupted, "how z'about 'nother whiskey ober here?"

"Yeah, how about it?" chimed in another.

"Chivvy with the Frenchman after closing, Annabel," a third suggested. "A man could die of thirst around here."

"Miss Riordan," one of the maids exclaimed as she erupted from the kitchen, "the saddle of mutton is burning."

"I swear," Annabel muttered, "if it isn't one thing it is another."

"Go," David ordered as he stood up. "I'll get this lot their drinks. You see to the food."

"Ye'll get them . . . ?"

"I can pour a glass full, for God's sake. Go."

Annabel stared at him for an instant before she abruptly did as he said. David watched until she disappeared through the kitchen door. He felt oddly pleased and wasn't sure why. Swiftly, he rolled up his sleeves and went to work.

❧ CHAPTER ❧
Thirteen

*C*AMERON had made tending the bar look easy but it wasn't. David had his hands full keeping up with a steady stream of orders. To his surprise, he enjoyed it. As he cracked a fresh keg of ale, spraying himself in the process, he laughed.

A buxom barmaid approached and asked timorously for two gins. He filled the heavy-bottomed shot glasses and set them on her tray. She smiled gratefully, as though he had performed a feat to marvel at.

Wryly, he wondered if commoners in general expected so little of the upper class. Were he and his kind considered so essentially inept that they couldn't be expected to perform the simplest task?

He had a sudden notion of a pyramid, the broad base representing the lowest and most common class, tapering upwards to a pinnacle occupied not by human beings but by elaborately clipped topiary statues such as were found in formal gardens. Should such a statue move or speak it would indeed be an occasion for wonder.

He thought the fumes from all the assembled bottles must be affecting him, he wasn't normally given to such whimsy. But then nothing was normal this day. He stood in disheveled clothes, free of most of the trappings of his rank, playing barkeep. All the while his eyes searched for the woman who should have been no more than slight amusement but was achingly far more.

Annabel. Sweet, enticing, stubborn, infuriating Annabel. Tomorrow she would be only a memory. That thought pierced him to the quick. He already had too many memories of people gone, never to be seen again. How dare she inflict yet another on him? How dare he do that to himself?

Deliberately, he turned his thoughts away, finding comfort in the most ordinary tasks. Beneath a steady rhythm, his mind lay still. Hours passed as he filled innumerable mugs of ale, developing a deft hand at settling the frothy head just so. Whiskey and gin were almost as popular. He found he had an instinct for noting who was reaching the limit of his tolerance and deflecting his interest to food.

Once the initial novelty of his presence wore off, men talked before him genially enough. They spoke of women and war, of work and worry. The fever that had struck David shortly after his arrival was still present in the city. A group of officers in the Civil Militia had been struck down by it, further complicating efforts to plan Washington's defense. The Congress remained in disarray, its members content to doze through the long days, or alternately, to hurl insults at one another.

Rumors abounded: the British were massing to march on the capital itself. The British were in full retreat. The war was lost, the war was won, the war had never really begun. No one knew and it seemed truly as if no one really cared. It was enough on that sultry, rain-soaked night to seize some fragment of good cheer, even if it could be found only at the bottom of a bottle.

David found that he, too, had a thirst. But he quenched it with clear spring water. The physical need was satisfied, only the emotional remained.

Not that all was grim and yearning. There were moments of outright levity, especially when poor old Pomfret came in for his supper.

Taking no notice of the man behind the bar, he ordered a large whiskey. David complied, setting it before him. The wizened apple-face glanced up, froze, and then crinkled into an expression of outright horror.

"*You . . .*" This, Pomfret seemed to say, went beyond all else. Was there nothing to which his master would not stoop? The world was turned upside down, all order banished. This strange, topsy-turvy America was as close to hell as a man of conscience would ever wish to get.

He downed the whiskey in a single gulp which caused him to cough and sputter helplessly. A barmaid, the buxom one, tried to lend assistance. She crushed Pomfret to her ample chest, pounding on his back and cooing to him in what was undoubtedly intended to be a soothing manner.

When the valet tried to protest, she redoubled her efforts until David had some doubts as to whether his servant would survive. He intervened then, sending Pomfret off to bed, but could not resist suggesting that the maid might want to check on him later. She indicated that she would, leaving David to imagine how his valet would receive such a visitation.

His own prospects for the night seemed a good deal dimmer. He could not bring himself to ask Annabel to share his bed. Yet it was highly unlikely—in light of what had happened between them—that she would invite him to hers. Across the crowded, smoke-filled tavern, they eyed one another like adversaries in an age-old battle. She frowned and looked away. He did the same. Moments later their gazes touched again. So it went through the long, seemingly endless evening. Had Washington ever been wetter, yet more consumed by thirst? Was the need for camaraderie so great that no one could even think of going home?

Annabel forced a smile as she reassured an old horse-trader that indeed, the vegetables were fresh, having been pulled only that morning from the earth. He appeared unconvinced but she remembered that he had lost his wife to the sweating sickness the year before and now with it back, though much less virulently, he would be thinking of her. She stayed beside his table, chatting about nothing in particular, until he seemed cheerier. Only then did she return to the kitchen.

A wave of heat struck her. The open hearth had been burning all day for the beehive oven where bread and pies were baked. The air was fragrant but stultifying. It closed around her like a suffocating blanket which she longed to throw off but could not.

Wearily, she bent over a large cast-iron kettle to stir the lentil soup. They should move more of the cooking outside into the side yard, she thought, but the bugs were bad there this time of year and she had an aversion to having them near food.

An old woman she had known in Ireland had been convinced that flies and their like carried diseases. Learned people laughed at the notion but Annabel still thought it possible.

She was straightening up, feeling faintly dizzy from the heat, when she became aware of someone behind her. Turning, she found David looking at her.

His lean, burnished features were suffused with concern. "Are you all right?"

Swiftly, she nodded. The motion set her head to throbbing. "I'm fine, just tired. Did ye need something?"

"Another keg of ale, but that can wait. It's an inferno in here."

"It will be cooler soon. The cookin' is almost done."

His mouth, the selfsame lips that had caressed her so maddeningly, narrowed to an ominous line. "You sweat in here so that mob out there will finally have its belly filled, and you think that's the way you should live?"

The throbbing increased, shooting down her neck as far as her shoulders. She closed her eyes for an instant. Rotating lights danced behind them. Frightened, she looked at him again. "If ye find the mob—as ye call it—so distasteful, there's no reason for ye to stay."

David didn't dignify that with a reply. He merely allowed the need that had been in him all along, growing stronger and more insistent, to take control at last. His hands were hard and unrelenting as he reached for her, but his mouth was all tenderness and sweet, enticing pleasure.

Annabel gasped. Her hands came up to ward him off and instead fell to caressing the steely span of his chest. Her body, which should have pulled away, drew nearer. Their breaths mingled, hearts pounding, tongues teasing. Restraint vanished, snapped like a fragile, overstrained reed before the storm's fury. They clung together, heedless of the swirling heat and the pounding rain. Nothing mattered except the taste, the scent, the feel of one another.

David's fingers tangled in the mass of silken curls tumbling down her back. Her head fell back, further exposing the vulnerable lines of her soft, white neck. His teeth grazed it, his tongue licking the tiny abrasion. Sensation enveloped him.

He could feel the pulse of her life's blood beneath his lips. Her natural fragrance—spices, soap, and young, vital woman—rose to tantalize him. Her slender form seemed almost to match his in strength, so urgently did she strain against him. But for the barrier of their garments they would have come together right then and there, standing in the rough-hewn kitchen, heedless of all those no more than a door-span away.

Even the garments might have proved no real impediment had it not been for a sudden sputtering of the fire. Unwatched, a clump of embers fell, some of them breaking loose to roll across the flagstone floor. One reached as far as the hem of Annabel's skirt. The smell of burning cotton suddenly filled the air.

"What..." She looked down, saw tiny fingers of fire reaching up her legs and screamed.

David didn't hesitate. He tore the skirt from her in a single motion, threw it to the floor, and crushed the fire beneath his feet. It was over in an instant. Annabel was left standing in her petticoat and chemise, her face white and her body trembling.

"Fire," she murmured, swaying on her feet. "I've always been afraid of it... ever since..." She broke off, swallowing bile.

Terrifying images from her childhood threatened to engulf

her. Thatched-roof cottages burning, dark waves of smoke blanking out the sky, the mute faces of broken men and women who had dared to rise against their oppressors and were being punished for it by seeing their homes destroyed.

She hardly knew when David gathered her close. Holding her high against his chest, he took the back stairs from the kitchen. Unseen by anyone, he carried her to the small room beneath the eaves. There he set her gently on the bed.

"You must rest." How frail she felt, as though the fire had taken all the life and confidence from her. Yet she clung stubbornly to pride.

"I canna," she said. "There is much yet to be done."

"Let the maids earn their keep. I'll instruct them."

That drew a soft, breathless laugh from her. "Ye? Since when do ye know how to feed a room filled with hungry men?"

"You put food on a plate and put the plate in front of the man. When he's done, you take his money and bid him good night. There's nothing complicated about that."

They both knew he was minimizing what was involved, but Annabel was too tired and numb to object. She did not resist when he pressed her down against the mattress and drew the thin sheet over her.

Her eyes fluttered shut. She was almost asleep when she thought she felt the brush of his lips on her forehead, more as a benediction than a kiss.

She woke uncounted hours later to cool, dry air and the silent depth of night. Sitting up, she glanced around uncertainly. She could not immediately recall how she had gotten where she was, but she knew something had been wrong. With a quick shock of fear she remembered.

A soft moan escaped her only to die away as she realized that she was no longer afraid. It was as though David's strength and protection still hovered over her, though the man himself was nowhere to be seen.

That was wrong. She needed to see him, to touch and be touched, to deny the inexorable passage of time that would soon part them.

Darkness lay over the room. She rose from the bed and reached for the thin robe hanging on the door. Softly, her feet soundless on the bare wooden floor, she left the room. It was the deep, hushed hour of night when nothing stirred. Even the air seemed to hang motionless. Instinct guided Annabel down the narrow steps and through the darkened hallway. She had avoided David's room since he came, but she knew it well enough.

The door creaked slightly as she opened it.

He lay in a pool of moonlight, naked but for that translucent glow. The sheet was at his feet, his arms were flung out with the easy abandonment of a child. His head had fallen to one side, and she noticed that his lips were gently parted. His powerful chest, lightly dusted with golden hair, rose and fell softly.

Annabel's throat was suddenly dry. Desire moved within her so consumingly that she could not breathe. Denied their sustenance, her lungs burned. She felt the discomfort absently, as though it was happening to someone else. Her being, her senses, her spirit were all focused on the man before her.

Slowly, never taking her eyes from him, she removed her robe and let it fall to the floor. Clad in her chemise and petticoat, she stood a moment longer studying him. He murmured faintly and turned his head.

Still watching, she loosened the laces of the chemise and drew it off over her head. Bare breasted, her lower body only half-concealed by flounces of filmy lace, she stood like an ancient goddess summoning her mortal lover.

No sound escaped her, no motion betrayed her presence. Yet David awoke.

He did not move but merely stared back at her, his eyes glittering with barely banked fires. Beneath his gaze, her nipples hardened. She shivered as the blood coursed more quickly through her, carrying away thought and reason, doubt and hesitation.

She had come this far...

The petticoat was held by a single strand of cotton knotted at her waist. Ordinarily, she had no difficulty undoing it. Tonight the knot stuck, defying her fingers.

David saw her difficulty. Without a word, he rose from the bed and came to her. His frock coat hung from the back of a chair. He reached a hand into an inside pocket. When he withdrew it again, the moonlight struck cold steel.

At Annabel's soft exclamation of surprise, he smiled ruefully. "An old habit." A flick of the long, pointed blade and the recalcitrant knot dissolved. The petticoat fell in a circle of whiteness, concealing her feet but leaving all else revealed.

He set the knife down on the table and returned to the bed. Seated there, heedless of his nudity, he studied her. Annabel fought down the natural inclination to modesty and met his gaze bravely. Before very long, she found that she enjoyed it. If nothing else, his boldness made her free to observe him in kind.

His voice touched her like a hand stroking down her body, claiming it utterly.

"Come here."

She crossed the room on legs that felt as though they would crumble at any moment. When she reached him at last, a long sigh of relief escaped her. It changed to an impassioned moan as he took hold of her around the hips and pressed his face to her soft, fragrant belly.

Pleasure too acute to be borne swept through her. She cried out and tried to push him away but he tightened his hold, letting her feel the iron will that lay beneath the warm, velvet-smooth skin. His strength, usually so rigidly held in check, startled her. She felt suddenly helpless, in the grip of something she could neither control nor elude.

Her hair tumbled around them, forming a dazzling cloud of fiery silk. David groaned deep in his throat. He raised his head, trailing hot, demanding kisses up along the shadowed indentations of her ribs.

His tongue stroked the satiny underside of her breasts, teasing, tempting, until she thought she would go mad from it. When his mouth at last closed around her nipple, suckling her urgently, she felt the tugging to the center of her womb and beyond.

The storm grew in intensity, but neither noticed it. They fell together onto the bed. Annabel's slender thighs straddled David's lean hips. She raised herself, her mouth curving in an ancient smile, and took him within her.

The world became the bed and their joined bodies moving upon it. Nothing else existed except the swift, rushing passion hurtling them into a darkness splintered by shards of blinding light.

From that pinnacle of supreme release, they slipped

effortlessly into sleep. Annabel did not wake again until the first gray fingers of dawn touched the clearing sky.

She lay for a long time propped up on an elbow, gazing at David. He slept like a child, but a child with secrets. A child who had learned at hard cost to guard himself from harm.

If she changed her mind and went with him, she would not merely be leaving the only world she knew. She would be entering into a relationship with a complex and in some ways contradictory man. There was nothing to say that such a relationship could long endure.

She had made her decision and she believed she would be wise to stay with it, whatever that cost her. But as she bent over him, her breath touching his lean cheek, tears slipped like broken diamonds down her face.

Softly, like the sigh of dying wind amid the trees, she whispered, "Goodbye."

❧ CHAPTER ❧
Fourteen

Washington, June 1814

SOMEONE was hammering outside the door. The sound reverberated through the darkened room, penetrating the dreams of the sleeping man.

Paul Delamare awoke at once. He sat up, instantly alert in the way of men who have lived through deadly times. His first thought was of Dominique but he then remembered that she was still in Boston with the children. She had wanted to come but fears of a British attack made Paul refuse to bring her when he returned to the capital a few days before.

He had been back and forth for most of the past year. Thanks to his efforts, the armed forces were in better condition medically than perhaps they had ever been. But that was scant comfort. Against the overwhelming British force, a healthy man was just as liable to be killed as a sick one.

If only Napoleon hadn't been defeated, the British would not have been able to turn their full fury on the former colonists. Odd, Paul thought as he got out of bed and reached for his robe, that he should be regretting the fate of his old enemy, but such was the way of the world. Everything turned round in the most unlikely directions.

Perhaps that would explain why Cameron was standing outside his door, looking pale and anxious. "Fer the love of God, mahn," the Scotsman said, "ye sleep like the dead. Another minute an' I'd 'ave knocked the bloody door down."

"What's wrong?" Paul demanded. Enough people had come to his door late at night for him to know what Cameron's presence meant. Someone was ill, possibly close to death. Weariness dropped away from him. This was an old battle but one he would willingly engage in time and again.

Even so, he wasn't prepared for the shock that cut through him when Cameron responded.

"It's Miss Annabel. Ye must come now."

Paul nodded. He asked no more questions but returned immediately to the room where he threw on the required minimum of clothing and seized his medical bag. No matter where he was or what the circumstances, the bag was always kept ready. He had needed it more times than he cared to remember.

"What's the matter with her?" he asked when they were out on the street. Cameron had brought two horses. He mounted one while Paul took the other. Within seconds, they were galloping down the empty street.

The horse's hooves rang sharply on the wood planks that spanned the dirty trench cut into the red soil. There was talk of putting down cobblestones but so far that was all it was, talk.

With characteristic obduracy, the Scotsman said, "She's ailin'."

"I concluded that for myself," Paul said. "Could you be more specific?"

As he waited for Cameron to reply, he thought quickly of his most recent visit to the Wild Geese. He'd stopped in there the day after he arrived in Washington. It was busy as usual but there was no sign of Annabel. One of the maids had said she was out of the city for a bit.

Now it seemed that she was back and ill.

"She doesn't know I went for ye," Cameron said. "And she won't be likin' it when she finds out. So I'll leave the rest fer you an' her to sort through."

That was hardly what a doctor wanted to hear as he prepared to deal with an emergency, but there didn't seem to be anything to be done about it. Cameron had sunk into morose silence. There was no sound except the pounding of hoofbeats and the far-off cry of the night watch announcing all's well.

Paul grimaced. They'd undoubtedly be calling out the same false good cheer as the British marched into the city. Even as the war intensified and American losses mounted, the citizens of Washington had become no more realistic. They continued to argue and dither, to debate and proclaim, but in essence to do nothing. The city was as undefended as it had been almost a year before. If the British came that very night, they would meet virtually no resistance. The Revolution—and all the proud hopes it had represented— would be crushed under the load of apathy and disorganization.

But that was not his concern, at least not at the moment. He had a patient to consider.

At this hour, the Wild Geese was closed. A single light burned over the door. Another could be seen burning low in a top-floor room.

Paul took the stairs quickly. As he reached the uppermost landing, he heard a woman's sharp moan. Cameron had followed him. He opened the door to a room and stood aside to let Paul enter.

Annabel lay on the bed. Her red-gold hair hung in damp tendrils around her face. She was pale and her eyes were darkly shadowed. Her lips had been bitten to the point of bleeding. She twisted helplessly as her fingers knotted around the thin sheet.

Instantly, Paul was at her side. His hand touched her forehead gently. "Easy," he murmured, "let it come . . . ride it out . . . that's right . . . it's going now . . . good . . . let it go."

She exhaled deeply and sagged back against the pillows. A wan smile touched her lips. "Sweet Lord but it hurts."

"Yes," Paul said briskly, "I know it does." He stepped away from the bed and gestured to Cameron. "Get towels and more sheets, also a bucket of warm water." When the Scotsman hesitated, Paul said sharply, "Get on with it, man. We don't have all night and neither does she."

Beneath the sheet and the soft gown she wore, her belly moved. Hugely swollen, it seemed to have a life of its own, as indeed it did. A tiny bulge appeared—a hand, perhaps, or a foot—part of the child fighting to be born.

Paul returned to the bed. He bent over Annabel, watching her closely, trying to gauge how much of her strength was left.

"When did this begin?" he asked.

"Yesterday," she whispered, "early . . . in the *m-morning—aahhh*."

Another contraction seized her. Paul held her hand as it grew, murmuring to her gently, counting the seconds until it peaked. When it was done, he wiped her forehead gently.

"You should have sent for me sooner," he said.

"I didn't send for ye at all," she reminded him. He was relieved to note that despite her agony, she had not lost her spirit. "That Cameron . . ."

"Did the only thing he could," Paul countered.

"He was supposed to get Old Meg but her granddaughter took sick and she went to her instead-d *aaahhh* . . ."

Again, Paul held her hand and encouraged her through the contraction. He had done the same for Dominique in all five of her birthings and he had assisted numerous other women as well. Though he hardly claimed it as a specialty, he was known for the skill—and kindness—with which he helped to bring children into the world.

He would need both this night, as his swift examination told him. Annabel's labor had been going on for almost a full day; she should have been much further along. He suspected that the baby might be turned the wrong way but his fears on that score at least were quickly alleviated.

The baby was correctly positioned and seemed vigorous, but it also appeared to be very large. That was serious enough but he also sensed something in Annabel that worried him, a certain holding back which could not be defined but was present nonetheless. He had felt it before in women who were reluctant to give birth and he knew what it could cost them.

"You must want this child to come," he told her roughly. "You must will it into the world. Nothing else will work."

She looked at him for an instant, her eyes swimming in pain and fear. Then she turned her face to the wall.

Cameron returned. Paul gestured him to put the supplies down by the bed. Another contraction had seized Annabel. It seemed even deeper and more fierce than the others. Watching her, Cameron blanched.

"The pur wee lass," he murmured. "This shouldn't be happenin' to her."

"But it is," Paul said through gritted teeth. Annabel had seized his hand and was holding onto it with such desperate fierceness that he thought the bones might snap.

When she eased her grip a little, he turned back to the Scotsman. "Help me get her up."

"Are you daft, man? She canna stand."

"She isn't going to. She's going to kneel with our help. The baby's very large," Paul explained. "If she's upright, it will come more quickly."

If it came at all, he added silently. Such children frequently did not survive their births. Oftentimes, neither did their mothers.

Anger surged through Paul. He liked Annabel, he admired her spirit and her tenacity. She had survived much in her young life. He was damned if he was going to lose her now.

"Come on," he ordered. Together the two men lifted Annabel until she was crouching on the bed. Supported between them, she managed a wan smile.

"Ye both will be wishin' ye'd stayed in bed."

"And miss this?" Paul said. "I've always wanted to see a faery child come into the world."

" 'Tis no faery," Annabel whispered. Her head fell forward and her body clenched as another contraction hit her. When it had passed, she said breathlessly, "Tis a brash, brawlin' thing without the sense to know it shouldn't even be."

"But it is, Annabel." He leaned close to her, his voice so near it seemed to be within her. "It's real and it's alive, and it wants desperately to be born. Help it."

And suddenly, through the veil of her pain and anguish, she understood the immense, vital truth behind those words. The child she had tried to deny, the child who mocked her vaunted independence, was fighting for its life.

And only she could help it.

All that she was, the whole of her being, focused on the great struggle going on within her. She was in that moment not a single woman but all women, part of an endless, unbroken line stretching back through the millennia and far ahead into the fathomless future. She felt linked to a quicksilver thread running through the darkness of eternity, illuminating it with light and hope. She sensed the power that had existed from before the beginning and would still be there after the end to begin again.

The thread coiled, spinning tighter and tighter into a shining bead of light that darted behind her eyes, drawing her down a dark, pulsating tunnel. She felt tightness pressing all around her. She was afraid and she was elated. She was struggling and she was passive, following out of the warm, wet darkness into *light*. Her eyes flew open. After the darkness, the light was blinding. She could not see but she could hear the lusty, enraged cry of her newborn child.

She gasped and reached out her hands. Paul hesitated only an instant before he placed the red, mucous-stained bundle in her arms. Tiny fists flailed at her. The small mouth opened to emit another outraged howl. Crystalline blue eyes shot through with gold glared at her.

"A fighter, this one," Cameron murmured admiringly. "He looks mad enough to take on the world."

"An' why shouldn't he be?" Annabel asked against the rising tide of her own exhaustion. She gathered the child closer, cooing to him softly. "Pur wee bairn, tis a hard time ye had. But tis over now and look at ye, fit as any fiddle."

The child paused in mid-yell and appeared to regard her solemnly. He must have been satisfied with what he saw, for after a moment, he began rooting for her breast with the ferocity he had already demonstrated.

Annabel blushed. She knew little about such things; indeed, she had deliberately kept herself ignorant over the course of her pregnancy as a way of denying what was happening to her. There was no chance of any such denial now. Her son had arrived, hale and hearty, and unmistakable in his demands.

Paul stepped in to smooth the way. Having safely delivered the afterbirth, he turned his attention to the child. A quick check satisfied him as to the baby's health. As Cameron discreetly withdrew with the soiled sheets, Paul issued matter-of-fact instructions that shortly had the desired result.

Despite her instant attraction to the baby, Annabel remained uncomfortable with her new-found role. She felt awkward and uncertain, not familiar sentiments for her. The child, however, seemed to have no such inhibition.

Staring at the downy head anchored firmly against her breast, she murmured, "He's very... vigorous, isn't he?"

Paul laughed gently. "I haven't seen many bigger or stronger, that's for certain. You did very well."

She looked up, startled, as though the suggestion that she had done something admirable would never have occurred to her. "There's more than a few who wouldn't agree with ye," she said.

Paul sat down on the side of the bed. He knew he had to tread carefully but he was determined to say what needed to be said. "Is that what you're afraid of, what people will think?"

"I'm not afraid," Annabel insisted. More softly, she amended, "At least not that way. People will think what they will, but they'll still need to eat and drink. Besides, the sort that comes to the Wild Geese doesn't care much about such things."

"Then what troubles you so?" Paul asked gently.

"I . . . never expected this. I never meant to do as women usually do. I thought . . . I don't know exactly . . . but I wanted to be freer." She broke off, too weary and befuddled to go on.

She didn't need to. Paul made no claim to understanding exactly what it meant to be a woman, but he too had yearned after freedom, following it like a will-o'-the-wisp almost to his death. In the end, only love had saved him.

Quietly, he said, "Life has a habit of taking us unawares. You must rest now. We'll talk again later."

He waited the few moments it took her to slip into exhausted sleep, then gently removed the infant. The baby, his stomach filled, looked up at him calmly. Paul chuckled. He had always liked babies and since siring five of his own, he felt he knew a thing or two about them. But this one had brought his own set of complications into the world.

Together they settled in a nearby chair—the big, hard

man and the newborn infant. Gazing down into the small, perfectly formed face, Paul sighed ruefully.

He had not asked Annabel who had fathered her child, because there was no reason to do so. If his own sensitivity to the currents that flowed between individuals had not been enough, the child himself proclaimed his heritage. His proud, strong features bore the unmistakable stamp of the de Montforts.

David would have no difficulty recognizing his son.

"I canna," Annabel proclaimed. She was sitting up in bed, clad in a fresh nightrail, her russet hair brushed until it shone like glistening silk, and the color restored to her cheeks. She looked, Paul mused, remarkably beautiful. She was also angry.

"Tis my responsibility to care for this child. I'll do it on my own without anyone's interference." More gently, she added, "Not that I don't appreciate all ye've done. Ye're as good a friend as any man or woman could ever hope to have. But I don't think ye realize how unusual ye are, Paul Delamare. Precious few men think as ye do. I'll be subject to none of them, thank ye very much."

"I'm not suggesting that you sell your soul," Paul murmured dryly. It was morning now and he, unlike Annabel, had not slept. He was very tired but his mind was perfectly clear. He could see what had to be done even if she could not.

Bluntly, he said, "David has to be told."

"Why?" Annabel demanded. "Because he happened to be in the wrong place at the wrong time—with the wrong woman? He's thousands of miles away now with a life of his own. The most he could do would be to send money and that"—she added fiercely—"I'll be havin' none of."

"Is that the most?" Paul countered softly. "If you really believe that, you don't know David at all. He's still a young man but he's experienced more loss in his life than most people will ever know. Almost everyone and everything he's cared about has been destroyed in one way or another. Now you want to deny him even the knowledge of this child. His *only* child unless I am very much mistaken."

"How could ye know a thing like that?" Annabel scoffed, trying to quell the shock that rippled through her. Somehow she had never thought that David might have other children. Despite Paul's assurances, the notion was distinctly disturbing. "Women must have been throwin' themselves at him since he was a wee lad."

"True enough," Paul acknowledged. He was pleased to see her flinch, it helped to confirm his suspicions about the depth of her feeling for David.

"Nonetheless," he went on, "I am quite certain this lad is his only child. After all," he paused pointedly, "David is a man of the world. He knows perfectly well how to avoid unwanted pregnancies. Indeed, I confess to being surprised that he didn't take such simple precautions with you."

Annabel froze. Her eyes widened in disbelief. Torn between her desire to appear in control and her fierce need to know the truth, she asked, "What do ye mean?"

Paul managed to appear surprised. "I thought you would already have realized. There are methods a sensible man can use to prevent unwanted accidents. Indeed, women can avail themselves of them as well. I rather thought David would have ... or failing that, you would have ... but it seems neither of you ..."

"*Me*," Annabel exclaimed. "I was as green a girl as ever came out of Eire. While he. . . ." Her voice dropped to a low, fierce murmur. "That bloody, deceivin' blackguard. If I ever get my hands on him, I'll . . ."

"Write to him," Paul interjected. "Tell him of the child. He's every bit as responsible as you are. It's only right that he do his duty."

Having observed the child now for several hours, Paul privately thought the "pur wee bairn" capable of taking just about anything from life that he happened to desire, but he forbore saying so.

He was equally unconcerned about having exaggerated the case regarding effective precautions against pregnancy. For all he knew, David had made use of them. As he knew from his own experience—being the father of an unexpected fifth child—such precautions were not always effective. But let Annabel believe they had not been used. She would be far more ready then to do what was right.

Offering a silent prayer from one man to another that his brother-in-law would forgive him, Paul said, "If you will write the letter, I will see to its dispatch."

She stared at him for a long moment. Finally, she murmured, "I'll think on it."

Paul nodded. He was satisfied for the moment. She was an honorable woman and ultimately a sensible one. She would do what was right.

In the meantime, he had his own letters to prepare.

❧ CHAPTER ❧
Fifteen

Chateau de Montfort, late June 1814

A BEE was busy working its industrious way down a stalk of grass. As it went, it maneuvered its wings so as to keep a constant distance between itself and the surface which it contrived to never quite touch.

Stretched out beneath an oak tree that had been old when his great-grandfather was young, David watched the bee absently. He was glad of the chance to rest. Since before dawn, he had been in the saddle, riding over the vast lands attached to his estate. His purpose was to show himself to the people laboring there, *his* people, who needed to know that he was back and he was in command. Otherwise, they might be tempted to doubt it.

He had stayed with Napoleon to the end. There was some satisfaction in that, though less than he would have expected. He still woke sweating from dreams of the final battle at

Leipzig the previous October. He had been there when troops which up to that moment had been loyal to the emperor, suddenly turned their guns on him. History rested upon such vagaries of human loyalty.

Napoleon was fortunate to be alive although from the perspective of his exile on the Isle of Elba, he might not agree. David had returned home to Montfort with the humility of a man given a second chance at life. He was not ashamed to admit that he had wept when he first set his feet again on its firm black soil. He felt it now beneath his fingers, sun warmed and filled with the promise of the harvest to come. Beneath his shuttered eyes, in the privacy of his own thoughts, he reviewed what he had found since his return.

At first there had been a certain laxity, not unexpected considering how long he had been away. That had changed swiftly enough once he had made his intentions clear. He was master here, this was his land, his holding. Men of his blood had ruled it since remembered time. The shakily restored monarchy was in no position to contest that.

The de Montforts were a tenacious lot. They failed to recognize the passage of eras, the disintegration of other families like their own, or the increasingly strident demands of the modern world which thought them obsolete. They had survived war, famine, drought, revolution, personal misfortune, and public calamity. They were, in short, indomitable.

He ruled. The words suggested much but even that was only a tiny fragment of what they truly meant. This was not merely his land but his world, the only one he wanted.

He put his head back and gazed up at the cerulean sky. The air was scented with the heavy, langorous scent of the vineyard. Beyond it lay fields of wheat ripening in the sun, orchards heavy with apples and pears, rippling streams bursting with fish, and more.

A bird seeing Montfort from the sky would observe a canvas of gold and green, blue and silver, punctuated by white blossoms and red fruit. All centered around the manor house itself, dozing beneath the sun.

Home. After a lifetime of battles, the word had a special poignancy for David. This was the place of his earliest memories—before the final gilded days at Versailles, the imprisonment at the Tuileries, the guillotine. Here he had come into the world and here, God willing, he would leave it. But not any time soon. He had a great deal of work to do first.

Slowly, he stood and brushed the fine dark soil from his breeches. His horse—a fine roan stallion—nickered softly. "Tired, boy?" he asked. "You've earned a rest."

There would be no such thing for him. He had records to go over, part of his ongoing effort to acquaint himself with all that had happened during his absence. His steward was impeccable but David still felt the need to know everything for himself.

Later, in the silence of the long summer night, there would be a quiet dinner taken alone. He had kept almost entirely to his own since his return, by choice. He had no desire for diversion in any form. He wanted to let France— that cursed, seductive beauty of a nation—go its own way. He had his life to put in order. Until he found Pomfret waiting for him in the vast marble entry hall.

The valet's presence, rather than the steward's, told him at once that something was not right. Bad news was generally left to the body servants to communicate, their intimacy with their masters being a presumed protection.

Silently, David held out his hand. Pomfret sighed exaggeratedly, as was his wont, and placed a thick envelope in it.

"From America, sir," he said.

David nodded. He walked the distance to his study and shut the door behind him without any awareness of his actions. All his attention was focused on the boldly scrawled handwriting.

Paul. If something had happened to Dominique or Nicole, his brother-in-law would certainly write. But the stamps placed across the top of envelope bore the notice that it had been mailed from Washington. If either of his sisters was ill, Paul would not have left them in Boston.

That left only one other possibility, the same one he had shied away from considering these past ten months. Annabel had been ever in his dreams but rarely in his thoughts. At her first appearance in the unguarded night realm of his mind, he had resolutely thrust her aside. And at every appearance thereafter. A hundred times? A thousand? He had vowed not to think of her, then made a mockery of that vow.

She was as persistent a specter as had ever haunted any man, all the more so because the real flesh-and-blood Annabel had no reason to know of his suffering. She, undoubtedly, was going gaily about her chosen life, wallowing with the ale-swilling, garlic-belching peasantry she so enjoyed. Damn her to hell and back.

He scanned the heavy vellum sheets with mingled disbelief and astonishment. She had given him a child. A baby... a son. Born three weeks before and alive all these days without his even knowing. As his fields swelled and prepared to give up their fruit, his child had already been in the world.

He turned to stare out the tall windows toward the garden planted by some remote ancestress and still maintained in perfect bloom. His child. Everything was changed. Even the light from the sun looked different.

"Pomfret."

The door opened reluctantly. A wary Pomfret poked his head in. "Sir?"

"Pack. We are returning to Washington."

Had he announced his decision to visit Hades, the valet could not have been more dismayed. His small, wizened face turned red and he appeared to have difficulty breathing. "But sir..."

"To your tasks, Pomfret, and I to mine. I must find out when the next vessel is sailing."

Dazed and morose, Pomfret withdrew.

Montfort was located close enough to the coast to have the benefit of a weekly news sheet which listed departures and arrivals. David scanned it quickly. With the British blockade of the Americas still in effect, travel remained difficult. But as had been the case a year before, numerous captains were still willing to take the chance for a sufficient fee.

Swiftly, David dispatched a message to the stables to inform his grooms that he would require a carriage the following morning. He then sent for his steward.

Gerard Blanchard was a large, strapping man. His black hair, blue eyes, and burnished skin radiated health and energy. He was one of the very few at Montfort who unfailingly looked David in the eye. Blanchard was not insubordinate but he was proud. David liked that.

"I am going away for a time."

Gerard said nothing but he managed to convey by the tension in his big body that he disapproved of any such action. "A few more weeks and it'll be reapin' time," he pointed out.

"I hope to be back by then." David paused. It was not his way to take any man into his confidence, much less a servant. Still he felt he owed his hard-working and impeccably honest steward some sort of explanation. "It is . . . a personal matter of great urgency, otherwise I would not go."

Gerard nodded slowly. Like David, he was a veteran of Napoleon's wars. He had barely survived the Russian campaign and still limped because of it. His family had been at Montfort for uncounted generations. He considered it was as much his own as any man's though he was wise enough to know that the bond would mean nothing if David himself chose to sever it.

"I will return," David went on, "as quickly as possible."

"Certainly, sir," Gerard murmured. "Be assured everything will be well cared for in your absence."

"I expect no less." David paused for a moment, studying the young man. Quietly, he said, "We live in difficult times, Gerard. Your dedication does not go unnoticed . . . or unappreciated."

The steward nodded somberly. He made none of the gestures common to his class—no tugging of the forelock or ducking of the head. Instead, he eyed David squarely, one man to another.

"It's the land that counts, sir. Properly tended, it goes on forever."

David nodded slowly. He felt the same way himself. There had always been men like Blanchard on the land. They were as necessary to it as sunshine and rain. But there had also been de Montforts, to rule by wit and sword, to stave off other, greedier men, to keep the land pure and safe. Forever.

Quietly, he said, "I go to claim my son."

Nicole laughed softly. She lifted the baby, watching his small face crinkle with pleasure, and felt a matching surge of delight coil through her. It was unexpected. She had learned of Annabel's situation just as the school term was ending. It occurred to her that she would be at loose ends with time on her hands, just when another woman was torn between work and caring for her child who happened also to be Nicole's nephew. The solution was obvious.

Never mind that neither Annabel nor Nicole knew much of anything about babies. They were learning as they went along. Cameron was proving a godsend.

"Nine brothers and sisters, I have," he had explained as he deftly changed a nappy. "Be a bit strange if I didn't know which end was which."

"We're not that bad," Annabel replied.

"Nay," he allowed with a grin. "Ye know which end to feed and which end to wipe, I'll give you that. The rest will come."

And so it did.

Nicole lowered the baby gently. He snuggled against her,

his head fitting exactly into the curve of her neck. She inhaled the soft, fragrant scent of him and smiled.

"Ah, little Louis," she murmured. "What a way you have about you."

He had been named for the dauphin of France, the doomed friend of David's childhood. Annabel had made that choice herself without telling anyone else. She claimed to merely like the sound of it. Needless to say, no one believed her.

The baby emitted a fragrant belch and promptly fell asleep.

Nicole laid him gently in his cradle. A young maid poked her head in the door. "Miss Annabel said you might be wantin' a bit of rest, ma'am."

Nicole accepted gratefully enough. She loved her nephew but even she admitted that he was a handful. How any child of less than two months managed to turn the world on its ear the way he did was beyond her. Of course, there was the fact that he didn't like to sleep—at least not as most babies seemed to. He liked to eat and to be entertained. Not much else interested him.

Annabel was below in the kitchen. She had recovered swiftly from the birth and had wasted no time resuming her usual activities.

Seeing her, Nicole sighed. The happiness of being with her nephew faded. It was time to talk about less pleasant realities.

Quietly, she entered the kitchen and took a seat at the worktable. Annabel glanced up but said nothing. She was busy rolling dough for pies. Her slender arms, bared to the shoulders, were speckled with flour. Her simple dress and wide white apron were similarly festooned. She looked absurdly young and utterly determined.

Softly, Nicole said, "You must leave."

Annabel pretended not to hear her. They had had the same conversation three times in as many days. There was nothing new to be said.

Still, Nicole felt bound to try. "It is only a matter of time before the British attack Washington. Do you imagine they will be sweet and gentle about it?"

Annabel's hands clenched. She turned away from the table, still refusing to look at Nicole, and thrust a pan of dough into the oven.

"I imagine they will be as they always have been. But we will survive—as we always have."

"How can you be so sure? More to the point, how can you risk your child's life? It would be bad enough if it were only your own, but a baby's . . ."

Annabel stood, straight and proud, beside the fire. She did not turn, nor did her voice give any hint of her feelings. With rigid control, she said, "Ye have been a good friend, Nicole. I appreciate that. But ye're wrong if you think I'll ever put Louis at risk. He's all I have."

Nicole was silent for long moments. She could not pretend to understand the bond between a mother and child, although she had seen it often enough. Dominique would undoubtedly have died to protect her children. Or she would have killed. And she was the gentlest of women. Annabel was anything but. Nicole did not doubt that she would go to any lengths to protect her son.

Reassured, she asked, "Then you don't intend to stay?"

Annabel hesitated. She truly did appreciate Nicole's help, but even more she appreciated the woman herself. She had appeared unexpectedly a week after Louis's birth, brought apparently by a letter from Paul to his wife and sister-in-law. With her usual no-nonsense manner, Nicole had explained that she was free for the summer and happy to help.

And help she had. Annabel wasn't quite sure what she would have done without her. Now more than ever she had to keep the Wild Geese going. She had her son to look after. He would need clothes and toys, books and tutors, a fine horse and the means to travel. Someday he would take his place among the ranks of gentlemen to which he assuredly belonged. But all that required money.

With every plate of mutton and every tankard of ale, she thought of the baby lying upstairs, snug and unknowing in his cradle. Please God, let the world be better for him, she prayed. A simple prayer, the age-old entreaty of mothers everywhere.

Slowly, she said, "I intend to watch...and to listen. When the time is right for leavin', I'll go."

Nicole was far from satisfied but instinct warned her she would get no further, at least not at the moment. Her young friend was indomitably stubborn. In her mind's eye, Nicole likened her to a beautiful, graceful willow standing proudly against the storm. She only hoped that Annabel would have the sense to bend rather than break.

With a sigh, she left the kitchen and went out into the side yard to check on the laundry that had been left there to dry. She was testing the sun-scented sheets to judge whether they were ready to come down when she saw Cameron emerging from the tool shed.

He had spent the morning repairing the white rail fence in front of the tavern. A fine sheen of perspiration shone on his hard features. His plaid shirt clung to the broad sweep of his chest. As he moved, Nicole could see the muscles move with fluid ease.

Her mouth was suddenly dry. She swallowed hard and managed a faint smile.

"Good afternoon, Cameron," she said softly.

He hesitated and for a moment she thought he was going to turn away. Only then did she realize that he wasn't wearing his eye patch. She had noticed before that it seemed to chafe him, at least enough for him to take it off when he was doing hot, heavy work. Now he reached automatically for his pocket.

"Wait." Without pausing to consider her boldness, Nicole stepped forward. Her hand closed over his. Unflinchingly, she stared him full in the face. "There's nothing wrong with the way you look right now."

Beneath his almost silvery hair, his brow furrowed. He studied her warily. "There's not many who would agree with ye."

She smiled gently. "Is that supposed to trouble me?"

He was silent for a long moment before he said, "Do ye not care then for the opinion of others, Miss de Montfort?"

"I care, but I care more for my own opinion." Her cheeks warmed with embarrassment or excitement, it was impossible to tell which. "Does that make me sound awful?"

His gaze still on hers, Cameron shook his head. "It makes ye sound like a rebel. But I must tell ye, ye don't look like one."

She took a quick, sharp breath, aware of the sudden triphammer beat of her heart as she stood before this big, hard, unexpectedly gentle man. "What do I look like?" she asked softly.

His mouth quirked and a deep, male laugh rumbled up in

him. "Ah, now, if I be tellin' ye that, ye won't be thinkin' anything good about me."

Nicole swallowed with difficulty and lifted her head. "Is it that terrible?"

Cameron watched the faint pulsation of her throat beneath ivory skin that looked impossibly smooth and delicate. He imagined his mouth pressed to that skin, tasting and caressing it. The thought hit him with the force of an immense wave. It rocked through his body, tightening every muscle in response.

"Nay," he said slowly, "not terrible but foolish. Very... very foolish."

Nicole's lips parted. The air seemed much warmer than it had even a few minutes before. She was suddenly aware of the constriction of her clothing and had to repress a mad impulse to be free of it.

They were alone in the side yard but someone might come at any moment. Even if no one did, they could be easily seen from the tavern's upper windows.

The lack of privacy aside, they shouldn't even be having such a conversation. She was a lady—educated, refined, genteel. He was a rough-edged working man, a wanderer with no firm roots and no clear intentions. There could be no possible future for them.

And yet she was drawn to him in a way she had never before experienced. This big, scarred Scotsman with his cautious manner and restrained strength affected her far more powerfully than any of the fine solid burghers of Boston or the dashing cavaliers of Paris.

"Long ago," she said softly, "kings kept fools to make them wise. Those prancing jokesters in bell-jangled hats saw truth more easily than plain, sensible people."

She looked up at him again, her eyes deep pools of green in which the wariest of men might drown. On the sweet, fragrant air, her voice touched him like a breath of light. Far off in the distance, he could almost hear the mocking, teasing sound of bells dancing ever out of sight but always there.

A shaft of pain cut through him—pain for lost worlds and lost years, for those he had loved who were gone forever and for those whom he had thought never to love. He took the pain for what it was, let it blossom within him, and let it go.

In its place was peace—and firm, unwavering purpose.

In the spirit of both, he drew her to him.

❧ CHAPTER ❧
Sixteen

DAVID stepped onto the pier near Washington's Green-leaf Point scarcely an hour after dawn. Although the sun was still barely visible in the heat-hazed sky, the wharves were thronged with people, including many in uniform. He saw the outfits and insignia of at least a half-dozen regiments, the members of which all seemed to be waiting for transport. So did dozens of civilians clustered around a handful of harried men, the shipping agents for the few lines still sailing.

The British blockade and the threat of direct attack had finally convinced many of the citizens of Washington that the time had come to leave. For many the decision was made too late. There were far fewer berths available than would-be customers. The bidding was fast and furious, with voices raised and fists clenched. An air of impending panic hung over the proceedings despite the efforts of many to maintain calm.

Behind David, carrying their two valises, came Pomfret. The valet glanced fearfully in all directions. He clutched the cases as though expecting a regiment of British dragoons to appear at any moment. He had developed a nervous tic over one eye and had taken to sighing with even greater force than usual.

David ignored him and waved down a passing brougham. As he set his foot on the running board, a tall, bearded man in a blue captain's uniform approached him. Kayes was master of the *Seafarer*, the ship that had carried David from France. The two men had struck up a pleasant acquaintance during the crossing.

Kayes was convinced that the long-awaited British attack on Washington was finally about to occur. For that reason, he intended to stay only until the tide turned. *Seafarer* would sail that afternoon with whoever had the sense to be aboard her.

"You'll not reconsider then, sir?" the captain asked.

David shook his head. He appreciated Kayes's concern but he was not about to be swayed by it. "My business is too important. I must remain until it is concluded."

The captain shrugged. "The Bible tells us we are our brother's keeper, but there's only so much a man can do. If you're determined to stay, God be with you."

On the verge of entering the carriage, David hesitated. He glanced back at Pomfret standing behind him. The little man was the picture of dejection. He stood with his head bowed, a long-suffering expression on his face and an aura of hopelessness hovering about him.

David turned back to the captain. "I won't be returning with you but my man here will. Go on, Pomfret," he urged as the valet's head jerked up and he stared at his master open-mouthed. David reached quickly into his wallet and handed him a thick sheaf of bills. "This should take care of everything. Return to Montfort and await me there."

"But sir . . ." Pomfret murmured, all but overcome.

"I shouldn't have brought you," David said. "It wasn't right. Go on now and see to matters at home for me." With mock sternness, he added, "I will expect to find everything in order when I return."

Pomfret straightened his shoulders. His hangdog manner fell away as though it had never been. With somber dignity, he said, "As indeed you shall, sir, for Gerard Blanchard will see to it. I am not needed in that capacity. My place is to serve you. To do so, I must be at your side."

Caught unawares by the man's sudden courage, David said, "That is generally so, but under the present circumstances . . ."

"It is doubly imperative that I remain." Lowering his voice, as though to impart a fact too horrible to be blared about, Pomfret said, "I don't think you fully appreciate, sir, precisely how difficult it will be to maintain proper standards here. It was bad enough before, but should there be an actual battle . . ."

He trailed off, as though unwilling to contemplate even more closely the consequences of a British attack to David's wardrobe and grooming.

The marquis restrained a smile. "Should that occur, don't you think standards might be relaxed . . . just a little?"

Pomfret bristled, a dark flush staining his round cheeks. "Absolutely not, sir. I realize that before I entered your employ, you experienced certain periods of—shall we say— laxity in these matters, but there is no reason for that to occur again."

It was true, David thought wryly, that while in flight from the Reign of Terror, he had paid little attention to his dress. And during the Russian campaign, he had let it slip altogether, being less concerned with how he looked than with not freezing to death. Undoubtedly, had Pomfret been along then, the valet would have contrived some means of keeping him both properly accoutered and alive.

"You realize," David said gently, "that this business is liable to get rather messy before it is done?"

Pomfret shrugged manfully. "I will contrive to do my best, sir, whatever may occur. My personal preferences make no difference in the performance of my duty."

Captain Kayes frowned. He respected courage above all but only where it was legitimately called for. "There's no shame in taking a way out of this if you can get it."

Pomfret eyed him stonily. "We of the old school have certain standards I don't expect are understood over here. Suffice to say my mind is made up." He hefted the valises once again and looked pointedly toward the interior of the carriage.

There was little David could do except relent. He nodded farewell to the captain and stepped into the brougham. Pomfret followed and they set off at a rapid clip toward the destination David had already given the driver.

The long months since his last visit to the Wild Geese seemed to vanish as the carriage rolled to a stop in front of the tavern. The white clapboard building looked unchanged. There was the same neat path leading past the gate to the Dutch door, the upper part of which stood open.

Leaving Pomfret to pay the driver, David moved quickly. He could feel his heart pounding, driven by the twin forces of anticipation and anxiety. Was his son here?

Annabel had written her letter almost two months before. In that time, anything might have happened. Paul's accompanying note had assured him that the child was healthy, but had he stayed so? Infants were frequently snatched away almost as soon as they were born.

His hand on the door, David hesitated. He had faced moments of crisis often enough before but none quite like this. The pull of the unknown child was irresistible. But so, too, were the feelings he still had for the boy's stubborn, independent, enticing mother. Indeed, at that moment he could not have said which he yearned for more.

Taking a deep breath, he thrust the door open. Beyond lay the taproom, empty and silent. He could smell the aroma of ale and sawdust. Sunlight filtering through the windows sent dust motes dancing on the air. A fat gray cat lifted its head from the bar and gazed at him lazily.

"Where is everyone?" David murmured as he scratched the cat's ear. The beast meowed approvingly and flicked the ear toward the kitchen door. From beyond it came the rich, yeasty aroma of baking bread.

But the kitchen itself, like the taproom, was empty. Although here at least were signs of recent occupancy. A familiar white apron hung neatly over the back of the chair railing. A bright-yellow bowl held apples waiting to be pared. Tin plates stood in a row, waiting to receive pie crusts. All reminded him forcefully of Annabel; only she herself was missing.

Voices reached him from the side yard. He heard a woman's soft laughter and the deeper response of a man. Annabel?

Raw, primal jealousy shot through him. He had little experience with the emotion and no practice in controlling it. The effect was akin to that of a red flag dangled in front of a bull.

Before he could question himself, he was outside in the yard, scattering a flock of hens in the process. After the darkness of the tavern, the sunlight was all but blinding.

He could make out little but the silhouetted forms of a man and woman standing close enough to be touching. Had it not been for the frantic clucking of the chickens, they would not have noticed him. When they did, they started guiltily and drew apart.

"David . . ."

Not Annabel. That realization flowed through him with the sweet balm of relief. He all but sagged as he recognized that the voice was not hers, for all that it was familiar.

"Nicole, what are you . . . ?"

The man stepped out of the shadows. Sunlight struck his silvery hair.

"Cameron."

The Scotsman nodded cordially. "Welcome back, de Montfort. Ye've been expected." But not, if the look on his sister's face was anything to go by, at that precise moment.

Nicole hastily smoothed her hair. She looked younger than David remembered and less confident. She also looked very happy.

Cameron appeared much as always—big, solid, imperturbable. Only the lambent light of his blue eye betrayed hastily controlled passion.

David was torn. On the one hand, as Nicole's brother he felt called upon to make some appropriately stern comment. On the other, he was keenly aware that to do any such thing would be hypocritical in the extreme. He least of all was in any position to lecture on the subject of morality. Instead, he opted for discretion—and his own immediate objective. "Where is Annabel?"

Nicole shot him a quick look of relief but it was Cameron who spoke. "If she isn't in the kitchen, she must be upstairs with Louis."

David looked at them both as the reality of what he was dealing with suddenly settled over him. His son was not some anonymous amorphous creature. He had a name, an identity. He existed. "L-Louis?"

Nicole took a step forward and touched her brother's arm gently. "Your son, Louis David Riordan."

"Riordan?" he repeated. His mouth tightened and a look came into his eyes that men who had faced him on battlefields would have recognized, had any of them still been alive to do so.

"Oh, no," he said with lethal conviction. "Not Riordan. He is a de Montfort and so he will be named."

Leaving the pair staring after him, he walked swiftly from the yard. He took the steps two at a time straight to the third floor. But there he paused, held in place by the sound of a woman singing.

The words were in no language he understood, but instinctively he realized that they must be Gaelic. Annabel was singing to the baby as she must have been sung to in her own childhood.

She was also nursing him. That much was evident the moment David stepped within. He stopped just over the lintel and stared at the scene before him.

Annabel sat with her back to the window, the light streaming in behind her. She had left her hair unbound so that it fell over her bared shoulder and the white folds of her chemise. At her breast, suckling vigorously, lay the golden head of a child.

David stood transfixed. He had seen mothers nursing their children before but never with such a sense of what it truly meant, of life being given and received, of the cycle of all things flowing onward one generation to another despite all the stupidity and brutality of which man was capable.

It was such a simple act, ordinary even if one considered how many times it was done in all places of the world. And yet for all that it was eerily beautiful. For an instant he had the sense of gazing beyond the physical to a realm far surpassing it.

His child. Whole, safe, and here within his grasp. Without hesitation, he stepped farther into the room. Annabel had gasped softly at the first sight of him. Now she stiffened and made ready to draw back. Only pride stopped her. That and the look in David's eyes.

He looked like a man stunned by the force of his own emotions. His powerful features had turned ashen and his hand trembled as he reached out hesitantly.

Putting her own fear aside, Annabel said softly, "Go ahead. He won't break."

David looked as though he doubted it but he managed to lightly brush a finger over Louis's cheek. The baby did not pause in his suckling but he did open his eyes to gaze at his father.

David did not move or breathe. He watched wonderingly every flicker of his son's eyelids, every soft rise and fall of his chest, every sweet, suckling motion of his mouth. Until at last the tiny lips fell slack as the child was at last satisfied. His eyes fluttered shut again and he drifted into sleep with the effortless ease granted only to the purely innocent.

Only then did Annabel stir. She lifted the baby to her shoulder and sighed in exasperation. "I did it again. He's not supposed to go to sleep without burping first. Cameron has told me that a dozen times but I canna seem to get it right."

"Why does he have to burp?" David asked.

"Because if he doesn't, his tummy might get upset."

"Does it?"

"No," Annabel admitted. "At least it hasn't so far."

"Then there's no problem." Having come to his first fatherly decision, David felt relieved. He was not completely overwhelmed after all. Indeed, he felt an unexpected surge of confidence. Much of this baby business seemed to be mere common sense.

"May I hold him?" he asked quietly.

Annabel hesitated. She was clearly loath to give the baby up, yet there was no good reason for her to refuse. Cautiously, watching David's every move, she allowed him to take the child.

"He's heavier than I realized," David said as soon as Louis was settled in his arms. He slept on peacefully, unperturbed by the change.

"He's good-sized for his age," Annabel allowed. She was being modest. In fact, she thought Louis to be the strongest, handsomest, and certainly the brightest child she had ever seen.

And David was his father. There was no denying that even if she had wanted to. She had known from the beginning that Louis resembled his sire, but now seeing them side-by-side the similarity between the two was striking. Feature for feature, they were as alike as two peas in a pod.

For some reason she did not care to examine, that knowledge filled her with pain. She turned away lest David see it. He was too engrossed in the baby to notice. When she regained control of herself and looked back to him, he was smiling in what she could only think was an extraordinarily giddy fashion. Really, the man looked besotted. She certainly couldn't remember him ever gazing at her that way and doubted that he ever had at anyone else either. Yet she couldn't be totally unsympathetic. She understood the feeling well enough, being in thrall to it herself.

"Ye can put him in his cradle now," she said softly. She didn't begrudge David the chance to be with his son, but neither was she completely comfortable about it. Something about the gentle but firm way he held the child made her nervous.

While he complied and laid Louis back down, she took the opportunity to straighten her clothes. That done, she felt better able to face him directly.

"I am surprised to see ye," she said. "Are ye here to speak with the President again?"

David stared at her in surprise. Surely, she knew why he was here. She had written to him, hadn't she?

"Your letter . . ." he began before breaking off, uncertain of how to continue.

Annabel glanced away. She could feel the blush heating her cheeks and wished that she didn't give away her feelings so easily. "Paul insisted that I write to ye," she explained. "He said ye had a right to know about Louis."

"He was right," David said bluntly. He sent up a silent prayer of thanks to his brother-in-law. Without his intervention, heaven only knew when he would have learned of his son.

"Having told me," he went on, "what did you expect me to do?"

"I don't know," Annabel admitted. "I was afraid . . . ."

"Of what?"

"That . . . ye would send money, make a show of supporting him, something like that."

"And why," David demanded, "would that be wrong?"

They stood facing one another in the small, quiet room, alone except for the child sleeping so peacefully in his cradle. The child they had made together who was part of them both and who would link them forever whether they wished it or not.

Yet they could no more accept the inevitability of that than could two wild horses yoked together in tandem.

"Because," Annabel said, "he is my child and I am responsible for him."

"*Your* child? What did you do, conceive him immaculately?"

Annabel gasped in shock. "That is blasphemy."

David stepped closer to her. The space between them narrowed to no more than a hand's breadth. She could feel his breath on her cheek and see the angry pulsation of a nerve in his shadowed jaw.

"That is truth," he said. "He is my child as much as yours. Which reminds me, what's this nonsense about calling him Riordan?"

Very much on her dignity, Annabel said, "That is my name, in case ye've forgotten."

"I have forgotten nothing." A wealth of meaning lay beneath that seemingly simple statement. None of it escaped

Annabel. She knew exactly what he was recalling to his mind and her own—the heated tangle of their bodies, the passion neither had been able to deny, the incandescent joy they had shared and which had resulted in this child they both now claimed.

For she no longer doubted that was his purpose in coming. He meant to acknowledge Louis as his own, to have him bear his name, and perhaps benefit in some way from their relationship. Surely, she should be glad, yet the same niggling fear that had come upon her before made itself felt again.

Almost a year had passed since she had last seen David and even then they had only known each other a short time. Yet she understood him in ways a lifetime might not have provided. He 'was not a man to simply acknowledge something as his own and then walk away from it. What he had, he kept—and closely.

But not this time. No, surely not now. This was not a something or an it. This was a child, carried in her body, born of her. He couldn't think that she would let him take Louis from her. Could he?

From between compressed lips, she said, "A maid will be in to watch him. Let's go downstairs."

David nodded curtly. The young girl was waiting on the landing. She smiled at them shyly as she slipped into the room.

Downstairs, there was no sign of Nicole or Cameron. David knew he should be concerned about that, but he couldn't seem to manage it. All his attention was focused on Annabel.

She was even more beautiful than before. Motherhood had added a small amount of weight to her, rounding the gentle curves while taking nothing from her gracefulness. But it had also softened her in other ways. The light in her eyes shone more deeply, hinting of secret places he couldn't yet reach.

In the kitchen, she put on her apron and went back to work. He stood for a moment watching her before taking a seat at the big oak table.

Quietly, he said, "I wasn't sure you'd still be here."

"And where would I be?" Annabel demanded. "I've a business to run."

"So you've pointed out to me. But you also have a battle to avoid. The British are about to attack." He didn't know this for sure, though it seemed a common enough belief. But he spoke as though he was absolutely certain.

Annabel stifled an exclamation of impatience. It must run in the family, this thinking that she was daft. First Nicole and now her brother pointing out to her what she already knew quite well enough.

"Are they now?" she murmured with feigned surprise. "Faith and begorrah, I thought they were comin' for a party."

David wasn't about to trade sallies with her. Besides, she was undoubtedly better at it than he.

Coldly, he said, "It's time for you to go. The main British force is south of here near Baltimore, so I propose heading north. With luck, we can reach Boston in ten days or so. I'm sure Paul and Dominique will have no objection to our staying with them while we get this situation sorted out."

Oh, he had it all figured out, he did, the damnable man, Annabel thought. All neat and tidy like a row of numbers in a ledger and her supposed to be too dumb to see how they totaled up.

Go to Boston, he said, and then what? She'd wager everything she had that they'd barely get the dust of the road washed off before he'd be going to France. Napoleon was defeated, the wars in Europe were over. It was far safer there than in America. He'd tried once to convince her to go and now he was back, with more reason than ever to win this time. But now there was far more at stake than her own pride. Above all, she was determined to do what was right for her child. Nothing else mattered.

She wiped her hands off on her apron, squared her shoulders, and faced him.

"No one is sure right now where the British forces are. They may indeed be near Baltimore but there's substantial reason to think they're also blockin' the roads north of Washington. Until we know exactly where they are, it isn't safe to strike out in any direction."

"Then what do you propose?" David demanded. "It's never going to be possible to know exactly where they are."

"Oh, yes, it is. Ye've been in enough fightin' to know that there's one time when you can know absolutely where an army is—and where it isn't."

David's eyes darkened. He wanted to think that he hadn't heard her correctly but he knew all too well that he had. How a woman understood such a thing was beyond him, but she was quite right. There *was* one time when an army's position became clear beyond any doubt.

"That's why you're waiting," he said slowly. "For the British themselves to tell you where they are."

Annabel stood straight and proud, not a hint of fear about her as she squarely faced what was to come.

"We'll know the British position once they've actually begun the attack on Washington," she said. "Everything we'll need is already packed and I'm ready to leave on the moment. But I won't run before I know which way it's safe to go."

"You're playing it very close to the edge," David said.

"Aye," she agreed with a toss of her head. "But the stakes are too high for a coward's bet. Of course, if ye care to leave now, that's fine with me."

"Oh, no," he said. Despite himself, he laughed. Here he'd only been back a few hours and already he'd met his son, discovered the woman he still desired more than any other, and been challenged to prove his manhood, although not in the more desirable way. Whatever else it was, being around Annabel was never boring.

"I'll stay," he said. "If need be, until the redcoats are hammering down the door. But I hope, sweet lady, that you'll have agreed to leave a bit before then."

"That ye can be sure of," Annabel said as she went back to her pies. "I've no desire to tangle with the Brits meself."

She watched him out of the corner of her eye, thinking for sure he'd reply. Was he really giving in this easily? She'd expected him to argue and threaten, perhaps even to try physical force. Instead, he actually seemed to respect her opinion and to agree with it.

Obviously, he was even trickier than she'd thought.

❧ CHAPTER ❧
Seventeen

DAVID did not sleep that night. He waited until the tavern had emptied out, until he was certain that Annabel had gone to her room, and then he slipped away. He was dressed in the plainest clothes he could find, worn linen trousers and a cotton shirt Pomfret had tried repeatedly to throw away. His hair was disheveled and he was not precisely clean, thanks to a few artfully applied streaks of charcoal to his face and clothes. His aim was to blend in with the crowd of citizens and refugees thronging the city. If he moved among them unnoticed, he could gather valuable information. But before he could leave the confines of the Wild Geese, he was stopped.

"Ye're off then, are ye?" Cameron inquired as David stepped out a side door. The Scotsman appeared to be lounging there with no greater purpose than an enjoyment of the night air. Yet that night it was hot, muggy, and bug-ridden.

Drawn up short, David said, "I felt the need for a stroll."

"Tis a need you might think of postponin'. This isn't the safest of places, ye know."

"Perhaps not," David agreed, looking at the big, silver-haired man. Cameron was puffing on a fragrant pipe but he tapped it down now and stuck it away in his pocket.

"Ah, well, then," he said, "let's be off."

"It was a solitary walk I had in mind," David said pointedly.

"I'll just tag along to watch yer back," the Scotsman replied, making it clear that any suggestion to the contrary would bounce off his thick hide.

Resigned, David said, "All right then, but be warned, I intend to move fast."

"What is it, exactly, that ye be lookin' fer?" Cameron asked as he trotted after him.

"Information. Annabel believes we won't know for sure where the British are until they actually attack Washington. She may be right, but I wouldn't mind picking up a hint or two."

"Ye want the wharf rats then," Cameron said. "They know everything or they think they do."

David stopped and looked at him. "The wharf rats? Who are they?"

Cameron gestured down the hot steamy street. "Come along an' ye'll see."

The wharf rats were aptly named, for they lived in the place where real rats might well have dwelled. They had fought those competitors for their place and held it defiantly against all odds. Lurking beneath the wharves and around the warehouses, wherever there was a small amount of shelter and privacy from prying eyes, the wharf rats settled. They existed in every city in every country throughout the world.

Not all the grand philosophizing that had created America and not the noblest of intentions could prevent them from being a part of the new capital.

David reminded himself of that as he and Cameron made their way down the muddy river banks and around the barnacle-draped pilings. Here and there they surprised a shadow that darted away as soon as they appeared. Still, Cameron kept going, undeterred and certain in his purpose.

"They've a leader," he explained, "like almost everybody else. One of their own, but the strongest."

David nodded. He was having a hard time keeping his thoughts strictly on the business at hand. His mind kept straying to the memory of his small son tucked into his cradle, well-fed and safe despite the maelstrom swirling around him. In a better world all children would be the same. In the world as it was, some of them became wharf rats.

Their leader was a small, saturnine boy of no more than thirteen. He ruled, apparently, by wit rather than strength which was probably preferable. He received them seated on a piling of old wooden crates stowed beneath a bridge that crossed one of the numerous meandering streams in and around Washington. The stream wound down to the river where the ships came and went, where there were pockets to be picked and cargo to be lifted.

"Ah, Cam," the boy called when he spotted the two who approached. "Why did I think you'd be coming around? Maybe I've a touch of the faery gift your folk are always on about."

"And maybe ye're just a smart little bugger," Cameron suggested good-naturedly. He pointed at the boy and said, "This is The Badger, chief of the wharfies. Don't mistake the look of him. If they had him in that fine Congress they've been buildin', they'd be doin' a damn sight better than they have been. Of course," he added upon reflection, "they'd also be lucky to still be wearin' their pants, but that's another matter. Badger, this be . . ."

Before he could introduce David, the boy said, "I know who he is, Cam." His narrow, hunger-tight face lit in a grin that held nothing of youthful innocence and everything of canny wisdom.

"Do you think such a personage could come to our fair town without my knowing? This be the marquis de Montfort," he went on, his accent on the French words passable if not perfect. Addressing the children assembled around him, he explained, "He's a fine lord in his own land and he's here on some very important and personal business, if you take my meanin'. The bairn keepin' well, your lordship?"

"Tolerably," David replied. He was not about to let this boy see how he discomfited him. But he could give vent a little to his curiosity.

"Is there anything in Washington you don't know?" he asked, deliberately couching his question in the most flattering terms.

The Badger laughed. As soon as he did, the other children joined in. They made a far greater joke of it than it really was, until he cut them off with a quick slash of his small, dirty hand.

"I know Miss Annabel right enough, run errands for her sometimes. In case you're wondering, everyone figured you for the father even though she never said anything." On a note of wonder, he added, "A lady, she is, never mind where she comes from."

All around him, the others nodded. David heard their murmurs of agreement.

"Does she know about you?" David asked quietly.

The boy frowned. "That we're wharf rats, you mean? Naaah, she don't know, why should she? Got enough on her own shoulders without any of us crying on them, right mates?"

Again the heads moved, this time as though attached to a marionette's strings. David frowned, knowing how wrong they were. Had Annabel known of their plight, she would undoubtedly have tried to intervene.

Yet a combination of pride and hard common sense kept them from accepting help from people like her. No single person, no matter how well intentioned, could make any true difference. But she could, however inadvertently, make them all too aware of how badly off they were. The wharf rats obviously thought it better to hide behind the mask of self-reliance and sufficiency and pretend that the world was really as one wanted it.

David had done that himself more times than he cared to remember. His physical surroundings had always been far more pleasant but when his survival was very much threatened, he, too, had pretended that everything was fine until at last he could pretend no more.

"Since you know Annabel," David said, "and you know her—our—situation, you must also know that we're thinking of leaving Washington."

The Badger chuckled. "You and everyone else, mate. Soon the only ones left here will be the real rats—and the Congress. By the time they think to leave, they'll be tied to the end of British ropes."

David suspected he was right but didn't say so. Instead,

he asked, "If you think the outcome will be that bad, why aren't you going?"

The Badger grinned and leaned back against his improvised seat. "We're too busy, see? The Brits are on the move. That means opportunity for us."

Behind David, where he could keep a careful eye on all, Cameron growled, "Speak yer meanin' lad, we've not got all night."

The Badger flushed but he didn't challenge the Scotsman. Alone he might have taken him on, with the help of the others, of course. But the Frenchie made it a different matter altogether. He had a look about him like tensile steel, as though he'd gone through the fire and half-enjoyed the experience. The Badger knew better than to tangle with that sort under any circumstances.

"The Brits are movin' up the Chesapeake," the Badger said. "They got into the Patuxent last night which means they're close enough for us to start runnin' a few little things down to them."

At Cameron's speaking glance, he went on hurriedly. "Nothin' bad, man. A little rum, a bit of tobaccee, a few scraps of lace to please whatever dolly they're slaverin' after. You know the drill."

Cameron did, as did David. Armies everywhere were made up of men and men had needs. Especially on the eve of battle, they liked to have those needs seen to.

The wharf rats were undoubtedly making a tidy profit, lifting what they could from the vessels tied up in the capital and running it across the lines to the Brits who were probably willing to pay double or triple.

His mouth set grimly, Cameron asked, "How far into the Patuxent?"

The Badger shrugged. He had the grace to look apologetic as he said, "Over near Bladensburg."

The Scotsman cursed, long and fluently and in Scottish Gaelic so that the words were indistinguishable. When he was done, he jerked his head toward the river.

"Let's go."

David didn't argue. He knew they had what they'd come for, even if he didn't fully understand it. As soon as they were away from the Badger's den, he asked, "Where's Bladensburg?"

"North of here," Cameron said, "on the Patuxent River. And a nice clean shot straight down to the capital. Not only that, but they've got the way blocked to Baltimore where a good part of the Militia is waiting, including my own regiment."

"I didn't realize you were in the Army," David said.

"I'm not," Cameron said as they scrambled up the bank once again. "I'm in the Militia."

David frowned. Normally, in time of war, there was no difference. When he said as much, Cameron laughed. "Tell that to the Congress. They can't agree on who any of us are or what we should be doing. I'll tell you since you're interested that there's the Army—maybe three thousand strong—and then there's the Militia with another fifteen thousand in the field and ready to go at the signal. We've been drilling regularly since last year." He smiled faintly. "I think Miss Annabel thought I was going off after a lady, though she never said as much. Unfortunately, I was slopping around in the mud and heat instead, learnin' how to fight redcoats."

David stopped dead in his tracks. All this time—when he had come to America before and after he'd returned to

France—he'd been presuming that the total force available to face the British was about the three thousand Cameron mentioned. He thought that because so did everyone else. No one had thought of any Militia, much less that it was truly prepared to fight.

"Ready, you say?" he asked.

"Aye, ready and chompin' at the bit. We thought we'd be sent into the field long before now but between one thing and another, no one could agree what to do with us. So here we sit, all more or less in the same place, waiting for the Brits to come a-callin'."

David straightened up, brushing the mud from his trousers, and glanced around at the silent, sleeping city. Far off in the distance he could see lights still burning and thought they were in the White House, though he couldn't be sure.

"Do the British have any idea?" he asked.

Cameron chuckled. "I very much doubt it. They think they've got us beat, you see, so they aren't likely to be worryin' too much about the details."

But perhaps they ought to be, David thought. Fifteen thousand men armed and ready, waiting to be unleashed at the most opportune moment.

He turned abruptly and faced Cameron. "Was this a plan or merely an accident, that you should be available when and where you are most needed?"

The Scotsman laughed again, the sound deep and rich on the fragrant night air. "Well you might ask, as I do meself. We won the first time when no one thought we could and grace be to God we will again. But make no mistake, it'll be a bad business along the way."

"I've no doubt of that," David said. "We must get back to the Wild Geese at once."

They returned shortly before dawn. David had been up more than a full day and was tired, but he shrugged that off. There was too much to be done. Parting from Cameron in the yard, he went quickly up the stairs.

Only two of the guest rooms on the second floor were occupied, there not being too many people anxious to stay in Washington. Nicole was deeply asleep but she woke immediately at David's knock.

Sitting up in the bed, she said, "What is it? Cameron . . . ?"

"The Scotsman is fine," David said with a hint of exasperation. "He's getting himself organized to join his regiment but I expect he'll be seeing you before he leaves."

"H-his regiment . . . oh, sweet Lord . . ." Without further ado, Nicole leaped from the bed. She darted behind a privacy screen where she hastily pulled on garments. Scant moments later, she was dressed and confronting her brother.

"I must see him . . . you understand, well, even if you don't . . . I must . . . Annabel is upstairs with the baby." Suddenly aware of all the implications behind what was happening, she asked, "What are you going to do?"

"Inform her that the conditions she required have been met. The British are on the march, we know their location, at least fairly well. There is no time to waste."

He regarded his sister gently. "Make your farewells quickly and join us below."

White-faced, Nicole nodded. She dashed from the room and ran swiftly down the stairs. David went back out onto the landing and banged on the second door.

"Wake up, Pomfret," he called. "We're leaving."

From behind the door, he heard a mournful sigh, sufficient reassurance that his valet was awake and on the job.

Swiftly, he mounted the steps to the third floor. He wasn't

absolutely certain what Annabel's reaction would be but as it turned out, he needn't have worried. She had awakened sometime before. An uneasy sense she could not identify itched at her. She checked Louis in his cradle and found the baby sleeping peacefully.

Unable to return to bed, she paced back and forth across the small room until in the midst of her pacing she found herself gathering up the last of her belongings that needed to be packed. Then she knew, although how she could never have said. Some fey faery sense, the breath of hidden glens and ancient standing stones, stirred within her.

When David opened the door she was already dressed with Louis in her arms.

"It is time," they both said. The words hung in the air as they stared at one another, trying to comprehend this moment of shared understanding. Abruptly, they shook themselves. David picked up the bags standing by the door. He led the way down the stairs.

Cameron and Nicole were below near the entrance to the tavern. They stood very close together without speaking. As Annabel and David approached, Nicole reached up and gently touched the big Scotsman's face. He covered her hand with his own and bent his proud head. Softly, their lips touched.

When he straightened, he looked at David directly. "Ye'll see them through safe then?"

Quietly, David said, "On my life."

Cameron nodded once, looked again at Nicole, and was gone.

Annabel had been thorough in her preparations. Not only had she packed everything she thought could possibly be needed, but she had also arranged to dispatch those of her employees who remained to safety.

The young maid who had helped care for Louis left them with a tear but also with relief. Along in the wagon with her went the stableboy and a strapping farm youth stranded in Washington by events and glad of the ride. He listened attentively to the route Annabel outlined for him and promised he would exercise great caution.

That done, she at last felt free to climb into the second wagon. Nicole was already there, holding Louis on her lap. Pomfret sat behind them surrounded by bags and bundles as well as his own and his master's valises. David came last.

As he swung up onto the seat, Annabel's eyes widened. A leather strap ran diagonally across his broad chest. Attached to it was a holster from which protruded the gleaming hilt of a hunting knife.

"Where did you come by that?" she asked, trying without great success to mask her surprise at seeing him with so purely functional and ruthless a weapon. A grand dueling sword would have been no surprise, nor much use where they were going. But a knife that had only one purpose—to kill in the most efficient way possible—was unexpected.

He smiled faintly. "I've had it so long I can't remember."

She didn't believe him but neither did she want to pursue the subject. A shiver ran through her as she considered how little she knew him. She had lain in his arms, borne a child by him, and yet there was so much about him that she did not understand. The knife for instance and the conviction she had, without having to ask, that he knew precisely how to use it.

David tapped the reins lightly to start the horses moving. They had taken less than a handful of steps when they heard a single rider coming down the darkened street. He appeared almost at once, a young, weary man in the uniform of an American captain.

Seeing the group in the wagon, he said quickly, "Is this the Wild Geese?"

Annabel nodded. "It is, but you're too late to find anyone. They've all left. We're the last."

The young man grimaced. He drew off his hat and wiped an arm across his sweat-stained forehead. "I was afraid of that."

David loosened his hold on the reins. He had a vague sense of premonition, the feeling that he knew what the young man would say before he spoke again.

"Who are you looking for?" he asked.

"A Frenchman, name of David de Montfort. He arrived yesterday on the *Seafarer*. Apparently, he stayed here last year so the baron thought he might . . ."

"The baron?" David broke in. "You mean de Plessis?"

The captain nodded. "That's the one. Are you de Montfort?"

"I am, but what's happened to Bertrand?"

"Nothing, but he thought you ought to know. Your brother-in-law, Paul Delamare, was wounded several hours ago in a British ambush."

The young man looked from one to the other gravely. With sincere regrets, he said, "I'm sorry to tell you that he is close to death."

❧ CHAPTER ❧
Eighteen

*A*NNABEL straightened slowly from her position beside the bed. Paul did not stir. He remained unconscious, his face gray and his breathing labored, the most outward signs of the musket ball he had taken in his right side.

The details of what had happened were still not clear but it appeared that he had returned to Washington the day before and had been south of the city, assessing the medical needs of the troops stationed there, when his party was attacked by a British patrol. Two of the men with him had died. The others in the small group who survived had managed to get Paul back to the capital, but the hospitals there were understaffed and disorganized. When de Plessis learned of his condition, the baron had concluded that he would be better off in the hands of friends. He had arranged for him to be brought to the Wild Geese.

Annabel approved although she was close to despair over

what to do. Paul was more than merely her friend. He had helped her at a time when she had never needed it more. It was probably no exaggeration to say that he had saved both her life and the life of her child. She hoped she would be able to do the same for him.

Her eyes were burning. She passed a hand over them wearily as she stood up. For the moment, there was nothing more she could do except pray.

Behind her, Nicole opened the door. Softly, she said, "I'll sit with him now. Louis needs you."

Annabel nodded. She was more grateful for the other woman's presence than ever before. Despite her own anguish, Nicole was a tower of strength. She even managed a faint smile as she took her place beside her brother-in-law.

"I would try to send word to Dominique in Boston," she said quietly, "but there's no way for it to get through. Besides, somehow I think she knows."

"They love each other very much, don't they?" Annabel asked.

Nicole nodded. "More than I have seen in any other couple." She leaned closer to Paul, covering his hand with her own. Her beautiful face was suffused with concern as she saw how weak he remained.

"If the worst happens . . ." she murmured, "I would fear for Dominique, were it not for the children."

New to motherhood though she was, Annabel understood. Dominique would make any sacrifice for the sake of her children, even continuing to live in a world that no longer held the man she loved more than life itself.

Her hands clenched as she wondered what it must mean to share a love like that. Surely, it was something she would never know. Every moment she spent beside Paul's bed, thoughts of David haunted her. She was grief-stricken enough as it was; how would she feel if it was the proud, insufferable marquis lying there? The man who had invited her to be his mistress, whom she had scornfully refused, still tempted her more than she could bear.

Damn him. And damn the whole stupid situation. Her plans were thwarted, she was trapped in Washington with who-knew-what consequences, and she had to cope with the father of her child who seemed to be nurturing plans she didn't care to contemplate.

All in all, it had not been a good day, but not beyond the measure of a feisty Irish girl who could muster the strength of ten—make that a hundred—when she had to.

Louis was in the kitchen, watched over by Pomfret who had been pressed into that service simply because there was no one else. He was managing it surprisingly well, if his hesitant smile was anything to go by.

"I'm afraid he's hungry, miss," the valet said apologetically as Annabel reached the kitchen. He was holding Louis gingerly but with dogged determination.

"Give him to me," Annabel said. She took the baby and sat down as Pomfret discreetly left. As Louis nursed, she listened to the sound of hammering immediately beyond.

David was nailing the shutters closed across the windows. Pomfret had gone to help him. Earlier, they had brought the chickens, the goat, and the work tools in from the outside and secured them in a shed adjacent to the house. David had also filled every available pail with water for reasons Annabel did not care to question.

By the time they were done, the shirts of both men were damp with sweat. As an indication of how tense things were, Pomfret was too preoccupied to notice. He slumped down in the kitchen chair and accepted a mug of water from Annabel with a grateful smile.

"We've done all we can," David said quietly. "Now we must wait. How is Paul?"

"The same," Annabel told him. "The wound has stopped bleeding but he remains unconscious. I can't tell whether or not he has additional injuries, perhaps to his head. If only we had a doctor."

"We do," David muttered. "Unfortunately, he's in no condition to help."

Since the same thought had occurred to Annabel, she couldn't help grimacing. "Is there any way we could get someone else?"

David shook his head. He put down the hammer he had been using and went to look at Louis lying on a blanket on the kitchen floor. The child smiled at him and waved his hands. David's eyes gentled. He was about to reach out to him, but realizing how dirty he was from his labors, he restrained himself.

Quietly, he said, "Those who haven't left are with the Army. Word has spread that the attack is imminent."

Annabel's throat tightened. For a moment, she felt engulfed by fear. Only with the greatest effort did she manage to fight it down.

"What do we do now?" she asked softly.

David's eyes met hers across the kitchen. "We wait," he said.

Around noon, the air rumbled. It might have been mistaken for thunder except that the sky was clear. Looking north through the one window he had left unsealed, David saw puffs of smoke coming from the region around Bladensburg, a village near the capital.

Without saying anything, he closed off that last window and went back to the kitchen table. Annabel watched him out of the corner of her eye. She was trying to peel potatoes for their supper. Pomfret was upstairs watching Paul. He had reported a few minutes before that there was still no change.

Late in the day, long after they had all grown used to the sound of artillery from the north, the noise abruptly stopped. In the sudden silence that followed, the three adults glanced at one another. When several more minutes passed without any sound, David stood up. He uncovered the window again and looked out into the gathering twilight.

Annabel set the potatoes down and went to join him. Their bodies touched as she stood on tiptoe to look past him. "Who are those people?" she asked, seeing a group of men running down the street.

"American soldiers, I recognize their insignia." He had seen the same on the wharf when he arrived. Then the American soldiers had looked apprehensive but determined. Now they appeared to be in retreat.

He watched them for several minutes before he said, "They are giving up the city."

"No," Nicole exclaimed. "This is the capital. They would not do that."

"They would if they knew they couldn't defend it," David said as he closed the window again. "What counts is survival."

Annabel bit back a cry of dismay. The thought of her brave, young city abandoned to the enemy horrified her. But she feared that David was right.

"What should we do?" she asked.

He looked around at the shadowed kitchen growing increasingly torpid with the heated day, at the two women and the baby depending on him. Grimly, he said, "Stay calm and when they come, follow my lead. Whatever I say or do, agree with me. Understand?"

Nicole nodded at once, Annabel an instant later. Louis pursed his small mouth and gurgled. No one moved. Somewhere in the room, a trapped bee buzzed angrily. Otherwise, it was silent.

Until the silence was shattered by the distant boom of an explosion, followed by the whine of a rocket. A dull thud shook the air.

Her face strained and white, Annabel murmured, "Rockets . . ."

David stepped quickly to her side. "It makes sense that they would fire the Army's defensive positions. There is no reason to think they will harm civilians."

Actually, he had no such confidence, being fully aware of what armies could do to helpless populaces. But he was determined to keep her from thinking of that, at least so long as he could.

"Go upstairs," he said gently. "It's your turn with Paul."

Numbly, Annabel nodded. She gathered Louis and left the room. When she was gone, Nicole said, "Now tell me the truth, what do you think they will do?"

"It depends on how much resistance they meet," David said wearily. "If there is any real opposition, they are liable to do anything."

Nicole blanched. She was a courageous woman but the thought of being at the mercy of a marauding army terrified her. They were too much like the mobs of her childhood.

Brother and sister exchanged a look of understanding. Quietly, he said, "We have lived through worse. We can survive this as well."

"In that case, I am going to prepare supper."

David smiled, grateful for his sister's resilience. He sat down again at the table. "I didn't know you could cook."

She looked at him and grinned. "I can't. But this seems as good a time as any to learn."

Nicole burned the potatoes and completely forgot to season the beef, but it hardly mattered. Only Pomfret had an appetite. He finished off two helpings and belched apologetically before returning upstairs to relieve David, who was taking his turn with Paul.

Annabel had just risen from the table, intending to take the dishes to the sink, when an explosion tore the air. It was far worse than any that had come earlier. Puffs of dust loosened from the rafters overhead rained down on the room.

Nicole screamed and instinctively threw herself over Louis. As the air continued to reverberate, Annabel fought her way to her. Together, the two women crouched over the infant who awoke and began to cry.

Upstairs, David heard the sound and rushed to the window. The light was fading rapidly but to the south, where the immense Navy Yard was located, he could make out vast fires burning.

He stared at them, riveted, until a sound from the bed made him turn. Paul's eyes were open. He had raised his head off the pillow and was staring at David.

"W-what is that . . ." he murmured. His voice was hoarse and weak, but audible.

Quickly, David was at his side. He lowered the other man back onto the bed and spoke to him gently. "You have been wounded but I am delighted to see you conscious. How are you feeling?"

"As though an army marched over me," Paul said dryly. "But tell me . . . the fighting . . . what is happening?"

David hesitated only a moment before he replied. "The British are in the city and the Americans are in retreat. I believe they have fired the Navy Yard to prevent it being taken."

"Yes . . . they would do that . . . but why are you . . ." The realization came suddenly that if David was still there, so might Annabel and Nicole. "I thought you would get away before now."

David was not about to tell him that they almost had. Instead, he said merely, "There is no certainty that we would have been better off. You must rest now, don't try to talk anymore. I am going downstairs to tell the others that you are conscious."

Reluctantly, Paul nodded. The doctor in him knew that David was right, he must not tax his strength. But he was consumed with concern, deeply worried about those he loved, and apprehensive that his own ill luck would also prove to be theirs. He said as much when Annabel and Nicole hurried up to see for themselves that he was better. Neither of them would hear of it.

"Don't be silly," Nicole said tearfully. Her emotions were in turmoil. She was immensely relieved that her brother-in-law was better, but as the immediate worry for him eased, all her concern for Cameron returned tenfold. He was out there somewhere amid the burning buildings and the screaming rockets. Anything might happen to him.

Paul fell into a natural sleep a short time later. Pomfret offered to stay with him.

"You should also get some rest while there's the chance," David told the women. Nicole agreed; she was suddenly so tired that the effort to stay awake was almost beyond her. But Annabel knew she would not be able to sleep. With Louis nestled on her shoulder, she returned to the kitchen with David.

"It's going to be a long night," she said quietly. "If ye can hold him for a few minutes, I'll brew some coffee."

David took the baby from her a little clumsily but soon caught the way of it. Louis slept on, blissfully unaware of the tumult surrounding him. The fragrance of freshly ground coffee filled the warm, humid air.

David was struck by the sense of quiet domesticity so harshly at odds with the reality of what was actually happening. The inn had become a tiny refuge in the midst of a storm. He was grateful for that even as he knew it could not last indefinitely.

Indeed, it seemed as though the end came only moments later. There was a loud knocking at the door followed by a voice shouting, *"Open up."*

David handed the baby to Annabel and motioned her back. He unbolted the small spy hole in the center of the door and looked out.

"De Plessis."

"Who were you expecting, monsieur?" the baron inquired genially when the bolts had been undone and the door opened. "The citizens of this fair city are keeping to home tonight and the British are otherwise occupied."

"I'm glad to hear it," David said as he gestured him inside and shut the door again. "But what are you doing out and about?"

The baron shrugged. He inclined his head cordially to Annabel. The baby in her arms drew a tolerant but unsurprised smile. "Do you mind if I sit, Miss Annabel?" he asked. "All this excitement is a bit wearing."

At her quick nod, he lowered himself gratefully into a nearby chair. He had grown more stout in the last year but had lost none of his taste for finery. Despite the heat, and the inconvenient fact of invasion, he was sumptuously dressed in a brocade vest and frock coat with a tuft of lace beneath his portly chin.

"I should call Pomfret down to see you," David said with a grin, "except that I would never hear the end of it. He would use you for ever after as proof of his contention that the proper standards can be upheld even under the worst circumstances."

De Plessis laughed. He drew out a fine linen handkerchief and patted his forehead. "Ah, but Pomfret should know I am only a baron and a rather recently created one at that. I have no choice but to always look the part whereas you were born to the nobility and will never be taken for anything less."

The truth of that had never been more evident. In the dim light of the single lantern, David stood tall and proud. His golden head gleamed like burnished metal. His features were set and strained, but there was no hint of fear in him. He looked ready and able to deal with anything.

De Plessis took a long swallow of the ale Annabel set before him and eyed David cautiously. He set the mug down and said, "I came to warn you, my friend. The British are going house to house. Wherever they find something they don't like, they are firing the premises and sending the residents into the street.''

"How do they feel about Frenchmen?'' David asked. He managed to make it sound humorous though he was feeling anything but. Frenchmen and Englishmen had been fighting each other on the battlefields of Europe up to a few months before. It was unlikely that there would be any love lost between them now. Yet he couldn't see himself leaving Annabel and Nicole to their own devices, particularly not while they were sheltering an official of the American government whom the British might be only too happy to capture.

"I didn't try to ask them,'' de Plessis said. "But I won't be staying. I don't want to cause you any trouble.''

Annabel put down the coffeepot loudly. "Don't be daft, of course you'll stay. You can't be going back out onto the streets now. Besides,'' she added with a wicked grin, "Nicole made so much supper that we've plenty left over. I'll fix you a plate.''

De Plessis looked unmistakably relieved, at least until he saw the food. Hunger drove him to tuck in manfully and in the end he cleaned his plate, if only with the help of the ale that Annabel kept pouring.

"You should think of holding onto that,'' the baron said, gesturing to the ale. "There's no telling when you'll be able to get more and it's certain that the British will have a powerful thirst.''

"Then the less they have to drink the better,'' she muttered. She fanned herself with a corner of her apron and went over to check on Louis. He had just woken up and was fretful. Although night had fallen, it was still very hot. The temperature in the shuttered kitchen was close to intolerable.

"I'll get some water, " David said, rising, "and you can bathe him."

He slipped out into the yard with a bucket and returned a few minutes later, his face grim. "There are new fires to the west. It looks as though the British are burning the Capitol and possibly the White House."

Annabel said something under her breath and took the water. She was pouring it into a basin when they heard shouts nearby. David stepped in front of her as de Plessis rose. At the same moment, the door was struck by what sounded like the butts of several guns. An instant later, it flew open.

Two British redcoats ran into the room, muskets at the ready. They were followed by an officer in full regalia. He was a young man with narrow, supercilious features and a high-pitched nasal drawl.

"Don't move," he ordered as he surveyed the scene. His gaze flicked past Annabel and the baron to settle on David. "We are searching for contraband. You are advised to cooperate."

He gestured to the soldiers who obediently began to move around the kitchen, peering into cupboards and under the table. One deliberately knocked over a bushel of potatoes, apparently thinking that something else might have been hidden inside.

Without thinking, Annabel gave an angry exclamation and moved to clean up the mess. Instantly, the young officer drew his sword, slashing it through the air directly in front of her.

He smiled as he did so, relishing his power. "I said not to

move. It's time you bloody Americans learned to obey your betters."

A dark flush stained Annabel's cheeks. She lifted her head and glared at him. "Our betters? Is that what ye think ye are? Ye're nothing but..."

Before she could continue, the officer stepped forward, raised his hand, and brought it down hard across her face. She cried out. Knocked off balance, she fell, striking the side of the table.

She heard a rushing sound and for a moment could see only blackness. When her vision cleared, she was aware of David, grappling with the officer. He had launched himself at the other man in a fury and was close to wrenching the sword from his hand. But the two soldiers had lifted their muskets to firing position.

"For the love of God," Annabel screamed. She ran at one of the soldiers even as the baron grabbed for the other. The redcoats, both young and apparently inexperienced boys, hesitated. They could see their officer, locked in a struggle with David, and they knew what they were supposed to do. But they couldn't quite bring themselves to fire on what seemed to be an innocent family, complete with small baby.

David and officer fell against the wall. The officer's face was contorted with rage and fear while David looked icily, terrifyingly calm. Slowly, unrelentingly, he tightened his hold on the other man to the point where the bones of the officer's wrists began to crack.

"*Shoot,*" the Britisher screamed. "*Shoot, damn it.*"

Again, the young soldiers raised their guns. Looking confused and afraid, they hesitated with their fingers on the trigger.

White with terror, Annabel pleaded. "*No, don't.* I made a mistake. We've nothing here, for pity's sake, just go."

But the officer was having none of it. He was angry, embarrassed, and hurting. To yield to those for whom he had only hatred and contempt was unthinkable. He lashed out at David, trying to kick him in the groin.

David evaded the blow. He wrenched the sword from the officer's hands, sending it skittering across the floor, and threw him against the door. His head struck a wooden crossbar. He groaned as his eyes rolled back and he slumped unconscious to the floor.

Picking up the sword, David held it in both hands and snapped it cleanly over his knee. The two parts of razor-sharp steel clattered to the floor, bounced once, and landed in a corner.

"Get the hell out of here," David said grimly to the young soldiers. Gesturing to the officer, he added, "And take that with you. Put him somewhere he can't hurt himself or anyone else."

The young men needed no further convincing. They shouldered their muskets and, seizing the officer beneath the arms, dragged him from the inn. He was tossed unceremoniously into the back of a wagon which moved quickly away.

In the silence that followed their departure, Annabel put a hand to her mouth. She felt sick and ashamed. Her impulsiveness could have killed them all. If the British soldiers hadn't been fundamentally decent young men, tragedy would have been unavoidable.

"I'm sorry," she whispered brokenly. She was shaking badly and wrapped her arms around herself to try to stop it. Louis had begun to howl. Shocked and stunned by what had almost happened, she stared at him numbly.

Not so David. He looked worriedly at Annabel for a moment before quickly moving to his son. Picking the baby up, he soothed him gently. Whether it was his voice, the way he held the child, or merely his presence, Louis calmed almost at once.

The water David had brought from the well was still in a bucket on the floor. Anxious to have things return to normal as quickly as possible, he said to Annabel, "You sit down. I'll bathe him."

She nodded slowly and did as he said. It was just as well. Her legs felt barely able to hold her. Staring at the man and the child he held so tenderly, she had to fight back tears.

She had never felt more confused in her life, or more inadequate. All her presumptions about who and what she was, and what she was capable of doing, were cracking wide open. Nothing was certain any longer. A great darkness of the soul threatened to pull her down. She struggled against it even as she feared her strength would prove inadequate.

De Plessis cast her a worried glance. He sensed her turmoil and wanted to help, but he was himself caught in the fear that the worst was not yet over.

Only David and his son appeared untouched by it. Cool water flowed into the basin as the baby chortled. Outside, gunfire sounded. Nothing was certain except the man and the child, and the bond being inexorably forged between them.

❧ CHAPTER ❧
Nineteen

A CLAP of thunder reverberating through the sky woke Annabel from dreamless sleep. She sat up groggily and looked toward the window. It was getting on toward dawn. A sullen, yellow light heralded one of Washington's infamous summer storms. The tiny hairs at the nape of her neck rose. Quickly, she left the bed.

Last night, the British, David, and the officer all flashed through her mind. Despite the warmth, she shivered. Dimly, she remembered staying in the kitchen after the British left until finally weariness and fear overcame her. David had gathered her into his arms and carried her upstairs.

Apparently, he had also removed some of her clothes. She wore only a thin chemise and a cotton petticoat. Her skirt and blouse were hung neatly over a chair. Her shoes were set on the floor nearby. He had even taken the pins from her hair and made an attempt to braid it despite tangles.

Sweet heaven, was there nothing the man couldn't do? Soothe a fretful child, turn away an enraged British officer, care for a friend, and put a woman to bed as though he'd been doing the same tasks all his life? What had happened to the arrogant, spoiled, self-centered aristocrat who had first drawn her eye?

Maybe he'd never existed or maybe there had always been this other, far more complex man right alongside him. Whatever the truth, this wasn't the time to be worrying about it. She dressed quickly, pausing only long enough to splash cold water on her face, and hurried downstairs.

By the time she reached the main floor, rain was coming down in torrents. Beneath it she smelled something that made her stop in mid-step. Smoke. Or rather the soggy aftermath of it as when a fire is suddenly doused with water.

Last night, David had said the British were lighting fires, yet incredibly she had not thought much about it. She, who feared fire above all else, had fallen asleep as deeply as a child while parts of the city around her burned.

Try though she did, she couldn't ascribe that to simple exhaustion. It had been David's strong, calming presence that enabled her to forget what was happening and find the release of sleep. But now, with morning, she was consumed with the need to know what had happened.

"No," David said flatly a few moments later when she found him in the kitchen. "Absolutely not. No one is going outside."

"But we canna just stay huddled in here waitin' for the sky to fall," Annabel insisted.

He straightened from beside the fireplace where he had just set a few more logs, and said, "In case you haven't noticed, that's exactly what it's doing. Go out there now and you won't have to worry about the British. You'll drown before they ever notice you.''

As though to confirm his words, a further clap of thunder shook the room.

"*Mon Dieu*," de Plessis murmured. He was sitting at the table, looking tired and rumpled, with Louis in his lap. "I have never heard such a storm."

Annabel privately agreed but she wasn't about to say so. "We have them all the time in Washington. It'll pass over soon enough."

The baron looked relieved. "In that case, dear lady, I believe I shall take this opportunity to repair myself. If you wouldn't mind . . ."

She took the baby from him with a grateful nod. "We've plenty of rooms upstairs, if ye donna mind helpin' yerself . . ."

He assured her he did not. Louis stirred in her arms and began to root about. She smiled gently as she sat down and began unbuttoning her dress. Modesty compelled her to sit half-turned away from David, yet she could still see him clearly enough. He looked tired but not excessively so.

"Did ye get any rest?" she asked softly.

He shook his head. "There will be time for that later."

His stamina astounded her. She knew that her own strength was considerable but in this case, at least, it did not compare to his.

"How do ye manage?" she asked.

He looked surprised by the question. "Practice, I guess. There have been times before when I really couldn't sleep. I just got used to it."

She wanted to ask him more, to get him to talk about those times and share them with her, but at that moment she realized that Louis was having trouble. He was suckling well enough but his hunger was not being satisfied. His agitation increased until he let go of her nipple and bellowed.

Annabel was baffled. She had encountered some trouble when she first started nursing, but had put that down to her own inexperience. Once she got the knack, it had gone very well. Until now.

She turned more fully away from David and looked down at herself. Her breasts appeared smaller than was usual in the morning. But far worse, her nipples were dry. No milk was coming from them.

"Ah, no . . ."

Though she whispered the words under her breath, David heard her. "What's wrong?" he asked.

She shook her head. "Nothing . . . the storm . . . it frightened me, that's all."

Desperately, she prayed that she was right. Perhaps this sort of thing happened to women all the time. If only she knew more, but she had never paid much attention, thinking that she would never need to know. Now the hungry, crying child in her arms made a mockery of such false assurance. Blessed Mary, what could have happened to cause this?

David looked from her to the child, his forehead knitting in concern. "He's crying."

"I know that," Annabel snapped. "'Tis the nature of babies to cry. He'll be fine."

To her ears, at least, she sounded callous. But David saw nothing amiss. So far as he knew, babies did indeed cry. And there was no question but that Annabel was a competent mother as well as a very loving one.

"I need to check on Paul," he said after he had returned to stir the fire.

She nodded but said nothing. Inside she was wondering how she could have become so insensitive, not even to ask about Paul when she came down. Perhaps her aunt, the one who had taken her in, had been right. She had always minimized Annabel's accomplishments, telling her she was nothing near what she thought herself to be.

Annabel had been amazed to be left the inn, having presumed that a woman who found her so incompetent would leave her nothing. But her uncle had been different, trying whenever he could to soften his wife's judgment. He'd won through in the end but now Annabel wondered if he'd been right to stand up for her.

She was fearful, callous, and—it seemed—unable even to properly care for her child. She was also perilously close to self-pity, a possibility that filled her with disgust.

Giving herself a hard, mental shake, she stood up with Louis in her arms. Her milk had dried up. But she still had an infant to feed. Now how was she to do it?

Mercifully, at that moment the goat tethered in the nearby shed brayed. Annabel wasted no time. She had drunk goat's milk herself as a child and knew it to be safe. Louis couldn't subsist on it for any length of time, not at his age, but it would do until a substitute could be found.

Once she had milked the goat, who was plainly grateful, and fed her child, she felt better. Restored to his usual self, Louis chortled contentedly. Annabel began preparing breakfast, thinking the routine task would steady her nerves. Meanwhile, the storm continued to rage.

A short time later, David returned. Ignoring his own advice, he had gone outside and gotten soaking wet. His golden hair clung in sodden tendrils to his forehead. His linen shirt had turned almost transparent so that the powerful sinews of his chest could be clearly seen. His breeches were dark with water.

Accepting a towel from Annabel, he said, "The fires are out. It's very quiet."

"I'll bet it is," she muttered. "The Brits will be sleepin' off their kill."

"I'm not sure of that."

"Why not?" de Plessis asked from the doorway. Having restored himself with Pomfret's help, he was drawn back downstairs by the smell of food.

David looked at his son, once again peaceful and happy, and smiled. "I don't think they can hold the city."

Annabel stopped in the midst of stirring the porridge. "Why couldn't they?"

"Because they must give battle if they are to actually defeat the Americans. Your countrymen have too much sense to fight here. They will evade the enemy and find more favorable ground. The British can't afford the luxury of holding this city if it prevents them from winning the war."

"Do you think they will win?" the baron asked. The question might have seemed incredibly naive, given the events of the last few hours, but David hesitated.

"I'm not sure," he admitted. "The Americans are more clever than I'd expected."

De Plessis's round face split in a grin. "That's a surprise, isn't it? This rough-hewn, simple folk have a knack for preserving themselves."

"I wouldn't describe them quite that way," David said dryly. He thought of Madison, the President he had not seen in a year but whom he still remembered very well. The man was as cautious and diplomatic as any European statesman could hope to be. But more than that, he was fired by a vision so many others lacked. A vision he would die for.

And he was not alone. In his brief foray beyond the inn, David had heard murmurs of the American forces gathering on the heights near Georgetown, of an even larger force massing near Baltimore, and of the American Navy virtually on the rampage, hunting down and sinking British ships wherever they could be found. The Americans were—at long last—in a deadly fury. Surely, the burning of much of their capital could only strengthen that.

It was even rumored, though not confirmed, that the members of Congress had decided to put aside their incessant quarreling and at last get down to the business of saving the country.

"It's so quiet," Nicole said a short time later when she came down to the kitchen. Annabel had gone upstairs to sit with Paul and see if she couldn't coax some food into him. The thunderstorm was over. Nothing stirred in the street beyond the tavern. Even the birds seemed silent.

Except for trips upstairs to see Paul, the small group remained largely in the kitchen throughout the day. Occasionally, new fires could be seen burning but there was little gunfire to be heard. The city seemed to be settling down to an odd sort of peace.

They were almost becoming accustomed to their circumstances when suddenly toward afternoon, there was a deafening explosion from the direction of the Navy Yard. So powerful was it that for seconds no one could move or speak. Annabel thought she had gone deaf; she could hear nothing, not even her own breathing. The walls vibrated and pieces of furniture left the floor as though jerked by an unseen hand.

David recovered first. He threw the door open and went out, followed closely by Annabel.

"It's the Yard," she said, looking in the direction of a plume of smoke that rose thick and swirling to the sky. "But I thought there was nothing left there."

"Apparently not," David said quietly. "The British must have stumbled across something."

And paid for it with their lives if the shouts and screams they heard from that direction were anything to go by. David stood for a moment, hands clenched at his side, before he turned abruptly and headed for the stable.

"Where are you going?" Annabel demanded, running after him.

"To hitch up the wagon. If it's as bad as it sounds, they'll need help with the wounded."

"B-but . . . they're British."

He turned, staring down at her, his face darkened to burnished bronze in the fading light. Thunderclouds were appearing again and a cold, skittering wind blew over the city. It whipped at their clothes and made Annabel's fiery hair dance wildly.

David reached out a hand to capture it. He held the silken strands tenderly as he looked at her. "I don't expect you to understand, but I am part British and I've been a soldier. I can't just stand by and let them die."

Annabel stifled a curse. "Ye're a damn fool, Frenchman. They'd as soon shoot ye as look at ye."

"Perhaps," he acknowledged, "but that doesn't change anything." He turned to go only to be stopped by her sudden grip on his arm.

"I'm going with ye."

"No, you are not."

She bridled at his highhandedness. "I'm not some weak-livered little lady to faint at the sight of blood. Besides, I'll go anyway. whether you want me to or not."

"Why?" he demanded, glaring at her. "You hate the British."

At that moment Annabel wasn't entirely sure. She hated what some of them had done, but certainly she didn't hate the two young soldiers who could have killed them the night before but hadn't. They or others like them might have been caught in the explosion. They could be dying even now.

"What're we standin' around jabberin' for?" she asked. "Get the wagon hitched. I'll fetch the supplies we'll need."

David didn't argue further. He would have liked to but he sensed the futility of it. Either she would go with him or she would go alone. Given those alternatives, there was no choice.

He ran for the stables. By the time the wagon was ready, so was Annabel. She had thrown a shawl over her head to protect it from the still-swirling eddies of soot and the rain that promised to return. In her hand, she carried a bundle filled with whatever she could gather.

David lashed the horses to a gallop. With the streets almost empty, they made good time until they were almost at the Navy Yard. Then they were stopped by a teeming mass of horses, wagons, and carriages all milling around frantically. British soldiers were running in all directions but for the moment there appeared to be no one in charge.

"Where's your commanding officer?" David demanded of a man who was standing wide-eyed and ashen against the crumbled wall of what the day before had been a warehouse.

"Dead," he said numbly. "They all are. It's a carnage in there. The bloody Yanks . . . they must have set a trap for us . . . don't have the guts to fight like men . . ."

"You don't know they had anything to do with it," David said. "Spread rumors like that and you'll only cause more trouble than you've already got."

The man looked at him uncomprehendingly. He seemed incapable of moving or thinking. With a short, explicit curse, David leaned out of the wagon and grabbed hold of the soldier by his jacket. "For the love of God, man, pull yourself together. Are there drummers here?"

"D-drummers . . . ?"

"The signal drums. This is the British Army, isn't it? You are a British soldier, aren't you? Find something to serve as a drum and beat the assembly. This mob has to be sorted out if anything else is to be done."

Even as he spoke, David was handing the reins over to Annabel. "Just keep them steady," he said, grim faced and determined. "We'll get a path cleared in a moment."

He let go of the soldier, who stumbled away still dazed but reassured by the sense of his instructions. David jumped into the back of the wagon and stood upright. Hands on his lean hips, head high, face the very picture of disdain and disgust, he shouted, *'A-ten-tion, you bloody lot of fools. What in hell do you think you're doing? Form up, at the double, in ranks—hut, two, hut, two.'*

He spoke not in the deep, generally soft tones Annabel knew. There was no hint of the slight French accent that she remembered. Instead, his voice was that of an Englishman born and bred, and not simply any Englishman but one from the highest level of society. An aristocrat, a ruler, one to be instantly obeyed.

And obey they did. To her astonishment, the troops which a few moments before had been milling around in disarray began falling in. Without exception, the young, tired faces looked relieved to at last be told what to do. As improvised drums began to beat, they formed into neat, rigid ranks.

Only when they had accomplished that much did they take notice of the man who had assumed command of them. A few looked surprised to see that he was apparently a civilian, but most didn't seem to care one way or another. He sounded right, he looked—apart from his clothes—perfectly correct, and he clearly knew exactly what to do.

"You, you, and you..." David directed as he pointed out the groups he wanted, "find buckets and start fighting the fires. You and you... rig for stretchers. The rest of you, follow me. And," he added for good measure, "let the lady through. We'll need the wagon to remove wounded."

The next few hours passed in a blur. There was no time or strength left for fear. All that mattered was the shattered bodies of those young soldiers still left alive. Men who clutched at Annabel's hands, crying out for their mother, for God, for anything and anyone they thought might ease their suffering.

While David remained behind, Annabel and the soldiers delegated to help her loaded as many of the wounded as they could into the wagon. Not knowing where else to take them, she returned to the inn. Nicole, Pomfret, and de Plessis had been busy. They had cleared the tavern of tables and chairs so that the wounded could be laid out on the floor. Every bedsheet was put into service and torn into strips for bandages. As soon as the first group was unloaded, Annabel returned for more. She kept that up until at long last there were no other broken but still-living bodies in need of help. Weary and bloodstained, she made the last trip back to the inn with David beside her.

They arrived to find Paul out of bed despite his wounds

and supervising the care of the injured. He was undeniably pale and could not stand fully upright, but he was doggedly determined.

"You're going to kill yourself," David said.

"On the contrary," Paul replied. "Being useful is probably the best medicine for me. By the way, what happened to these poor devils? All I've managed to get are garbled accounts."

"I'm not sure," David said, "but I think the retreat from Washington has already begun. They were checking the Navy Yard on their way and discovered an unexploded powder magazine. They couldn't take the barrels with them so they decided to drop them down a deep well shaft. The barrels must have struck sparks on the stone siding. The explosion blew everything to hell."

Paul shook his head sadly. The accidental toll of war was often far greater than the purposeful one.

Three of the wounded soldiers in their care died during that long afternoon, but the rest—almost fifty altogether— were alive and improving when a senior British officer at last arrived at their door. He brought with him a detachment of troops and wagons.

Surveying the makeshift hospital, he said stiffly, "We are most grateful, of course. Very decent of you, this."

As the troops began removing the wounded, Paul raised a hand. He was slumped in a chair, too weak and tired to move, but still determined. Realizing what concerned him, David said, "Several of these men shouldn't be moved. Their wounds are too serious."

The officer hesitated. He was a middle-aged man who had seen a great deal in his time. It was clear that the tall, golden-haired man was correct. Yet he had a duty to his fellow soldiers.

Seeing his quandary, David said quietly, "Leave them here. We will be personally responsible for their safety. Once an armistice is declared, they can be exchanged for our own prisoners."

Slowly, the officer nodded. There was no point denying what was apparently obvious. The glorious victory of the day before—seizing the enemy's capital and burning its most treasured monuments—had turned out to be more costly than expected. The Americans had retreated in good order, taking few casualties, whereas the British losses were far heavier. The next few weeks and months promised to be difficult for all concerned.

With a curt salute, the officer turned on his heel, shouted the appropriate orders, and departed. The siege of Washington was over.

Twenty

A FAT drop of soapy water struck David on the nose. He pulled back slightly and laughed into the surprised face of his son. Louis grinned and splashed his chubby fists, sending sprays of water in all directions.

Watching them, de Plessis shook his head wryly. "Which one of you is having the bath?"

"Did you see how quickly he learned that?" David asked. "The first time was an accident but then he realized he could do it again."

"Amazing," the baron murmured. "A baby discovers he can make water splash. Fascinating."

David had the grace to look embarrassed, if only slightly. His son was an endless source of wonder to him. He couldn't get enough of the baby, especially not since he'd discovered that he could actually care for Louis himself.

Annabel's admission that she could no longer nurse

meant that David even got to feed him. So far the goat's milk was working well enough but they were trying to find a wet nurse. That was difficult since, a week after the end of the siege, life in Washington was still far from normal.

Wrapping the baby in a length of toweling, David sat down with him on his lap. The warm, sturdy weight of his child in his arms filled him with a sense of contentment unlike any he had ever known. It seemed almost inconceivable that he had lived so long without this elemental joy. When he gazed down at the baby, he felt a fierce joy and protectiveness that were almost overwhelming.

Watching him, de Plessis said quietly, "Does she know?"

It was pointless to pretend not to understand him. David's arm tightened around his son. "We haven't talked yet."

Although he had not yet confronted Annabel, he doubted she didn't realize what he intended. In the week since the British had left, she had kept herself so busy that he had scarcely seen her. Once or twice, he had found her holding Louis with a look in her eyes that made him want to reach out and comfort her. But she had always evaded him. She seemed satisfied to leave Louis to the care of his father and Nicole. All her attention was devoted to getting the inn running again.

But today David was determined she would avoid him no longer. He could not tarry forever in Washington. The matter had to be settled.

He was waiting for her an hour later when she returned from the market. She saw him but said nothing until she had supervised the unloading of supplies from the wagon. When that was done, she went into the kitchen, removed her bonnet, and hung it on a peg beside the door. Her movements were rigid, her back stiff. She was unnaturally pale.

"You need a cool drink," David said quietly. He went to get it for her without waiting for a response. She took it and drank, seated at the table, her eyes averted. The silence drew out between them. Only the humming of bees beyond the window could be heard.

Finally, David said, "I want to talk with you, Annabel. There is much that needs to be said."

Her mouth twisted. She bit her lower lip to stop its trembling and stared down at her hands. "That sounds very ominous."

He sat down beside her, wanting to touch her but knowing that would be wrong. In her present mood, she would reject any comfort he might try to offer.

"You don't have to see it that way. We both want the same thing, that is to say what's best for Louis."

What little color remained in her face now fled. Her eyes behind the thick fringes were deep, impenetrable pools. So softly that he could hardly hear her, she said, "I'm listening."

This was far more than David had expected. He had thought she would fight him every step of the way, but here she was at least indicating that she would consider what he had to say. Even as he wondered at what lay behind her tolerance, he moved to make use of it.

"As you know, I possess a fairly sizeable fortune, as well as an old, honorable name and an estate that has been in my family for generations. By all rights, any child of mine should receive considerable advantages and be raised to a station in life which many would find enviable."

He paused, thinking she would say something, but she remained silent. After a moment, he went on. "I realize that you are Louis's mother and that you love him. But you must recognize that there is relatively little for him here. In

France, he can have wealth, position, and a heritage of which he can be proud."

Annabel looked up, meeting his eyes. The surprise in hers was evident. "What exactly are ye saying, David? Children born out of wedlock are barred from the things you speak of."

"Ordinarily," he acknowledged, "but that doesn't have to be the case here. Louis can be legitimized. He is my only child and I intend to make him my heir."

Annabel's lips parted soundlessly. She had known for days that David would not willingly part from his son. She had expected him to say that he wanted to take Louis back to France. The advantages of that, even for a bastard child, were so evident that they had caused her much anguished soul-searching. But in all the long, dark hours of trying to decide what was best for her child, she had never considered that David meant to make him his heir. Any argument she could make, any case she could set forth for why Louis would be better off remaining in America, was gone.

Her throat tightened. She wanted to scream at him that Louis was her child. She had carried him in her body and given birth to him. What monster of a man would think to take him from her?

And yet she could not form the words. Too vividly, she remembered that she had not wanted Louis to be born. Her own fear and reluctance had almost doomed them both. And since then, how good a mother had she been? Others seemed able to care for him at least as well as she could. She couldn't even manage to nurse him. She was always running off, seeing to her business, where at least she felt as though she knew what she was doing. Did she truly have special rights where he was concerned?

She started to speak but her voice broke. She had to take a deep breath before trying again. "I—I do love him so much."

"I know," David said gently. He did reach over then and take her hands in his. Despite the warmth of the day, her skin was icy cold. He could feel the tremors shaking her.

Her eyes squeezed shut. From between the lashes, tears gleamed. "I want him to be happy," she whispered.

David's hard face gentled as he gazed at the woman before him. Long before he had known and loved his child, she had stirred him in ways he still could not fully understand. Her touch, her look, the sound of her voice were all precious to him. Even her prickly pride and stubborn independence had taken on an endearing aura.

That being the case the solution to their problem was obvious.

Quietly, he said, "Marry me, Annabel. Let us all return to France together."

She stared at him, stock still. Her lips moved stiffly. "Ye're mad."

He smiled and shook his head. "No, merely desperate. We can concoct some story to explain your sudden appearance. People won't necessarily believe it, but that doesn't matter. Louis will still be my heir, the future marquis de Montfort, and no one will be able to look down on him."

"Oh, really?" Annabel snatched her hands away. She stood up and walked to the far end of the kitchen. Her back to David, she said, "And what happens when he gets older and starts goin' out a bit on his own? He'll hear quick enough that his mother's no lady. How do you think he'll feel when people are snickerin' behind his back, talkin' about the fine marquise de Montfort with her shanty Irish accent and her uncouth ways? That'll do the lad a world of good, I don't think.''

"Who are you worrying for?" David shot back. "My estates are miles from Paris. If you're uncomfortable with society, you don't have to be part of it. But you can damn well do what's right for our child.''

Annabel whirled and faced him again. Her cheeks were stained with color and her eyes glittered, though whether from anger or from unshed tears he could not say.

"I know what's right for him," she said. "And I'll do it, damn ye.'' Her voice rose, taut with pain. "He'll not be a tavern brat. Take him. Go back to your precious France and raise him to be a nobleman. But God help ye if he's not happy with it.''

Her voice broke, the tears at last running down her cheeks. David took a step forward. He started to speak but before he could say a word, Annabel turned and ran from the room. He was left with only the sweet, tantalizing scent of her skin and the haunting fear that he had lost something more precious than he would ever know.

"You're mad," Nicole said. She had come hurrying into the taproom the next morning as soon as she heard the news and now she confronted Annabel angrily. "You can't possibly mean to let Louis go without you.''

Exhausted after a sleepless night, Annabel was in no mood to explain her reasoning. She said only, "It's best this way. David can give him things I never can.''

"Is that all you care about?" Nicole demanded. "Things? What about love?''

"David loves him," Annabel murmured. "Ye've only to look at them to know that."

"But so do you. How can you let him go?"

Annabel put down the cloth she was using to dry the bar. Her eyes burned and her throat hurt, so long and violently had she wept the night before. Nicole had asked the same question that had tortured her through the long, anguished hours. The question that still dripped like acid on her tormented spirit.

Wearily, she said, "My mind's made up. There's no point discussin' it further."

If she had thought that would be enough to discourage Nicole, she was disappointed. Like her brother, this de Montfort recognized few, if any, obstacles to doing what she believed was right.

Sternly, she said, "Oh, there isn't, is there? Well, it might still interest you to know that if you refuse to marry David, it's going to be that much more difficult for Louis to be made legitimate. David can adopt him, that's true, but it will make it clear to everyone that he was born a bastard. There are people who will never accept him because of that, no matter what his legal standing. And there are others who will use it as an excuse to speculate about his actual parentage."

"What are you saying? Why else would David adopt him if he didn't know him to be his son?"

"Because he needs an heir for Montfort. He has no other children, not in marriage or out of it. He's always been too scrupulous for that . . . at least until now. Oh, don't you see," Nicole went on, "by standing on pride and refusing to marry David, you're creating problems that can haunt all of you for the rest of your lives. Is that truly what you want?''

Annabel's head had begun to pound. She wasn't prone to headaches and had a tendency to disparage women who took refuge behind them, so there was some irony in her plight. The pain stabbed through her, making her catch her breath. Behind the confusion of discomfort and doubt, only one fact shone clearly—whatever she did, whichever way she turned, Louis had to come first. She wanted desperately to do the right thing, but she no longer felt certain what that might be.

"Where is David?" she asked finally.

"At the docks arranging for passage. He heard the ship he came on is back in port."

"I must speak with him."

"Then you'd best hurry. Berths still aren't easy to come by. It would certainly be a fine thing if there turned out to be no room for you."

That would be the last straw, Annabel thought as she grabbed her bonnet and headed for the door. If she did decide to go—sweet heaven, was she really considering that?—she certainly didn't want to wait weeks for a ship.

Darting down the cobblestone street, she struggled to gather her thoughts. Go or stay? Remain in the world she knew or risk one she could barely imagine? Be Annabel Riordan, tavern keeper, or Annabel de Montfort, wife, mother, lady?

Her heart was pounding by the time she reached the docks. People were milling around, looking for news, cargo, or berths. She had to strain over the heads of the crowd to catch sight of a proud, three-masted schooner riding at anchor.

A tall, bearded man in a captain's uniform stood at the bottom of the gangplank. He was talking with David. Pomfret was at his master's side, the customary, long-suffering expression back on his face. That was not altogether inappropriate considering that Louis was dozing securely in his father's arms, his head resting on the shoulder of David's impeccably tailored frock coat.

Several passersby stopped to look twice at the sight of a supremely aristocratic man matter-of-factly holding a baby. But the captain seemed to see nothing amiss. He was nodding as David spoke.

The nod turned to a polite frown when Annabel hurried up to them. Wearing her usual practical clothes and with her hair insisting as always on going its own way, she presented a startling picture. Lovely young women who accosted men on docks were usually more flamboyantly garbed. Jeremiah Kayes looked from Annabel to the child in David's arms. A smile touched his mouth as he considered the endless miracle of life and the varying ways the Lord took to bring it about.

"David, I must speak with . . ."

At the sound of her voice, Louis awoke. He blinked against the sudden light, then opened his eyes fully. A soft chortle escaped him. Twisting in his father's arms, he reached out for Annabel.

Twenty-one

CAPTAIN Jeremiah Kayes's black beard glinted in the sunlight. He stood ramrod straight in his best uniform, his weathered face solemn and benign. Between his hands he held the Book of Common Prayer that had been in his family for three generations. It was opened to the wedding service.

Annabel stared straight ahead, her eyes on the book. She was afraid that if she removed them for an instant, her nerve would desert her. The *Seafarer* had sailed that morning, less than a day after her decision to go with David. The hours in between had been taken up in a mad rush to leave some kind of order behind her.

Mercifully, Nicole had stepped into the breach. She had matter-of-factly announced her intention to stay in Washington.

"This is where Cameron will return," she said, "and this is where he'll expect to find me. I've several excellent teachers who can run the school in my absence, so there's no worry on that score. If you'll trust me with the Wild Geese, I promise you won't be disappointed.''

Annabel was delighted to do so. Nicole was the first true woman friend she had ever had; she felt toward her like a sister. And now she was to become that in fact.

Captain Kayes's deep voice reached across the deck to the assembly of crew and passengers gathered to observe the proceedings. Annabel continued to stare straight ahead. She was vividly aware of the man standing strong and unmoving beside her.

David held her hand in his, his burnished fingers curling around hers with possessive protectiveness. She had the very clear feeling that were she to try suddenly to pull away, he would not permit it. He would not hurt her, but neither would he let her go.

A warning drifted through her dazed mind: she had better get used to that sort of treatment. However pretty and high-principled they might sound, the vows they were exchanging effectively made her his property.

By marrying him, she was trusting him with her life, her happiness, and her future. Since she had been willing enough, however painfully, to trust him with her child, this seemed hardly more.

The captain stopped speaking. In the silence that followed, a sweet sea breeze still carrying memories of land touched Annabel's heated face. She was aware suddenly of an expectant hush.

David looked down, a sardonic smile playing around his hard mouth, a warning glint in his eyes. ''Say 'I do.' ''

Her throat was suddenly dry. She tried to moisten her lips and found that she could not. On a breath of sound, hardly audible, she complied.

A moment later, David said the same words, only far more strongly.

That same strength was evident as he turned her to him and with deliberate firmness, touched his lips to hers.

It was done, sealed by the words of God and the will of man. She was his wife.

Annabel stood as best she could the congratulations and laughter of those in attendance. Quickly enough, Captain Kayes sent the crew back to work, but the other passengers were naturally free to linger. Someone had brought up several bottles of wine. Toasts were offered to the new couple.

Many of the passengers on board the *Seafarer* were Frenchmen and Frenchwomen stranded in Washington by the turn of the war. They were delighted to at last be able to leave and were in a mood to celebrate. The unexpected wedding merely gave them an added excuse to do so.

Ordinarily, Annabel would have enjoyed it. But she was still far too shaken by the sudden turn in her life and uncertain of where it would lead. As soon as she could, she slipped away.

A young girl, the daughter of a family returning to France, had offered to stay with Louis during the ceremony. She smiled shyly when Annabel entered the cabin.

"He is such a good baby, madame," she murmured. "And so very beautiful. You must be so happy."

"Thank you," Annabel said. Instinctively, she responded in the girl's own language. Although she had rarely spoken French in the last few years, she was relieved that her understanding of it had not diminished. At least she would be able to make herself understood, once she was in France.

When the girl was gone, Annabel sat down next to Louis's cradle. She stared at the child for a long time, wondering how she could have seriously considered giving him up. Only the overriding desire to give him the best possible life had made her even consider it.

Frightened and confused though she was, she had to admit that David's alternative was better. Together as husband and wife they would raise their child in a secure place with all the advantages he could possibly need. Many would consider that ideal. Why didn't she?

"Always chasin' after the moon," she murmured under her breath. "Seekin' something that isn't there."

At the sound of her voice, however soft, Louis stirred. She smiled as he frowned slightly, then relaxed again without waking. Sweet heaven, how she loved him.

It didn't seem to matter that others had helped care for him or that she could no longer feed him herself. Merely to look at him was to feel the piercing strength of the bond between them. That love, at least, she would have. To yearn for David's also was the height of foolishness.

So she told herself and so she struggled to believe. The motion of the swaying ship and the sight of the sleeping child combined to dull her thoughts. She was worn out from the events of the last few days. Slowly, almost imperceptibly, her eyes fluttered closed.

David entered the cabin a few minutes later. He stopped just inside the door and gazed at Annabel. Even asleep, her hand rested protectively on their son's cradle. Her head drooped slightly, the fall of titian hair veiling her face. Through it, she looked young and almost unbearably vulnerable.

He stifled a groan. He didn't think of himself as a

particularly religious man but even he had been startled by the graphically irreligious trend of his thoughts during the wedding service. When he should have been concentrating on the holiness of their vows, he was thinking about the hard, driving hunger of his body.

Simply being near Annabel filled him with desire. In the days since his return to Washington, there had been no opportunity to even attempt to ease his lust. But now . . . now she was his wife.

He moved closer without taking his eyes from her. She was wearing a blue muslin dress embroidered with sprigs of violet. The dress had been a wedding gift from Nicole, there being nothing so festive in Annabel's own wardrobe. For all her bookishness, Nicole was a woman of fashion. The dress was cut low enough to reveal the swell of Annabel's breasts. They rose and fell slowly with each breath.

She was exhausted. He hardly needed blinding insight to recognize that. For a brief moment, conscience warred with lust. With a deep, regretful sigh, he lifted her from the chair.

The bunk was spacious enough for two. Alone in it, Annabel appeared even smaller and more fragile than before. She slept with the abandonment of a child, her lips slightly parted and her lashes thick against her cheeks.

David took a firm grip on himself and bent to loosen her clothes. He removed her shoes, then unfastened her dress. She did not wake as he slipped it from her. Underneath she wore a lace-trimmed shift and stockings of sheer ivory silk, also gifts from Nicole.

The stockings were held in place by white garters trimmed with rose buds. He slipped a finger beneath one and slowly slid it down her leg. When the other was also gone, he carefully removed each stocking. Her legs were slender and firm, tapering to slim ankles and delicately arched feet. By the time the first stocking was gone, his breathing was ragged. When the second leg was at last bared, he was hard with need.

Still, Annabel slept, as trustingly as a child. She should have known that he would want her. She should have been excited . . . concerned . . . something.

Maybe she had been. But maybe she'd simply been too exhausted to care.

Her skin was so enticingly soft. His fingers brushed over her calf, up across the back of her knees, to the inside of her thigh. She moaned faintly and stirred. The motion strained the fabric across her breasts. He drew a hard, rasping breath and pulled the blanket over her.

A moment later he was gone, the door closing sharply behind him.

If Pomfret found it at all odd that his master chose to share his cabin, he said nothing. There were two bunks, after all, and the marquis was no problem.

He stayed awake on deck until long after Pomfret was asleep and he arose again before the valet stirred. Indeed, Pomfret could not absolutely vouch that David slept at all during the three weeks it took to negotiate the eastward passage and arrive at Le Havre.

Certainly, by the time they debarked, the marquis was looking like a man at the edge of his limits. As for the marquise, though he had difficulty thinking of her as that,

Pomfret had to admit that Annabel was turning out to be a pleasant surprise.

She was very quiet, that was true, but when he did coax a word from her, she was invariably kind and thoughtful. Once he had even provoked a smile that had filled him with a sense of accomplishment for the remainder of the day.

Which made it all the more difficult for him to understand why master and mistress barely exchanged a word. Instead, they behaved like wary combatants, circling round each other, but never coming within arm's length. They even took turns playing with Louis, one or the other discreetly going elsewhere. On a small ship that hadn't been easy to manage. Pomfret sighed, supposing they would find it less difficult once they reached Montfort.

A carriage waited at the dock as the *Seafarer* dropped anchor. David and Annabel bade their separate farewells to Captain Kayes. To David, he offered a strong handshake and a respectful nod. To Annabel, of whom he had become fond, he gave a small book of poetry that had belonged to his late sister.

"You should not," Annabel protested softly. She had come to like the strong, stolid captain a great deal but she did not think that entitled her to anything that had such obvious personal significance for him.

"I insist," he said. "Elizabeth was a good woman—bright, loving, sensible. She would have liked you a great deal and I'm sure she would approve of your having this."

Annabel looked down at the little volume in her hands and blinked back tears. She wasn't normally a weepy person but lately her emotions were always on edge. It was a relief to leave the confines of the ship and make what she hoped would be a fresh start. But she was also concerned about where that would lead.

Now, as she sat in the carriage beside David, she looked down at the small reticule that held Captain Kayes's book and thought about what lay ahead. David was holding Louis.

The baby was awake and enthralled. His little head kept turning every which way in his determination not to miss anything. Watching him, David laughed softly. He seemed totally absorbed in his son and delighted by him.

Annabel permitted herself a small sigh. Whatever else they might face, she could not deny that David was an exemplary father.

He did things for his child that she knew men did not ordinarily do. As often as not, it was David who fed him from the bottle they had rigged up to hold the goat's milk. To their infinite relief, Louis was thriving on it, although he had recently indicated a preference for more solid food. The goat, who had made the voyage with them, might be put out to pasture soon.

But David did not draw the line at merely feeding his son. He also bathed and changed him, tended to him when he was fretful, and did in essence everything a mother would do. Moreover, he didn't seem to find anything unusual in this. Never by so much as a word or glance did he suggest that he deserved praise for taking care of his son.

He liked babies. Obviously, that was it. Some men liked dogs, others were mad for horses. David liked babies. There was no sense making more of it than that.

This, however, did not quite explain his consistent protectiveness and consideration during the trip to Paris.

They went not by carriage, as she had expected, but by the far more comfortable alternative of riverboat.

David seemed to be familiar with the family that owned the boat. The young man who greeted them showed neither surprise nor awe at having a member of the nobility aboard. Neither did his young wife who cooed over Louis and did her utmost to make Annabel comfortable.

"What a lovely babe," she said admiringly as she smiled at Louis. Shyly, she added, "I'm expecting one myself in the early spring."

"Congratulations," Annabel said and found to her surprise that she truly meant it. She felt a sense of communion with this young woman and could anticipate her happiness.

"We'd heard that the marquis had a son," the girl said. "They'll be celebrating at Montfort."

Seated on the wooden bench that ran along one wall of the galley, Annabel asked, "How did you hear?"

The girl shrugged. "Word spreads. I suppose a ship must have reached here ahead of yours with people who knew." Seeing Annabel's surprise, she added, "There's quite a few who care about the marquis. He's well thought of, you know."

Looking down at her hands, Annabel said, "No, actually, I don't. There's a great deal about him I don't know."

Had she issued an invitation, the girl could not have been more accommodating. She smiled eagerly and sat down beside Annabel. In a hushed voice, she said, "You do know that he fought with the emperor?"

"Yes," Annabel said slowly, "I had heard about that."

"I confess to having mixed feelings about Napoleon but be that as it may, everyone knows how bravely the marquis fought and how concerned he was for his men. More members of his battalion made it back from Russia than from any other. Indeed, it is said to have been with de Montfort is a sign of fortune's favor.''

Annabel smiled gently. She knew the feeling herself although she did not care to elaborate on it.

"Of course, he's always been like that,'' the girl went on. "My mother-in-law knew him as a child. Well, that is to say, they only met once, but when he returned to France much later, he got in touch with her. Wanted to make sure she was all right, he said. He's like that.''

"What do you mean, she met him only once as a child?'' Annabel asked.

"She and my father-in-law used to run a boat along the river. Not this one, one they had before. During the Terror, they helped people to escape, the marquis among them. Of course, he was only a child then. He got out along with his sisters and the good doctor. They were lucky. There's many another who died.''

Annabel nodded slowly. She had known about David's background but this brought it into clearer focus. The idea of him as a child escaping on a boat very much like this one moved her deeply. She thought of how loving he was with his own child. To go through such an experience and still retain the ability to love said no small thing about a man.

It was therefore all the more painful that he had said barely a word to her since their marriage. She knew she should feel relieved but she was not. Increasingly, the mere sight of him was enough to fill her with longing.

She was almost grateful that he kept to himself during most of the overnight journey to Paris. It was only the following morning, as they were alighting on the stone quay near Notre Dame, that he seemed to recall her presence.

"It won't be much longer now," he said quietly. He stood looking out at the city. It was very early. Few people were about. To the west, pale and ghostly in the gray light, stretched the vast expanse of the Louvre.

Annabel looked at it with wonder. Nothing had remotely prepared her for Paris. It was far larger and grander than either Dublin or Washington. Indeed, both those cities would have fit comfortably into a single corner of it.

Immense stone buildings, many of them obviously very old, rose all around her. The cathedral was the most familiar for she had seen many etchings of it. But she also recalled the graceful, three-story palace rising through stone colonnades to a slate roof. It had been a favorite illustration for tracts describing the bloody Revolution and the tragic fate of the royal family.

Softly, she said, "You lived there, didn't you, toward the end?"

David nodded. "You can't see the part where we were, it's around the other side. But yes, we did stay there for awhile."

"Have you ever gone back?"

He shook his head. "There is no reason. Everything that was is gone. Now it's only empty rooms occasionally populated by bureaucrats."

Annabel wanted to ask him how he had managed to stay away when Napoleon, whom he had served, had often held court at the Louvre. But she remained silent. Clearly, the place held too many painful memories for David. It was not really surprising that he had contrived to avoid it.

As he did now. The carriage that took them from Paris set off in the opposite direction from the great palace. They passed through the remnants of the ancient city walls to their modern counterparts, where they paid the toll required of all those leaving Paris. A short time later they were cantering along a broad country road framed by chestnut trees and fragrant with the scent of blackberries.

They stopped for lunch at an inn where David was known. The proprietor came out to welcome them effusively. His wife followed, beaming at Louis and Annabel. Since the day was warm, they chose to dine outside. Pomfret discreetly withdrew, removing the sleeping Louis with him. He had developed a fondness for the boy, not to mention a certain knack.

For the first time since their marriage, Annabel and David were left strictly alone. They sat across from each other at a table set with a fluttering white cloth and a handful of wild roses. A smiling maid brought a loaf of crusty bread still warm from the oven and a carafe of red wine.

David poured for them both. Annabel lifted her goblet to her lips but drank sparingly. Her stomach was empty and her head already felt light. As she reached for a piece of the bread, her hand trembled. She jerked it back, hoping David had not noticed.

He had. His eyes darkened as they swept over her. She had lost weight during the voyage and appeared slenderer than ever. The dress she wore, the same one she had been married in, no longer fit as well as it had.

The sea air had made her hair curl more than usual. She had endeavored to secure it with a length of blue ribbon tied at the nape of her neck, but stray tendrils had escaped. Her face was pale, the cheeks hollower than before. All in all, she looked beautiful but fragile—and almost unbearably young.

"You will be able to rest soon," he said quietly. "We will reach Montfort before nightfall."

Annabel nodded but said nothing. She wanted to speak, to chatter lightly and inconsequentially as though nothing in the world troubled her, but she could not manage it. In David's presence, she felt tongue-tied.

She stole a glance at him through her lashes. He looked almost unbearably handsome sitting there in the midday sun. The pure white of his shirt and stock contrasted with his deeply tanned face.

To Pomfret's dismay, he refused to follow fashion and powder his hair. It gleamed thick and golden like the mane of a proud, young lion. His frock coat and breeches were of the plain black broadcloth he favored. There was nothing of the effete aristocrat about him, only hard, unrelenting male strength and purpose.

Desire, so determinedly repressed during the long days and nights at sea, stirred within her. A fierce, hot sweetness moved through her veins. She was suddenly aware of her breasts, the nipples swollen and sensitive, pressing against the fabric of her gown. Between her thighs, deep at the center of her being, the memory of him made her ache.

She took another sip of the wine, feeling his eyes on her throat as the liquid slipped slowly down. His lean, blunt-tipped fingers tore a piece from the crusty loaf, exposing its inner softness.

His teeth gleamed whitely as he bit into it. She stared, fascinated by his mouth. Too clearly, she remembered how it had felt moving over her, the rasp of his teeth on her nipples, the quick, soothing lick of his tongue.

By nightfall, he had said, they would be at Montfort, within his home that must now somehow become hers. They were husband and wife, parents together of a beautiful chid. And they still shared at least something of the feelings that had brought them together at the beginning.

She had seen that in his eyes and felt it within herself. Perhaps, after all, there was a chance that they could make this work not only for Louis's sake but for their own.

The future suddenly did not seem so bleak. For the first time since making her decision on the quay in Washington, she allowed herself to feel a tiny measure of hope.

❧ CHAPTER ❧
Twenty-two

H OPE lay in tattered shreds scant hours later. *Montfort*, he called it. "Strong mountain" it meant. The name was apt.

She was not so naive as to have thought it merely a house. Her knowledge of the country had led her to expect a chateau, functional and pretty, with perhaps two dozen rooms built around a center hall, rolling lawns, and a nearby pond glistening in the soft evening light.

She found instead a palace, rising mighty and proud above the surrounding plain. Not even the Louvre in all its majesty could equal it. It was immense, seeming to go on forever.

This was no primitive medieval keep, although it might long ago have begun as that. Now it appeared as something from her much-loved legends of King Arthur, a magnificent, fantastical palace of white marble and high turrets from which fluttered her husband's banner.

Husband. She was a peasant girl from the bogs of Eire who had used all her strength and will to rise as high as tavern keeper. A chateau she might—just might—have been able to manage with, given a bit of luck and a large dollop of nerve. But this . . . this was a place for a queen.

Her throat tightened. She gripped her hands tightly in her lap as they passed beneath the portcullis into a vast central courtyard. Despite the late hour, at least a hundred people milled around.

They raised a cheer as the carriage appeared, and cheered again when David stepped out. He smiled in acknowledgement, then turned and offered his hand to Annabel. Gathering all her courage, she took her first steps onto Montfort soil.

A hush fell over the crowd. She could feel their eyes raking her, taking in every aspect of her appearance from her unruly hair to the dress that no longer fit properly. Undoubtedly, it was also not of the latest style. Fashion moved at too rapid a clip for Americans to ever be quite up-to-date. But great French ladies always were, for they set the fashion, as these people knew.

Her back straightened. She lifted her head and returned their gaze. Men and women seemed to have gathered in roughly equal number, with a good smattering of children tumbling around them. Most wore the hand-sewn clothes of farm laborers but they were all clean and neat. Interspersed among them were men who looked like merchants, even a few scholars.

A tall, solemn-faced young man stepped up to David. "Welcome home, my lord. You've been missed."

"Thank you, Gerard." Turning, David took the sleeping

baby from Pomfret. He gazed down at him for a moment, smiling, before lifting him cradled in his arm so that the people could see him.

With his other arm, he drew Annabel to him. "My wife," he said, his voice strong and firm, "the marquise de Montfort, and our son, Louis."

The silence shattered as a hundred voices rose in acclamation. People pressed around them, smiling and laughing, gazing admiringly at the baby. But still, Annabel could see, when their glances turned her way they became more reserved and assessing.

David was clearly adored by his people who were more than willing to accept his son. His wife was another matter. She was not at all what they would have expected.

Still, they were respectful enough as they cleared a path to the broad stone stair leading to heavy double doors. Glancing down, Annabel saw that the steps were worn as only generations of people coming and going over centuries could do.

She looked up again at the vast bulk of the fortress rising above her and felt at that moment the weight of ages made real and tangible within it. No wonder David valued his heritage so greatly. No wonder he had been willing to go to such lengths to secure his son as heir to it. It was a prize that only those born to it could ever claim.

She would never belong.

The certainty of that sank into her, making every step she took a struggle against deadening weight. She nearly jumped when the doors were suddenly flung open, a shower of light pouring out. Servants stood within, footmen in bright uniforms lined up in rigidly straight rows, struggling to look solemn despite their smiles of welcome.

She could hear David speaking, giving instructions, but she could not make out the words. Her senses were dazed by too much light and sound—and truth. She could only stand silent and wide-eyed until a firm hand grasped her arm.

"This way, Annabel," her husband said gently. He led her toward a beautifully carved staircase that curved upward out of sight.

"Louis," she murmured, instinctively seeking her child.

"Josette will bring him." David indicated a plump, smiling woman following behind them.

Seeing her son in another's arm, in this strange and overwhelming place, caused something to snap inside Annabel. Without regard for what anyone would think, she reached out.

"Give him to me."

The woman frowned and looked questioningly at David. Only his almost imperceptible nod convinced her to relinquish the baby and then only an instant before Annabel would have snatched him from her.

The child's warm solidness was a comfort as they continued up the stairs to a second-floor hall. Candles, thick as a man's arm and set in golden sconces, lit the hall. The floor beneath was covered by a worn but beautiful rug of Oriental design. It ran the entire length of the hall, disappearing around distant corners where other wings began.

"Tomorrow," David said quietly, "you will see it all but for now I think this has been enough."

He opened the door and stood aside to let her enter. Within was a chamber that had apparently been furnished for the queen who belonged in such a place.

A huge canopied bed dominated the center of the room. It

was hung with brocade draperies drawn back to reveal a silken coverlet and thick, down-filled pillows. Opposite the bed was a large fireplace with an inlaid table and several chairs set before it. A door at the far end of the room stood open to reveal a private bathing chamber.

Annabel sank down into one of the chairs. A silent footman, eyes properly averted, deposited her single bag near the bed. He had also brought the plain wooden cradle in which Louis had slept since his birth, but appeared uncertain as to what to do with it.

"Excuse me, my lord," the young man said softly, "should I take this to the nursery?"

Before David could reply, Josette said, "Of course not. The child will sleep in the de Montfort cradle." She turned to David. "When we received word of your arrival, my lord, the nursery was fully readied. Everything the little one could need has been provided."

She looked pointedly at Annabel as though to emphasize the inappropriateness of her keeping Louis from where he properly belonged and would be most comfortable.

Annabel flushed but made no effort to give up her child. Instead, she said, "Louis is used to this cradle. He can remain in it at least for the next few days until he has had a chance to become more accustomed to his new surroundings."

The nurse's small mouth pursed disapprovingly but she had clearly not expected this pale, silent girl to oppose her, especially not in her own language.

"Very well," she said grudgingly. "We will take the cradle upstairs." She stepped forward, thinking that now for certain Annabel would yield the child.

As well she might have if she hadn't taken such a dislike

to the nurse. "Put the cradle down here." Looking directly at the other woman, she said, "My son stays with me."

Josette stared at her in disbelief. "My lord," she said, appealing to David, "surely that is not permissible."

He frowned. Annabel's stomach tightened. She had not meant for any such confrontation to happen, especially not so soon. But if it must, then so be it. If David ordered her to relinquish the child, she would refuse and the consequences be damned.

With deadly softness, he said, "The marquise has given you your instructions, Josette." A slight smile played about his hard mouth. "That will be all."

The woman flushed, turning almost purple, but she did not dare to challenge him. In a flutter of skirts, she departed.

The footmen followed swiftly, undoubtedly eager to spread this juicy bit of gossip. The marquis had stood by his wife, true enough, but she had shown herself lamentably lacking in propriety. At least, so Annabel imagined them thinking. She was too overwhelmed to dwell on the matter. It wasn't as though she could have fooled them anyway. And she had far more immediate concerns, the chief one of which was standing scant yards away looking at her enigmatically.

She rose with Louis in her arms and looked at her husband. "Thank you." Deliberately, she spoke in French, the language she intended to use from then on.

His eyebrows arched. He replied in kind. "For what?"

"For sending that horrible woman away. I realize I've never been in a place like this and I don't know how things are done, but is it possible to find someone else to . . ."

"First thing in the morning," David interjected gently. "I thought Josette would be a good choice but she clearly has forgotten her place. Someone more amenable to you will be found.''

Forgotten her place. The phrase rang in Annabel's mind even as she tried not to apply it to herself. Stiffly, she said, ''I will need to feed him again soon.''

David nodded. ''I'll have one of the footmen bring some milk.''

Now everyone would shortly know that Louis's mother couldn't nurse him herself. There was no helping it. Being vastly rich and powerful undoubtedly had many advantages; however, personal privacy wasn't among them.

''In the meantime,'' David went on, ''perhaps you would like to get comfortable. The maids will bring hot water for a bath.''

After three weeks at sea, the thought of a thorough wash was delightful, even if it had to be in such strange and intimidating surroundings.

David smiled gently. She had such an expressive face, though he suspected she didn't know it. She seemed to spend a great deal of time trying to appear confident and in control when she was anything but. He suspected that what she needed most was to be left alone to accustom herself to her circumstances.

Quietly, he said, ''I'll return when you've had a chance to rest. We will dine informally.''

Annabel managed some appropriate response, though she couldn't have said what it was. Not until David had left the room did the tension abruptly ease from her. She almost sagged with relief.

Afraid that she might drop Louis, she made haste to put him in his cradle. Determined then to keep busy as a way of avoiding her thoughts, she unpacked her small bag. When her few possessions were laid out on the immense bed, they looked ridiculously small and paltry.

She was about to put them away in the gilt and marble dresser when there was a hesitant knock at the door. Opening it, Annabel found two shy young girls gazing at her.

"I am Patrice, my lady," one of the two murmured, "and this is Claire. We've brought water for your bath."

Thoroughly unaccustomed to being waited on—and being well aware of how heavy water was—Annabel almost reached out to help them. She stopped herself just in time.

The girls went on into the bathroom. Annabel followed them. She had barely glanced in there before and was astounded to discover a black marble tub large enough to hold two people easily.

Across from the tub was a gilded mirror and a table holding a washing basin. Soft, fluffy towels were piled up on nearby shelves. Annabel picked up a bar of soap and sniffed it. The spicy, masculine scent made her frown.

The room adjoined a chamber obviously intended for a woman yet it appeared designed for a man's taste. Hesitantly, she glanced toward a second door she had just noticed.

"Where does that lead?" she asked.

The girls glanced at one another. Claire covered her mouth and giggled softly. Patrice shot her a chiding look. "His lordship's room is through there, my lady. He had the bath installed so that it could serve this chamber as well."

"I see . . ." Annabel said slowly. She should have expected that David's room would be nearby, but she hadn't quite bargained on taking her bath where he could walk in at any moment.

Briefly, she considered locking the adjoining door. But

she could hardly do so in front of the maids and she hated to acknowledge her self-consciousness even to herself.

Perhaps she was even hoping that he would come in on her.

When the tub was filled, Patrice turned to help her undress while Claire went to sit with Louis. Annabel allowed the maid to undo the buttons down the back of her dress, a task she had been managing for herself but which was awkward and difficult. As soon as it was done, Annabel said, "Thank you, I'll take care of the rest."

Patrice took a quick step back. She looked surprised and uncertain. "D-did I do something wrong?"

"No, of course not," Annabel said hastily. "You've been very kind, it's just that I'm used to managing for myself."

Still Patrice hesitated, clearly not certain that she hadn't done something to earn the new marquise's displeasure.

Seeing her concern, Annabel said gently, "I'll be fine, really, but I wonder is there any possibility that you could press the green dress on the bed? It's all I have to wear that's clean and presentable, and David—that is, the marquis— said something about supper."

Instantly, Patrice brightened. Her small face was wreathed in a relieved smile. "Of course, my lady, I'd be happy to and when you've finished bathing, if you'd like me to dress your hair, I can do that, too."

Tired though she was, Annabel did not fail to pick up on this. She knew that a grand lady was expected to have a lady's maid but had no idea how one went about acquiring such a personage. It appeared that Patrice might be able to solve the problem for her.

"You do hair?" she asked.

Patrice nodded eagerly. "I do, my lady, and I can sew, as

well. I can also give facials and massages. And I keep up with fashion although I must admit it's not easy, what with styles changing as fast as they do.''

"That's very impressive," Annabel said with a smile. "However do you manage it?"

The maid blushed, overcome by her own boldness. "My aunt taught me, my lady. She's maid to Madame Gaudin who has the adjoining estate."

"I see..." Annabel said slowly. "I'll be needing a lady's maid, Patrice. Would you like to give it a try?"

"Oh, yes, madame," the girl exclaimed. She clasped her hands but could not stop herself from bobbing up and down with delight. "There is nothing I would like better."

Satisfied that she had made a wise choice, Annabel nodded. "That's fine then. Off with you now before this water gets cold. I won't be long."

Patrice obeyed instantly. A moment later, Annabel heard her talking to Claire in an excited, happy whisper, undoubtedly relaying her good fortune. As she removed the rest of her clothes and folded them neatly over a stool, Annabel reflected that at least she had managed to make one person at Montfort happy.

The water was blessedly hot and welcome on her tired body. She leaned her head back against the edge of the marble tub and closed her eyes. A moment later, they shot open.

Above her, on the ceiling twelve feet away, a naked nymph smiled cheerfully at the leering satyr chasing after her. Precise attention to anatomical detail left no doubt as to the pursuer's intentions.

Annabel smiled. A soft laugh broke from her. It sounded good especially after all the weeks of tension and doubt.

She stayed in the tub until the water grew tepid. Patrice had left a crystal vial of foaming oil with which Annabel washed herself and her hair. When she was at last done, she rose dripping and bundled herself into a large towel.

Having wrapped it around herself and dried her hair as best she could, she went back to the bedroom. Patrice and Claire were both there. They had spread a blanket on the floor and were playing with Louis. He was awake and eager despite the relatively late hour. When he saw his mother, he waved his chubby arms and grinned.

"What a good baby he is," Claire said softly. "And so smart. He can roll over both ways already. Only my littlest brother could do that at his age, not any of the others."

"How many brothers do you have?" Annabel asked.

"Six, my lady, and four sisters."

"Claire is the oldest," Patrice chimed in. "She's helped look after all of them. There isn't much about babies that Claire doesn't know."

Claire looked pleased but embarrassed. "I'm sure Madame knows much more. After all, I've never had a baby of my own."

"You'd be very young for that, wouldn't you?" Annabel asked gently. She was beginning to get the idea that the girls hadn't been sent to her by accident. It would be like David, after seeing her difficulty with Josette, to single out the two he thought most likely to suit her and set them in her path.

"I'm seventeen, my lady," Claire said softly.

Four years younger than Annabel herself but seeming much more so because of her diffidence. Yet there was no doubt that she loved babies and was well versed in their ways. When Louis tried to grab a corner of the blanket and failed, Claire saw and pushed it closer before he could even begin to cry.

Annabel smiled as she watched their antics in the dressing table mirror. Patrice combed out her hair, murmuring admiringly at its color but frowning over the condition of its ends.

"Would you mind if I trimmed just a bit, ma'am?"

Annabel shook her head. She had never quite known what to do with her hair. If Patrice did, she was content to leave it in her hands.

A half-hour later, she sat back and looked at herself. It wasn't quite clear to her what the young maid had done, but it was undeniably successful.

Softly curling tendrils drifted gracefully around her face. The rest was pulled up high on her head and secured with a jeweled band, from which it fell in a thick, gleaming coil. The effect was elegant and sophisticated, yet seemingly without artifice.

Annabel slipped behind a privacy screen to don her shift and stockings. When she emerged, Patrice held out the dress she had ironed. If she found anything amiss about the simple cotton frock, she gave no sign of it.

"You look lovely, my lady," Claire said admiringly.

Annabel thanked her but glanced critically in the mirror. She thought she looked pale and tired.

A moment later, there was a knock at the door. Patrice hurried over to answer it. A footman stood rigidly at attention.

"His lordship requests that you join him in the sitting room, my lady."

Annabel took a deep breath to still the fluttering beneath her breast. She turned to Claire.

"Will you stay and look after Louis, please?"

The girl appeared surprised to have been asked rather than told but she nodded at once. "Don't you be worried, ma'am. I won't take my eyes off him."

With that taken care of, there was no excuse to linger. Squaring her shoulders, Annabel left the room.

❧ CHAPTER ❧
Twenty-three

WHAT the footman had described as the "sitting room" was in fact a large, exquisitely furnished parlor occupying a back corner of the house overlooking the gardens. Floor-to-ceiling windows stood open to admit a breeze scented with roses and honeysuckle.

Candles gleamed in the crystal chandeliers. There were couches covered in washed silk, marquetry tables, and at one end of the room, an elaborately fashioned harpsichord. Along the wall were portraits in gilt frames of de Montfort ancestors. They were without fail attractive men and women although Annabel had to admit that some looked a tad forbidding.

None, however, rivaled the man who stood beside the harpsichord, his fingers lightly tracing a tune. He looked up as Annabel entered. He had also bathed and changed but had dressed with what she suspected was deliberate simplicity.

Deliberate and devastating. His unadorned white shirt

was left open at the neck exposing a triangle of darkly burnished skin. Snugly fitted black breeches tapered down to gleaming boots. She wondered for a moment if they were the same pair he had struggled to remove the first time they made love.

His eyes as he gazed at her were hooded and watchful. She hid her hands within the folds of her skirt and smiled coolly. "It's a lovely instrument. Do you play?"

He shook his head. "My mother did and Dominique learned, but Nicole and I never had the opportunity."

No, of course they wouldn't have. The Reign of Terror had not been a good time for music lessons.

"What about yourself?" David asked.

"I can play the harp a bit," Annabel admitted. "I was taught as a child but I've always thought the harpsichord had the loveliest sound of any instrument."

"You could take lessons if you liked," he said. He stepped away from the small dais and came toward her. "It wouldn't be difficult to arrange. There are many skilled music teachers in need of employment."

Annabel nodded, not trusting herself to speak. He spoke so nonchalantly of things she could never have even dreamt of doing. He could command desires to be fulfilled and whims satisfied, and think nothing of it.

His hand touched her arm lightly. "I hope you won't mind, I had supper set up on the terrace."

She quickly realized that informal dining consisted of a wrought-iron table set with the finest linen, plates rimmed in gold, and goblets of exquisite crystal. Silent, discreet servants presented an array of dishes, each more enticing than the last, while off in the distance, hidden somewhere behind the fragrant bushes, a violinist played.

As cool, tart champagne slipped down her throat, Annabel felt sweet languor lapping at her senses. Fear and apprehension were dissolving. Whether from exhaustion or merely in self-defense, she let herself relax.

The man seated across from her seemed intent on being a charming companion. Certainly, David spared no effort to see to her comfort. He solicitously inquired if she found the food and wine pleasing. Did she enjoy the music? Was she either too warm or too cool? And her quarters, did she approve of them?

"How could anyone not?" Annabel asked languidly. The wine was having its effect. Wrapped in darkness lit only by candle and moon, the world was taking on a decidedly benign appearance.

"I've never been anyplace so beautiful," she said candidly. "Has it always been like this?"

David shook his head. "An ancestor of mine in the reign of Louis XIV took what had been a rough-hewn fortress and transformed it into this. He spared no expense but then he didn't need to. The king had granted him patents for importing silks and brocades from China. The nobility were mad for them; he did quite well."

Annabel struggled to contain her surprise. She didn't want to sound gauche but she couldn't resist commenting, "I didn't think aristocrats liked to dirty their hands with trade."

David laughed. He was enjoying the play of soft light over her hair and skin. She looked unbearably lovely but very, very fragile, far more than he suspected she knew. He was worried about her, about how well she could adjust to her new surroundings and about how much of a wife he could expect her to be. It was all complicated by the heated, demanding desire he felt for her.

Wryly, he admitted the truth to himself. The setting, the meal he had arranged, his concern for her well-being all came down to one thing—he wanted to seduce her. He didn't know if wives required seduction but then he had never been in such a position before. All he knew for certain was that if he couldn't bury himself within her sweet, yielding body soon, he would go mad.

She was his. With every word she spoke, every tilt of her head, and every smile, he remembered that. From the top of her gleaming head to the bottom of her slender feet, down the length of a body dreams were made of, she belonged to him.

He had the right to her. On the high seas, in the confines of the ship, there had always been some excuse to stay away from her. But now he was under his own roof, on the land he ruled, with his wife at hand and his desire urgent.

A footman placed succulent raspberries dotted with sweet cream before them. Annabel lifted her spoon. Her small tongue took one of the raspberries on its tip, savoring the sharp, heady taste with innocent pleasure.

David put down his glass. He was about to speak when a footman appeared suddenly at his arm. A silver tray was extended along with an apologetic cough. On the tray was a heavily embossed envelope.

David took it and slit the flap with his knife. Inside was a paper bearing a few lines of neatly penned words. At the bottom was a signature he recognized all too well.

Tallyrand. The wily foreign minister who had grown rich and powerful in service to Napoleon until the emperor grew weary of his advice and caused him to flee. Now he was back, a supporter of the Bourbon restoration and a trusted confidant of the king, Louis XVIII, brother of the guillotined Louis XVI and uncle of the doomed dauphin who had died in prison.

Tallyrand was a conniver of the first rank, but he was also a man of odd, unexpected honor. He had always admired the de Montforts and was not ill disposed to helping them.

David's eyes narrowed as he scanned the note. He folded it and placed it carefully in the pocket of his breeches. With an apologetic smile, he said, "Forgive me. It is from an old acquaintance who has learned of my return."

Annabel wondered if the acquaintance might be a woman but she would not stoop to ask. Instead, she devoted her attention to the raspberries which were surely most deserving of it. When she had finished the last of them, she raised her eyes to find David staring at her. A slow flush spread across her cheeks.

"What is it?" she asked.

He rose and held out a hand. "Walk in the garden with me."

She went willingly, as though in a dream, while behind them the swift, efficient servants carried away the remains of the meal. Beyond the terrace, amid curving paths and rolling lawns, all was still. An owl hooted high in an ancient oak tree. In the silver lake, bathed in moonlight, a heron fluttered its wings as it settled down to sleep.

Softly, David said, "It is good to be home." The words were simple but the emotion behind them had never been more heartfelt. Never had he felt so completely bound to Montfort, one with its fertile soil, its graceful hills, and its proud forests. His land and—one day—his son's, to nurture and protect so long as land and time existed.

He turned, Annabel's hand in his, and looked back at the magnificent fortress rising above them. Mists were forming near its base, making it seem to ride upon a cloud. He smiled ruefully. Montfort did no such thing. Its survival was rooted in hard, cold realities.

But they would still be there tomorrow and they could wait until then. Tonight was a time for owls and mists, for promises and for dreams.

For Annabel.

He raised her hand to his lips. Her skin was cool and lightly scented. He felt the tremor that ran through her and smiled inwardly.

"Are you cold?"

Annabel shook her head. Far from being chilled, she was on fire, but she could hardly tell him that. He was still so much a stranger, this husband who had sired her child and carried her off to a new land. And yet for all the strangeness there was an aching familiarity to his nearness. She breathed in the clean, male scent of him and remembered it imprinted on her body in the aftermath of their lovemaking. Her eyes scanned the large, powerful hands that had held her so tenderly. She had lain naked against that broad, muscled chest. Her hair had flowed over his loins and thighs. Their legs and arms had intertwined. They had shared the most shattering pleasure she could ever imagine.

Was she to forget all that?

She swayed slightly and reached out a hand to steady herself. Her fingers brushed the thin cotton of his shirt. She could feel the heat coming from him and from herself.

She took a shuddering breath and closed her eyes. David groaned. He wrapped an arm around her waist and drew her to him. The other hand went to the velvet band around her hair. He freed it with a hard, unrelenting jerk that sent a shower of fiery gold tumbling over her shoulders.

His fingers tangled in the silken tendrils, pulling her head back to expose the slim white column of her throat. He groaned again, deep in his chest, and bent to claim her.

A delicious, throbbing pressure moved through Annabel. Before it, reason fled. She clung to him with all the fierce strength of her womanliness. His hands, moving over her buttocks and hips, thrilled her. She arched her back, clinging to him, and gave herself up to the storm within.

For one wild, insane moment, David considered taking her then and there on the soft ground of Montfort. But he could not forget her vulnerability and the fragileness she strove so hard to conceal. He wanted her in his bed, naked on silken sheets, with all the night to explore and savor her beauty and her passion.

With a quick, effortless motion, he lifted her high against his chest. Annabel gasped. Her head fell back against his shoulder. Through eyes slumbrous with desire, she gazed at him. His powerful features were taut with the same need that consumed her.

A quiver of purely feminine anticipation ran through her. His immense strength and will made any thought of resistance absurd, as did the fact that he was master here. No one would attempt to stop him no matter what he did.

And yet she was not afraid.

He might infuriate and bewilder her, and force her to confront conflicts within herself that she was still far from understanding. But she knew he would never hurt her.

Nestled in his arms, secure within his embrace, she was carried swiftly into the great house and up the curving marble stairs. There on the second floor David hesitated for barely an instant before pushing open the door to his room.

Later there would be time to make love to her in the graceful, feminine chamber that was hers. But on this night he wanted her in his bed.

As he carried her within, Annabel said, "The baby... ?"

"Claire will see to him." David set her down gently on the bed and knelt before her. His hands slipped beneath her wide skirt, the roughened palms stroking possessively up her legs and to the apex of her thighs. Swiftly, he stripped away her shoes and stockings.

She gasped as he seized a slender ankle and raised it to his lips. Holding her gaze, he ran a finger along the sensitive sole of her foot, making the toes arch in response. He laughed and pulled slightly, causing her to fall back onto the bed in a tumble of skirt and petticoats.

She lay unblinking, her hair spilling out around her, as he undressed. His powerful shoulders and chest gleamed darkly in the starlight pouring through the high windows. She stared, fascinated, at the tensile ridging of muscles below his ribs and across his abdomen. A finger of golden hair ran down past his navel to thicken at his groin, his manhood...

She inhaled deeply. His manhood was straining. Annabel thought of him within her and felt her body tightening with desire so intense as to be painful.

When his hands urged her onto her stomach, she did not resist. He unfastened her dress and slid it down her arms, exposing the graceful line of her back. Through the thin chemise she wore beneath, his mouth and teeth traced lines of fire.

She moaned and tried to turn to face him but he would not let her do so. He cupped her breasts from behind, his thumbs rubbing over the aching nipples. Her skirt was pulled up along with her petticoat to expose her bare bottom. She felt his manhood pressing against her.

"*David . . . please . . .*"

His laugh was deep and husky against her ear, but it turned to a gasp a moment later as she deliberately rotated her hips.

"You're maddening me," he murmured. "Are you sure you want that?"

"Oh, yes," Annabel whispered. Nothing less would do. She wanted him as wanton as she herself felt.

A moment later she was on her back. David's eyes glinted like steel wrapped in fire. He stripped the dress to her waist. His hot, demanding mouth captured her breast, suckling and licking until Annabel cried out hoarsely.

A hard, hair-roughened thigh thrust between her smooth, white legs. He lifted her from beneath, fitting her to him, and entered her with a single, breath-dissolving thrust.

"I can't stand this . . ." she gasped. Her body strained to accommodate him, yet she felt only pleasure. Wild, engulfing, soul-shattering pleasure.

David loomed above her, unrelenting and indomitable. "I can never have enough of you. You are mine."

The deep, pulsing rhythm filled her. She clung to him, afraid that if she let go she would splinter into a thousand gleaming shards. Waves of sensation radiated outward from her womb. She sobbed his name as the world exploded.

When the darkness cleared, David was still within and above her. He withdrew slowly and she heard him give a deep sigh, but she could not tell what he thought or felt. His face, wreathed in shadows, was inscrutable. He seemed suddenly almost a stranger, this man with whom she had just shared the heights of intimacy.

She still wore the now-crumpled green dress but it had been pulled up to her waist and her breasts freed so that she felt unbearably exposed. She drew her legs together and moved to turn onto her side.

"Lie still," he ordered. Swiftly, tolerating no resistance, he pulled the dress over her head and tossed it onto the floor. With it went her chemise and petticoat. When she was completely naked, he drew a sheet over them both and gathered her into his arms. Huskily, he murmured, "Rest, Annabel, but not for long. My hunger for you is immense."

As he proved through the long, heated night. Again and again, he loved her until she was mindless with pleasure. Their bodies clung, they could not get enough of one another. Far in the back of her mind, Annabel was astounded by her own daring. In the darkest, most private hours, her husband drew from her a capacity for passion she had never thought she possessed.

And in the end, when the first gray light of dawn edged the horizon, it was she who held him safe and cherished within her heart.

Twenty-four

A NNABEL stared at the boldly scrawled words on the sheet of paper. She was sitting at her dressing table. Patrice stood behind, combing out her hair. Louis was playing on the floor with Claire. Outside, the day was brilliant with sunshine and late-summer breezes. But Annabel barely noticed. Her husband's note held her attention fully.

Gone to Paris? What could have prompted him to do that and without even saying goodbye? He offered no clue as to his reasons, nor when he might return, nor how she was supposed to occupy herself in his absence. He had simply left her in the still hours of morning as though nothing at all had occurred between them.

Given what had in fact transpired, she thought she could be forgiven for feeling a tad annoyed. But she was bound and determined not to show it. Lifting her chin, she said, "I will see the house today."

Patrice widened her eyes but said only, "In that case, my lady, I suggest you wear your most comfortable shoes."

Annabel did as she advised but as she was about to leave her room, doubt assailed her. Certainly, she could wander through the house on her own.

If she became lost, as was almost certain to happen, someone would eventually find her. But she would learn relatively little from such a solitary venture. She needed the help of someone not merely a part of Montfort, as Patrice or Claire were, but knowledgeable about the whole of it.

As though Providence had stirred itself to provide, Gerard was waiting outside her door. The previous day he had discreetly absented himself after welcoming David home. But now he appeared ready and willing to be on hand.

"Good morning, madame," he said softly. "Monsieur le Marquis left instructions that I am to assist you in any way possible. Your maid tells me you wish to see the house. If I might escort you . . ."

"That is very kind," Annabel said.

Gerard's smile deepened. He appeared young for his responsibilities but also highly intelligent and sensible. "Where would you like to start?"

"With the kitchens," Annabel said. She saw his surprise, quickly masked, and smiled in turn. "I know a thing or two about kitchens, you see, so I thought I'd feel most comfortable beginning there."

"Of course." Gerard found the request more amusing than inappropriate. It confirmed certain rumors that were already floating about concerning the new marquise. Obviously, she didn't come from the usual ranks of noblewomen.

Her bearing was much too natural and her appearance, while lovely, far too uncontrived to allow any misconceptions on that score. Besides, she was an American, which was sufficient to explain anything she might say or do no matter how odd.

There was also another fact to consider, one which Gerard had been at pains to communicate to the entire household staff first thing that morning. In his instructions prior to leaving, *monseigneur* could not possibly have made it plainer that he expected his young wife to be treated with the utmost respect. She was to be given anything she asked for and allowed to do anything she wished, so long as no harm could come to her.

Yesterday, some might have been surprised by that. But it was already known in the servant hall that the marquis had taken his wife to his bed and kept her there all night. Clearly, this was no marriage of convenience for the sake of the child. Annabel pleased her husband. That meant she had influence—and power.

Besides, Gerard decided, he liked her. Her smile, the light in her eyes, the easy way she walked and spoke all suggested a person who would be pleasant to deal with. He also knew she was just a little afraid.

Annabel paled slightly when they entered the immense space that ran the entire length of one wing of the house. Here, amid stone walls and brick arches, lit by the windows made possible by the sloping lawn, were the kitchens of Montfort.

Annabel stood gazing around her. The vast expanse she looked out on was easily three or four times the size of the entire Wild Geese inn. Enough pots and pans hung from the ceiling to feed an army in a single sitting. There were baskets of onions, potatoes, and bright red apples. She saw sacks of wheat, kegs of butter, and mounds of eggs.

Everything was meticulously clean and well ordered. There was nothing she could possibly have improved.

"In the old days," Gerard said quietly, "it wasn't unusual for a half-thousand guests to attend the great fêtes that were held here. They rivaled anything the monarch himself commanded at Versailles. Whole boar were roasted"—he gestured to a fireplace large enough for a man to stand in—"the ovens were capable of baking a hundred loaves of bread at once. A minimum of three chefs were on call at any given time."

"It must have been very exciting," Annabel said. Privately, she thought that the effort must have been immense but had it been worthwhile? Had the gloriously garbed lords and ladies given any thought to those who labored below, sweating and straining so that they might languish in pleasure?

"Of course," Gerard said matter-of-factly, "the Revolution changed all that."

"I'm glad to hear it," Annabel said.

Immediately, she knew she had erred. Or at least, she had said something highly controversial. Gerard stiffened. He stared at her as though he thought his ears had betrayed him. "Madame . . . ?"

"I meant . . . that is to say . . ." Her shoulders straightened. She knew what she'd said and she'd stick by it. "Look, Gerard, I wasn't exactly to the purple born. I'm glad my son will have a better start than I did, but I don't want him to grow up thinking that other people are there just to see to his comforts. Most folks have a lot better things to do or they certainly ought to."

"A novel idea, madame."

"Is it now? I'd have thought people would be getting used to it, seeing the way things have been around here."

Gerard coughed discreetly. "You must understand, madame, under the emperor a great deal of the old order returned. With the king we have now that has continued.''

Annabel shot him a smile. "You mean we'll be roasting boar again?"

Dryly, Gerard said, "That is a distinct possibility."

Discretion had never been Annabel's strength. She found it far simpler—and ultimately more effective—to speak her mind. "The marquis supported Napoleon. Where does that leave him with King Louis . . . what number is it?"

"Eighteenth, madame," Gerard murmured. He looked as though he was either going to cough again or choke. But he was getting the point. Beautiful she undoubtedly was, but the marquise also possessed a brain. "We're not absolutely clear on that," he admitted.

"Which is why he's gone to Paris?"

"We think so, yes."

"I should have gone with him."

Now Gerard really did choke. Ever willing to help, Annabel pounded him between the shoulders. Red-faced and tearing, he backed away. Uppermost in his mind were his master's final and most important instructions—under no circumstances was Madame to venture from Montfort. She was to remain where he knew she would be safe or there would be hell to pay.

"Paris is unsettled, madame," Gerard said when he was able. Grasping at straws, he added, "Besides, there is a great deal for you to do here."

"Such as?" Annabel demanded. She wasn't about to be fobbed off with easy excuses. Let him explain what was so important to keep her in the country while her husband confronted who knew what enemies?

Gerard swallowed hard. He was getting the distinct impression that he was in over his head. Still, he tried manfully to remedy the situation. "Such as seeing the house."

It took the entire day. Through room after room, corridor upon corridor, they proceeded. Several times, Annabel was tempted to give up; they would never get to the end of it. But she persevered, stopping only for a light lunch. Her feet hurt and her legs ached, this despite the fact that she had spent most of her life working from morning to night.

They walked acres of marble floors, peered into a hundred and more silent chambers, gazed out uncounted expanses of windows. There were assembly rooms, music rooms, ballrooms, solariums, libraries (two), pantries, wine cellars, bathing chambers (David had apparently installed a gross of them at one clip), and bedchamber after bedchamber. Montfort could have housed the entire populace of a good-sized village. Indeed, she wasn't sure that it didn't.

"How many people live here?" she asked at last when they had stumbled out into one of the gardens (she had no idea how many of *them* there were).

Seated on a stone bench beside her, Gerard mopped his brow. "I'm not sure," he hedged.

"You are the steward, you must know."

"It varies," he assured her. "During the spring and summer, there are perhaps a hundred servants in occupancy. But in the winter, there are probably half-again that number."

He paused, wondering if she would grasp the implications of that.

She did. Winter was the quietest time in any household, the time when people were least likely to be coming and going, and when all the work of preserving food should already have been done. The time when the fewest number of servants were needed. Employers concerned uppermost with their purse were likely to dismiss extra workers then, not acquire more of them.

Slowly, she said, "My husband . . . he is considered a kind man?"

Gerard turned and looked at her. She had a way of getting to the heart of things, this American. "Very kind."

She nodded, satisfied with the explanation—and with the situation. Obviously, David could afford to care for these people. Therefore, it was only right that he do so.

"Well," she said at length, "I suppose since we are outside, we should take a look around."

Gerard repressed a moan. He would pit his strength against any man, but trailing after the marquise had exhausted him. "Today, madame?"

Her eyes twinkled. "Perhaps not, if you are too tired."

"Tired? Not at all, I assure you . . ."

"Never mind, Gerard," she said softly. "We've done enough for the moment. Tomorrow will do for the rest."

The next day was given over to touring the dependencies. These ranged from the gardens and greenhouses to the forge and the mill, the tanner and the wheelwright, the stables and the granaries, the whole vast panoply of life and work on the great estate. In addition, there was the village with its ancient stone church and beyond it the patchwork quilt of fields that stretched as far as the eye could see.

Everywhere she turned, everywhere she looked, Annabel was within her husband's suzerainty. He was master here, as no one doubted. In a bygone era, he would have been a ruler in his own right. Now he was called a marquis but the title was misleading. He was as wealthy and as powerful as many a prince would wish to be.

Although suitably impressed, Annabel refused to be awed. Lying awake in her huge bed, wondering where David was and what he was doing, she told herself that she would adjust. Yet nothing she had seen supported that. She could see no place for herself at Montfort, nothing that she could make her own.

She stared up at the ceiling, feeling the keen edge of panic. All her life she had been busy. There had rarely been a chance to think, much less to relax. Now time stretched before her with no direction or purpose.

She could care for Louis, that was true. But she couldn't look to her child to fill her days. That would be a terrible burden to put on him.

Ladies in her position went to court where they flirted and conspired, advanced their husband's interests or their own, and generally amused themselves. She smiled into the darkness. What a fine spectacle that would be, Annabel Riordan arriving at court in her ill-fitting blue dress or perhaps the green, sporting her Irish accent and her American ways. She'd give everyone a good laugh, that was for sure. Except her husband who had a right to better.

Ah, well, there was always embroidery. Or she could take up gardening. She might even learn to ride a horse and explore the neighborhood. It would be a good life if only David were there. But he was away, in a place she feared to go. Beside that, nothing else mattered.

The next day passed slowly, as did the following. Annabel played with Louis as much as she could, but he was a baby and had to sleep sometime. When he did, she wandered alone through the vast corridors and endless rooms, or she went outside and tried not to be conspicuous. Occasionally, she caught a servant's sympathetic glance and looked hastily away. Above all, she could not stand to have anyone feeling sorry for her. Especially when she had more than she'd ever imagined in her life and every reason to be happy.

A week had passed since her arrival at Montfort when she returned from a garden stroll to find a visitor.

Madame Gaudin smiled charmingly when Annabel joined her in the sitting room.

"So kind of you to receive me, dear, especially when you are just settling in."

"Not at all," Annabel murmured, looking at the middle-aged but still beautiful woman, gloriously attired in a gown of Pompeian red that set off a still-slender figure. Her golden hair was perfectly coiffed into tiny curls brushed high at the back of her head. She held a fan folded between her graceful hands, their nails buffed until they shone like pearls. Her posture was regal, her voice cultured. But her smile appeared completely natural and unforced.

"My name is Babette Gaudin," she said. "We are neighbors. I heard of your arrival and thought I should come over to get acquainted. I would have waited longer," she added with a twinkle in her eyes, "but my curiosity got the better of me. I must say though, you are every bit as beautiful as rumor claims."

Annabel flushed. She couldn't believe that this exquisitely elegant creature found *her* beautiful but she was hardly in a position to argue. "May I offer you refreshment?" she asked as she gestured for her visitor to sit.

"Most kind," Babette murmured. She settled herself on the settee and glanced at her young hostess appraisingly. The green dress was atrocious; it lacked both style and quality. But clothes could be remedied easily enough. How like David to go off without thinking of that. Not that he didn't have more immediate problems, from what she heard. Still, something had to be done for this girl. She couldn't be allowed to simply rusticate.

Well aware of Annabel's uncertainty, Babette set out to soothe her. Chatting easily, she said, "I do so love this particular region of France. It has enchanted me ever since I was a child."

"Were you raised here?" Annabel asked. Polite social chatter had little appeal for her, but she did not want her guest to think her completely inept. Besides, it was nice to have someone new to talk with.

"I came from Toulon originally," Babette said, "but I had . . . a friend from this area. In the old days, people were forever visiting one another. I attended several fêtes held at Montfort and a few smaller events at the house that ultimately became mine." She smiled again, amused by the memory. "Life can work out in the most surprising ways. My great ambition back then was to own a residence in Paris, but ultimately the country came to have much more appeal for me. When the Delamare residence became available . . ."

"You bought Paul's house?" Annabel interjected.

"Ah, you know him? Such a splendid man and a truly dedicated doctor. It was a shame for this country that people such as he were forced out—or killed. Still, he was very good about selling me the house. Some people wouldn't have, even under those circumstances."

"Why not?" Annabel asked. She couldn't imagine how anyone could refuse this gracious, charming lady.

The obvious innocence of her question made Babette

laugh. "Let us just say that I had a habit of enjoying the benefits of marriage without its legal encumbrances. It was, to be frank, my profession." She looked directly at her young hostess. "Does that shock you, my dear?"

As a matter of fact, it did. Annabel had some difficulty accepting that a woman who seemed the epitome of propriety had, by her own telling, been far less. However, being shocked did not mean that she disapproved. It did not occur to her that she had any right to make such a judgment about Babette—or anyone else, for that matter.

"I see," Annabel said quietly. "Well, there's some say that's the world's oldest profession, so you're in good enough company. Myself, I kept a tavern before coming here. The same fine folks who wouldn't have sold a house to you undoubtedly wouldn't have wanted much to do with me either."

Babette studied her for a long moment. She appeared to come to a decision.

"You are a good child," she said. "But if I may be frank, your situation is difficult."

Annabel was far too relieved by such honesty to be offended. "That it is, and I've no idea what to do about it."

"Well, I do," Babette said firmly. "That is, if you wouldn't mind a bit of advice?"

David dismounted from his horse. He turned with a cautious smile, eying the wife he had last seen a month before. During the long nights when he had lain awake weary but unable to sleep, he had thought that he fully remembered her beauty and its effect on him. But now he realized that memory held only a pale shadow of reality.

Standing at the top of the stone steps, her hair flying freely in the breeze, she was magnificent. Her cheeks were flushed, her eyes glowing. A bolt of heat shot through him. He forgot to be concerned about what her mood might be after his protracted absence. He handed his reins to a groom and took the stairs two at a time.

"Madame," he said. His gaze held hers as he raised her hand to his lips.

It was on the tip of her tongue to ask him what he thought he was about, going off and leaving her for so long with nothing more than a poor parcel of notes saying all was well. In a pig's eye, it was. If he thought he could treat her like so much chattel to be forgotten whenever he had a mind, he would soon know differently.

Her thoughts dissolved in an onslaught of sensation. The fading sun struck David's bare head like a crown of ruddy gold. His broad shoulders and chest blotted out all else. She felt the heat of his body, the tensile strength, the proud, compelling masculinity. Unconsciously, she swayed toward him.

Around them, people exchanged startled glances that gave way quickly to amusement. It was early evening, supper had not even been served. Hardly the time to bundle one's wife off to bed, yet it seemed the marquis was about to do exactly that. Not that any man could blame him, nor any woman help but envy Annabel. Tolerant of nature's demands, they slipped easily away.

"Come," David said. The word was half-command, half-plea. Proper people did not behave like this. They exchanged polite pleasantries, concealed their feelings, and waited for an appropriate time. They did not return from an absence of a month and hasten their wives into bed with hardly a greeting.

So much for propriety. David drew her so quickly down the corridor to their rooms that she tripped over the hem of her new yellow silk gown, which, Annabel thought, he had not so much as noticed. He muttered an exclamation and swept her up. Moments later, they were in his room, the door firmly closed behind them.

"Too long," he rasped under his breath. "A month has been too damn long."

"You could have come back sooner," she pointed out tartly.

He stopped for an instant in the midst of setting her on the bed and stared at her. "No," he said, "I could not have."

And that, it seemed, was that. He showed no inclination to say another word about his absence. Or about anything else, for that matter. His face was dark and intent as he began to unfasten her dress.

Belatedly, she remembered the exquisitely fragile fabric, little more than a gossamer breath. "Be careful, you'll tear it."

He laughed huskily. "Since when have you cared about that?"

"Since I spent most of the last three weeks being poked and prodded by that slave-driving dressmaker," Annabel shot back. "And if you had a gnat's worth of sense, you'd care too. I've spent a bloody fortune."

There, it was out, she'd said it. Babette had sworn that he wouldn't mind, that he in fact expected it. Now they'd see.

David paused in the midst of disrobing her. His gaze took on a watchful gleam. "Have you indeed?"

Annabel forced herself to take a deep breath and met his eyes calmly. "I have and what's more, I didn't do it to impress the good folks of Montfort who need no such impressing anyway."

A finely arched eyebrow rose. "Then why did you do it?"

She hesitated the merest instant, then plunged. "Because the next time you go off to Paris, I'm going with you."

He started to speak but she rushed on. "Before you tell me I'm not, Babette has been explaining a thing or two. I know you've got trouble with this fellow Louis who's on the throne now. He's bound to be upset about you having been for Napoleon. I can understand your having to smooth things over with him, but it won't hurt to have another pair of eyes and ears, if only to watch your back."

David did his best to suppress a smile and failed. Indeed, he went further; he laughed out loud. "Sweet Annabel, I'd no more take you into that den of vipers than I'd set you down bare-assed naked in the middle of Boston. You'll stay here, woman, and I'll not hear another word about it."

Of all the patronizing, insufferable bonnyclabber . . . "*Ooohhh*, you're every bit as highhanded as you ever were. I'm not about to sit here while I could be helping the both of us, not to mention Louis as well."

David had heard enough. He rolled over, trapping her beneath him. Looming above her, ruthless and determined, he said, "You will do exactly as you are told, madame. I will not have my wife interfering in my affairs, endangering herself as well as me. Do you understand?"

Only too well. He was going to be one of those autocratic, heavy-handed husbands she had always feared. The kind who had made her decide never to marry in the first place.

Pain twisted in her only to be flushed out by a healthy dart of anger.

"Aye," she muttered, "you've made yourself perfectly clear."

He stared at her, trying to gauge the sincerity of her apparent capitulation. Her eyes remained stormy, her cheeks flushed. Somehow, he thought he hadn't heard the last of this. But for the moment it was enough. He had other matters to pursue: the loveliness of her breasts, for instance; the exquisite softness of her skin; the way she moaned and arched her back in the throes of pleasure; and the explosive, enticing joy he found within the depths of her body.

"Annabel . . ." he said. The harshness was gone from his voice. His eyes were hooded, his mouth gentled. He smiled faintly as his hand moved over the slender curve of her hip toward the joining of her thighs.

She gritted her teeth against the onslaught of pleasure. Insufferable man, to think that he could trample on her feelings one moment and seduce her the next. She'd show him otherwise. He'd have no satisfaction from her, at least none willingly given. No matter what he did, she would remain unmoved. She would be like ice, like the cruelest frost, like a statue . . . She would . . .

A moan broke from her. His mouth had found her nipple through the thin fabric. Cool air touched her legs as he pulled the skirt up. She heard a stitch pop, then another.

"The dress . . ."

"Damn the dress," he grated. His fingers grazed her breasts as he grasped the neckline. There was a sharp, rending tear. An instant later she was bare from throat to ankles.

"Ah, Annabel," he murmured, "don't be angry. I want

only for you to be safe. You are so lovely . . . so precious to me . . ." The words burned her skin as his hot mouth searched her avidly. She closed her eyes against a searing wave of passion.

Her last coherent thought was that she must get the couturier back to replace the dress and perhaps make a few others.

She would need them when she got to Paris.

LOUIS XVIII, king of France, restorer of the Bourbon dynasty, heir to a legacy of unrivaled power and glory, was not pleased. He sat in his stiffly brocaded chair, a portly man, plagued by gout, who at first glance appeared to be the epitome of self-indulgence. Yet this was the man known far and wide for his exquisite courtesy and impeccable scholarship. The man who had risen above enormous personal tragedy to be a voice for reason and compromise in an overheated world.

Ordinarily. At the moment, he was having difficulty containing his impatience. The Tuileries Palace, where he had felt compelled to take up residence, was dank and drafty. Suffering its late autumn chill gave him renewed sympathy for his late brother who had been imprisoned there.

What a frightful place. He would have much preferred Versailles but his advisors agreed that the glorious extravaganza of a palace would set the wrong tone. With the vanquishers of Napoleon conferring even now in Vienna to decide the fate of France, it behooved the recently acknowledged monarch to appear as humble and unobtrusive as possible.

He heaved a sigh. The capon he had eaten at supper had not agreed with him. The wines had been mediocre, the conversation tedious. What was France coming to?

Not that it was completely without bright spots. His eye fell on the young woman who had just entered the assembly room. A smile played over his broad mouth.

This business between the proud marquis de Montfort and his lovely wife was most amusing. He obviously did not want her at court, there were even rumors that he had forbidden her to come. She just as obviously had every intention of staying.

Louis raised a hand. He smiled benignly as he gestured for Annabel to join him. She looked startled but recovered quickly. As she crossed the marble floor to his side, he reflected that she looked lovelier every time he saw her. This evening she was wearing a gown of soft green-gold silk that perfectly complemented her hair and eyes.

The gown was sufficiently low-cut to be distracting but not so daring as those worn by some of the other ladies. In rejection of the fashion that decreed shorter hair for women, her own was caught up high on her head and allowed to fall in a riot of curls past her shoulders. Wide bands of lace fell over her hands. Beneath them, her fingers danced with the fire of emeralds and diamonds. The same gems gleamed at her slim white throat.

The marquis's annoyance with his wife had apparently not extended to forbidding her the Montfort jewels. They shone gloriously in the candlelight from a half-dozen crystal chandeliers.

"Do sit, my dear," Louis murmured. He patted the chair beside him. "I have been shooing off people all evening and I am most frightfully bored."

Annabel did as he bid. She smoothed her skirts, folded her hands, and looked out calmly at the assembled aristocrats. They stood about in clusters, pretending to chat among themselves while keeping a nervous eye on their sovereign. Several frowned at her.

After two weeks at court, Annabel knew enough to realize that nothing she did would please these peacock-garbed lords and ladies, except possibly disappearing off the face of the earth. They were aloof, arrogant, nasty, and just plain scared. Her origins made her a constant reminder of the mob they feared. Her refusal to be anything but straight-forward threatened the fragile facade of their security. Now the monarch's inexplicable favoring of her would put them in a tizzy.

Not that she could blame them.

She glanced at Louis covertly out of the corner of her eye. Was he truly just bored and seeking diversion? Or did he have some other motive in mind when he summoned her to his side?

He leaned closer, smiled charmingly, and said, "I understand you are getting to know Paris. What do you think of it?"

Annabel stifled her surprise. She had heard that the king employed a staff of secret police dedicated to looking after his interests. It stood to reason that they would report any unusual actions by a member of his court. Sadly, strolling through Paris for the sheer pleasure of it fell into that category.

"I think," Annabel said tartly, "that I must have been leading a parade these last few days and didn't even know it."

Louis's bushy white eyebrows rose. "Whatever do you mean, my dear?"

"Whoever you've had keeping an eye out has also been following my husband's servants who in turn follow me. If we hired a brass band, we could do this up right."

Louis laughed. The sound was so unusual for him that for a moment it seemed as though he was choking. His big, fleshy body shook with the effort. His face turned red and his eyes moistened. At length, he regained his composure.

"I can see David's problem now. Any sane man would have packed you back to the country but I suspect you are far too engaging to do without. My sympathies to the poor fellow."

Annabel flushed. She could have told him a thing or two about exactly how "engaging" her husband found her. The "poor fellow" had been annoyed enough by her turning up at court against his orders, but that hadn't stopped him from sharing her bed. He merely ignored her the rest of the time which had a tendency to raise her hackles and make her reckless.

"I'm an American, Your Highness," Annabel said. "We're a stubborn lot."

Louis laughed again though more softly. "The British would certainly agree. I gather they've bitten off more than they expected."

Annabel smiled just a bit smugly. The news from home delighted her. Although the war continued, the tide had turned. Since Washington, nothing had gone right for the British. They had suffered defeat after defeat, to the point where people were beginning to seriously wonder if the Americans might not win.

Best yet, she had received a letter from Nicole telling her that she and Cameron were well. So was the Wild Geese, which was flourishing as never before. They had offered to send the profits to her but Annabel declined. She had no need of money and she didn't feel right about taking what others had earned.

Although there were times when she thought nostalgically about the tavern and her life there, it seemed farther and farther away. Her life was here now, in a Paris torn by rumor and controversy, with a husband who baffled her and a monarch who was not at all what she had expected.

"Nonetheless," Louis continued good-humoredly, "if David really wanted to send you away, he would do so. As your husband, he certainly has the authority. Even as king, I would be hard pressed to stop him."

Annabel shot him a cautious glance. He had hit on the contradiction that puzzled her the most. Did David want her there or didn't he? And if he had changed his mind, why didn't he simply admit it?

"Frankly," she said, "he knows I don't fit in here."

Louis leaned back in his chair and eyed her gently. "What makes you think anyone does?"

"I don't understand . . ."

"Let us continue to be candid with one another, madame, if only for the novelty of it. No one knows what will happen at the Congress of Vienna. We cannot be sure what condition France will be in when her conquerors finish with her. Every one of those gloriously garbed ladies and gentlemen watching us could be in very different circumstances a year from now, or even a month.

"As for myself," he continued, "I occupy what is surely the least secure throne in Europe. Whatever I do, I am guaranteed to anger a large portion of the population. And we all know what happened the last time a French king proved so annoying."

Annabel shivered. He spoke so matter-of-factly, even with a touch of humor. Yet she saw the dark reality beneath his words. Was this beautiful country poised for yet more disaster?

Louis observed her silently. He was a cautious man, completely lacking in illusions. Yet he had a knack for surviving that few could equal.

Quietly, he said, "So you feel uncomfortable at court, yet you remain, despite your husband's disapproval. And he allows it, although he obviously thinks it would be more prudent to send you elsewhere. Can it be that the two of you care for each other?"

Annabel inhaled sharply. She had not anticipated so personal a question nor the effect it had on her. For a moment, she felt almost unbearably vulnerable. She stared over the king's shoulder into the obscure and safe middle distance.

"I cannot speak for my husband."

"Ah, of course not. And I don't really expect you to reveal yourself." At least no further than she had already done. The beguiling flush of her cheeks and the slight tremor of her exquisite mouth were enough to tell Louis what he wanted to know.

"Speaking of the marquis . . ." he said.

Annabel stiffened. She followed the direction of his

glance to find David standing dark and forbidding near the entrance to the salon.

Louis smiled cordially but his voice was hard. "Did you know Tallyrand wanted him in Vienna but he refused?"

"No . . ." Annabel said. She could not quite follow the direction of the royal thoughts, but she had an ominous sense that she would not like where they were leading.

"De Montfort is not an unpatriotic man," Louis murmured. "Modesty aside, he must know that he could make a difference in the negotiations there. Yet he remains here. He makes no particular effort to be pleasant, so he can't be thinking of advancing himself with me. He comes and goes around the city so skillfully that his movements cannot be traced. And he keeps you close, *very* close, as though he believed it better to have you near at hand, not miles away where it might be difficult to reach you in a crisis. To be frank, madame, I suspect him of being involved in something that could turn out to be very bad."

Annabel paled. She wanted nothing so much as to get out of her chair and leave before she heard anything more, but she did not. The monarch's reasons for summoning her were now clear. He wanted to use her to send a message to David.

Faintly, she said, "He is a loyal Frenchman, Your Highness. There is nothing his cares for so much as this country."

"I don't dispute that. What matters is how he thinks this country can best be served."

Louis leaned closer. So softly that only she could hear him, he asked, "They say the climate on Elba is pleasant and that the Corsican has everything he could require for his comfort, but when did Napoleon ever care about that? He lives to make war. I am determined to give this country peace, no matter what the cost. Tell your husband that.''

Slowly, Annabel rose. Her stomach was in knots and her knees felt weak. Out of the corner of her eye, she saw David approaching.

''Why don't you tell him yourself, Your Highness?'' she asked daringly.

Louis's small, dark eyes flashed with appreciation. ''Because, madame, it will sound so much more pleasant coming from you.''

''What will?'' David asked. Seeing Annabel talking with the king, he had thought to join them immediately. But he had been delayed by a government official he suspected had been delegated to prevent any such interference. Only with difficulty had he managed to brush the man aside.

Now he stood staring from his monarch to his wife. Annabel looked very pale. Her hand trembled slightly as she raised it to his arm in a gesture that in another woman might have been of entreaty.

David placed his hand over hers and pressed gently. His blue eyes glinted as he said, ''The marquise and I will be returning to Montfort, Your Highness.''

Louis blinked. He thought that over for a moment before he said, ''But you will be returning shortly, will you not? After all, it will be Christmas before we know it and Christmas at court is not to be missed.''

However literally Louis meant that, David did not take the hint. He shook his head. ''We have a very young son, Your Highness. A quiet family holiday seems best.''

''I see . . . Well, then, I won't detain you. Enjoy your stay in the country. I trust it will be . . . peaceful.''

They took their leave a few moments later. David bowed

courteously to his monarch but there was nothing subservient about his behavior. A hundred pairs of eyes watched the departure of the tall, golden-haired man and the beautiful, pale woman. Barely had the double doors closed behind them than a hundred tongues began to wag.

David had disdained the quarters offered to them in the Tuileries. He preferred the far more luxurious and comfortable apartment he kept a short distance away. Although the hour was far from late, the cobblestone streets surrounding the palace were almost empty. But then there were rarely as many people about as Annabel would have expected. Many Parisians seemed to be secluding themselves indoors, as though they expected trouble at any moment.

Annabel drew her ermine and velvet cloak more closely around her. She glanced at her husband, sitting silent and preoccupied across from her. Quietly, she asked, "Why are we leaving?"

He smiled in the darkness. "Don't you believe what I told Louis?"

"No, not entirely. By the way, he knows you're up to something."

"Indeed? Is that what he told you?"

"Essentially, yes. He wanted me to tell you that he will do anything he has to in order to keep the peace."

David leaned back against the tufted carriage seat. He stretched out his long legs so that they brushed against her full skirts. He looked perfectly relaxed. Only the pulse beating in the muscled column of his throat revealed otherwise. With his eyes closed, he said, "He may not have any choice."

Annabel wanted to ask what he meant, but caution stopped her. She sensed that he was holding onto his temper by the thinnest of threads and did not wish to snap them. Instead, she remained silent until they reached the apartment.

A gloriously garbed butler saw them in. Perhaps sensing their mood, he promptly made himself scarce. Alone with her husband in the exquisitely furnished anteroom, Annabel said, "I am going to bed now."

After a moment, when he had not replied, she wondered if he had heard her. Without a word, he walked into the parlor and poured himself a brandy. From the door, she saw him take a long swallow.

"David . . . is something wrong?"

He turned and looked at her. The smile he gave held nothing of tenderness and everything of deadly rage. "Go to bed, Annabel," he said.

She took a step forward. "Please . . . if I can help . . ."

"I said go to bed." The order cracked harshly in the stillness. She stiffened but held her ground. Two weeks ago when she arrived, she had braced herself for his displeasure. Instead, she had encountered merely annoyance tempered by resignation. Apparently, that had been misleading. His anger had not been avoided, merely delayed.

Bravely, she faced him. "I'll not be sent off like some errant child. I think the king was right, something bad is happening, and I want to know what it is."

He took another swallow of the brandy and stared at her. His eyes were hooded, the expression unreadable. Slowly, he said, "Louis is smarter than I thought he was, but he shouldn't have involved you. We will leave for Montfort at first light. Get some rest while you can."

The abrupt disappearance of his anger left her more

bewildered than ever. What warring forces were at work within him? She could not tell. He had turned his back on her. She was shut out as effectively as if she were not even there.

Her throat tightened. Aware that she was close to tears and determined that he would not see them, she picked up her skirts. A moment later she was gone, the door closing softly behind her.

✦ CHAPTER ✦
Twenty-six

---

*A*NNABEL stood on the battlements high above Montfort. Below her, a light dusting of snow covered the
fields. She could see wisps of smoke rising from
the village where people were having their evening meal.
High above, in the leaden sky, a late-hunting falcon
circled.

A gust of wind blew over the battlements. It tore at her
cloak and ruffled the soft tendrils of hair around her face.
Absently, she pushed the hair away and continued looking.

David had gone north to the coast several days before. As
had been the case since their return to Montfort, he had
refused to tell her why he was going. He seemed determined
to protect her from information which might prove harmful.
She tried to appreciate that even as her ignorance rankled.

Christmas had passed quietly, as they both wished. The
new year had come on the cusp of a bad storm that kept
everyone inside for days. Since then there had been little to

do except stay close to home and wonder at the preparations David was making.

Quietly, without fanfare, men had been coming to Montfort. Some were young, others middle-aged. Some came from the nearby villages, others from much farther away. All were soldiers. They had fought with David in Russia. They seemed to feel that they owed their survival to him. And they came to do his bidding.

Whatever that might be.

Annabel stifled a sigh of impatience. She knew that she should go back downstairs where it was warm but she could not get herself to move. Far off in the distance, down the long road, something was moving.

Her hands grasped the thick stone wall as she leaned forward, straining to see. In the fading light, it was difficult, but after a moment she realized that she was not looking at a solitary horse and rider. It was yet another wagon coming to Montfort the same way the men had, quietly.

A week before curiosity had overcome her and she had peered under the tarpaulin covering a similar wagon. She would not do so again. She did not need to see yet another load of muskets and ammunition to realize what they meant.

Montfort was preparing for war.

In the vast basements below the kitchens, food was stockpiled to the rafters. A new well had been dug in the central courtyard. No one had thought a new one was needed in more than a century. A new, larger bell hung from the highest tower. Everyone in the village knew that when the bell rang, they were to come inside the walls immediately.

Wearily, Annabel shook her head. She tried to find comfort in the letter she had received that morning from

Nicole. News of the astonishing American victory against the British had reached France already but details were few. Nicole provided them along with word that all the Delamares were well as was Cameron. He had gone back to his regiment to fight in some of the last skirmishes, then returned to Washington to ask Nicole to marry him. They had wed quietly on the last day of the year.

With the letter, Nicole had sent the signed copies of the document that transferred ownership of the Wild Geese to her and her husband. Her girls' school near Boston was simply going to have to get along without her, although she mentioned that she might start something similar in Washington. There was certainly need for it, especially now that it seemed America was actually going to survive.

Was France? Annabel sighed and turned away. It seemed pointless to tarry on the battlements any longer. Slowly, she went down the steep stone steps to the nursery.

Louis was sleeping peacefully with Claire watching him. The young nurse smiled when she saw Annabel.

"That new tooth isn't giving him any trouble at all, my lady. He's such a brave little soul."

Annabel nodded as she knelt down beside her son's cradle. He never had moved into the far more elaborate one Josette had wanted, but he didn't seem to mind. He slept peacefully, curled on his stomach with his knees pulled up underneath him and one small fist stuffed into his mouth.

Gently, she smoothed the cover over him and turned to Claire. "I'll stay with him for awhile. You go and have your supper."

The girl nodded appreciatively. The marquise was an unfailingly kind and considerate mistress. If only she didn't also seem to be so sad. But then she missed the marquis and was worried about him—with good reason if the rumors were to be believed.

Claire pulled her shawl around her and forced such thoughts from her mind. She preferred to concentrate on the hearty stew and fresh-baked bread awaiting her below.

Annabel had no such luxury. For her, there was no retreat from the pressing fears that grew stronger each day. Even snug in this small room, rocking her son in his cradle, she felt them closing in around her.

A single tear slipped down her cheek. She brushed it aside impatiently. Down below in the courtyard, she heard a shout and the clank of iron as the portcullis was raised.

Instantly, she was on her feet. From the nursery window, she could see little, and she didn't want to leave Louis alone. Gathering him up, she hurried from the room. He did not wake, not even when she reached the great hall. The doors had been thrown open. Snow swirled against the lintel. Outside, torches flared. Inside, the softer light of candles prevailed. They sent huge, dancing shadows against the walls.

"David . . ."

He turned, his cloak swirling around him. Fatigue etched his face yet his eyes lit with pleasure when he saw her. He came to her and held out his hand, only to remember how cold it would be. With an apologetic smile, he tucked it away.

"It has been quiet?" he asked.

Annabel nodded. "Are you hungry?"

"Ravenous," he admitted.

Annabel gave quick instructions to a servant. Claire was summoned and returned with Louis to the nursery. Others were dispatched to fill a bath.

By the time David had eaten his fill, the tub was ready. With Annabel's help, he stripped off his sodden clothes. She suppressed a cry when she saw the livid bruise running across his back. He shrugged it off.

"A fall, nothing more. I've have worse."

"How did it happen?"

"I was riding too fast. My horse slipped on ice."

Alone on what at this time of year would have been an empty road. She trembled to think what would have happened if the mount had been less well trained or the injury more serious.

"What was so important," she asked as he slipped into the water, "that you had to take such a chance?"

For a moment, the blessed heat made it impossible to reply. He groaned softly as the tension of the last few days began to ease from him.

Annabel turned to fetch him a brandy but he shook his head. It was vital to keep his mind clear.

Softly, without expression, he said, "Napoleon has left Elba."

Three days later, the messenger came. He was a young, handsome man with an aura of suppressed excitement. Dismounting in the courtyard, he solemnly handed David a sealed packet.

"From the emperor, sir."

Annabel inhaled sharply. She wanted to shout that there was no emperor, that the vainglorious, power-mad tyrant who had laid waste to much of Europe should never rise again. He was the direct opposite of everything she believed in. But he was also the man her husband had pledged to serve.

David had turned away to open the letter. When he looked at them again, his face was grim.

"Where is Napoleon now?"

"Somewhere between Lyons and Paris, sir. His army grows by the hour. He landed near Antibes and from there marched to Grenoble. The citizens threw open the city to him. He went on to Lyons where he was also received with acclaim. He has declared the restoration null and void. It is his intention to march on Paris."

Annabel could keep silent no longer. "How could this happen?" she demanded. "Hasn't France had enough of such insanity?"

The young man looked at her as though she were the insane one. Annabel ignored him. Her plea was solely to her husband.

"Surely, you won't go?"

He took her arm and led her a short distance away. Quietly, he said, "Do you have any idea what has been happening in Vienna? France is in danger of being destroyed as a nation. Louis lacks the basic loyalty of the people; they will never rally to him in this crisis. If Napoleon has learned anything from the past, if he is willing to seek peace instead of war..."

"He has never sought that. Why should he try now?"

"I don't know, but so long as there is a chance..." He broke off, gazing at her. She looked so exquisitely beautiful in the cold morning sun, this stubborn American girl he had made his wife. If only she could understand and accept the forces that drove him. But their backgrounds were so different, for all that bonded them to one another.

Resigned, he raised a hand to gently touch her cheek. "I must go." Before she could speak, he went on firmly. "And you must stay. This time there can be no question of that. If there is war, Montfort will be one of the few safe places to be. The people here will be depending on you to hold things together."

"That is nonsense. They trust only you for that."

He smiled, touched by the innocence that made her believe that. "Not any longer, Annabel. They have you."

A sob rose in her throat. She tried to fight it down but it escaped anyway. A moment later, she was in his arms, held fast against his powerful chest. She squeezed her eyes shut, blocking out all thought except the single, desperate prayer that time would somehow stop and leave them like this forever.

It did not. Within the hour, David was gone, riding hard for Paris. Annabel forced herself to do what she knew was expected. She went about the vast house, checking on everything yet again, and letting herself be seen. She spoke reassuringly to everyone she met. She ordered a special ration of wine to be served with supper, suspecting that they could all use a jolt of courage.

At noon, she asked the young priest in residence to say Mass in the central courtyard. More than two hundred people turned out for it, many coming up from the village. The service was simple but moving. It lightened Annabel's spirit, if only for a little while.

The next few days passed quietly. That ended toward the close of the week when a train of merchants came by. They were fleeing Paris, seeking the safety of the countryside.

Annabel offered them sanctuary but they demurred, saying that they would press on for the coast.

Before they went, they gave what news they had. Napoleon was in Paris. Louis and his court had fled. Rumors abounded that France would soon be at war again. Young men were hiding themselves as best they could, hoping to avoid a draft that would almost certainly send them to their deaths. The country was in chaos. What would happen next was anyone's guess but there was overwhelming certainty that it would not be good.

Of David, there was no sign. With mail service stopped and the roads uncertain, it was not surprising that he hadn't been able to send word. But Annabel was still deeply worried. At night she lay awake, tossing in her bed, desperately courting sleep without success.

The last snowfall melted and was gone. The wind blew more softly. Beneath the hard-packed earth, the first tentative stirrings of spring began.

Annabel found no joy in them. She needed hard, distracting work to sap her strength and enable her to find some semblance of peace. But with so many people domiciled at Montfort and everyone anxious to keep busy, there was nothing for her to do.

Until the night when a small, frantic boy appeared at the main gate, begging for admittance. He was let in and brought to her where she sat in the solar trying to divert herself with needlework. With relief, she put the mangled canvas down and smiled at him reassuringly.

"What is wrong, lad?"

Nervously, he clasped his cap between his hands and stared at the floor. "There's an old man who came to the village this morning, seeking someplace safe, I guess. He seemed fine at first but all of a sudden he had some kind of terrible fit and fell down on the floor like he's dead, except he isn't. His eyes are rolled way back in his head and he's frothing at the mouth. Most everyone's afraid to go near him. They say he's possessed by devils. My mother's afraid he'll die but she doesn't know what to do, so she sent me to get help while she watches him.''

Annabel stifled a curse. She was familiar with this falling sickness, having had a customer at the Wild Geese who suffered from it periodically. Certainly, it could be frightening to those who witnessed an attack but that was no reason to refuse help.

"Devils, indeed,'' she muttered. "The only devil they need to worry about is their own ignorance.''

She reached for the cloak she had left folded over a nearby chest. "We'll bring the man here and care for him. Come, show me where he is.''

"You, my lady?'' Patrice exclaimed. She had been keeping Annabel company in the solar. The thought that her lady would leave on such a mission appalled her.

"Send the soldiers, ma'am,'' Patrice advised. "They can deal with the situation well enough.''

"But they probably won't want to,'' Annabel replied. "They will be afraid like everyone else.''

"But what about yourself? If you become ill, *monseigneur* will never forgive us.''

Annabel smiled faintly. She did not doubt that Patrice had become fond of her, as she had become of the younger girl. But the first and foremost concern of everyone at Montfort was still what David would think. Even absent, he dominated their lives.

"I won't, this isn't the kind of disease people can catch.

All the man needs is a little care and kindness, and he'll recover perfectly well.''

At least she hoped he would, if she got to him in time. Gently, she urged the boy from the room.

In the courtyard, she ordered a wagon to be quickly made ready with a bed of straw in the back and blankets to cover the man. But before it could be done, several men from the guard came running out.

"Lady," one of them said, "you cannot go alone."

Annabel wasn't about to waste time arguing with them. "All right, but don't get in the way."

They nodded grimly and ran for their mounts. A few minutes later the little party clattered out under the portcullis and down the long road toward the village.

It was getting on toward sunset. Long shadows loomed on either side. Annabel started when she saw a dark gray shape moving in the underbrush not far from the road. With people staying much closer to their homes, the wolves were becoming bolder. She shivered and looked away.

They reached the village without incident. A small crowd stood outside the tavern.

"He's in there, my lady," a burly young man said when he had recovered from his first surprise at seeing Annabel. "Had the fit come on him while he was quaffing a pint." Growing bold, he looked around at the others. " 'Course it might not be devils after all. Might have been the ale!''

The crowd laughed nervously. They stepped back quickly to let Annabel enter. Left with no choice, the guards followed anxiously.

The man lay on his back on the sawdust-strewn floor. He was about sixty with gnarled features and a gray beard. His back was arched like a bow. As the boy had said, flecks of foam shone near his mouth. His eyes were open but sightless. He gave every appearance of being dead until his body jerked violently.

The guards leaped back as did the boy. Only Annabel approached the man calmly. She knelt on the floor beside him and put two fingers to his throat. The pulse of his life was weak but steady. She debated what to do. Some said it was best to set a piece of wood in the mouth to prevent choking, but others warned that a victim could bite down so fiercely as to splinter the wood and die from it.

Uncertain, she followed the tenet that the old woman in Ireland, the one who had been so certain that flies spread disease, had told her. *First, do no harm.* The old woman had said it was an ancient saying and a wise one. Annabel agreed.

Quickly, she straightened and slid her arms underneath the man's shoulders to lift him.

"You'll never manage that, lady," one of the guards said gruffly. He hesitated an instant before stepping forward to help her. Not willing to appear less than he, another did the same, and another. Within moments, the old man was carried from the tavern and laid carefully in the back of the wagon. Annabel swung up quickly behind the horses. She was anxious to get back to Montfort. Dark was coming and the old man needed care. They started back down the road and had gotten halfway from the village when there was a sudden flurry of movement off to the right.

From the concealment of the trees, a band of horsemen emerged. They were riding fast and brandishing weapons. A musket's flare cut through the gloom. An instant later, one of the guards toppled to the ground.

Annabel screamed. She slapped the reins, trying to force

her horses into a gallop, but they were panic-stricken and refused to obey. The bandits swarmed over them. The two remaining guards fought bravely but the odds were overwhelmingly against them.

A dark, leering face loomed over Annabel. The stench of unwashed clothing, garlic, and sweat engulfed her. Hands grabbed for her. She fought back and managed to break free but the effort knocked her from the wagon. She landed hard, the breath knocked from her. Sharp, gleaming hooves slashed the air inches from her face. She closed her eyes against an overwhelming sense of terrible loss. Uppermost in her mind was longing for David and their son. If only she could see them one more time . . .

A blood-chilling cry reverberated through the darkening wood. Hard on it came the sound of pounding hoofs. The bandit who had been about to bring his sword down on Annabel froze. His face filled with terror.

Out of the long shadows galloped a single horseman. He was dressed all in black. His right hand held a sword, not the narrow rapier favored by duelers but a much thicker and far more serious battle sword. It was etched along its length with ancient symbols, as was the solid gold hilt he grasped. The weapon had served his ancestors well down through the long, violent centuries. Now it would serve him.

Annabel stared at her husband in disbelief. Only once before had she seen him as he was now—with the British officer—and even that had been only a pale reflection. His hard, burnished features were set with deadly rage. His golden hair, come loose from the black ribbon that usually held it, fell to his massive shoulders. He looked like a warrior from another time, shorn of the trappings of civilization and intent only on death.

Emboldened by their master's appearance, the outnumbered guards surged to the offensive. They cut and slashed their way against the bandits, but it was David who overwhelmed them. He seemed to be everywhere at once, fighting now against two, now three. Men panicked and fell before his merciless assault. Only those with the greatest presence of mind thought to escape. They dug their heels into their horses' sides and took off down the road as though fleeing all the demons of hell.

Within minutes it was over. Annabel got slowly to her feet. She stood dazed and uncertain as David dismounted. His eyes never left her as he crossed the space between them.

"You are unharmed?" he asked. His voice was deep and husky. It moved through her like the most intimate caress.

Mutely, she nodded. His shirt and breeches were stained with blood. His blue eyes were hooded, his expression implacable. For a horrible moment, he looked like a stranger.

A wave of dizziness washed over Annabel. She swayed slightly. Instantly, David reached out to her. Mindful of his state, he held her a little distance from him. His arm was an iron bar across the small of her back. Thickly, he said, "My love, if you had been hurt . . ." The thought was too agonizing to complete.

Annabel's vision cleared. She gazed up at the man who, stranger no longer, looked at her with love and concern. Slowly, a smile of infinite gentleness touched her mouth.

"My love," she said. How sweet the sound. How true the words.

They gazed at each other a long moment before they remembered their surroundings. Softly, David said, "We must see to the others."

Annabel nodded. Later there would be time for them. He was here, he was safe, all things were possible.

Miraculously, the man in the wagon had not been injured during the assault. Annabel checked him quickly, seeing that he had slipped from unconsciousness into a more natural sleep. Reassured that he did not need her immediate attention, she turned to the wounded guard. He had taken a deep gash across the chest but the bleeding was slow and he did not appear to be in grave danger.

For the bandits, nothing could be done. Except for the two who had escaped, they were all dead. David gave quiet instructions to one of the guards who set off at once for Montfort. Annabel gathered from what she overheard that a large troop would be sent out immediately in pursuit. The odds were strong that the bandits would not live to see morning.

By the time they reached the great house, the gates had been thrown open and torches lit in the courtyard. The entire population of Montfort seemed to have turned out to greet them, alerted by the guard.

Patrice and Claire reached Annabel first. They flung their arms around her, sobbing.

"Thank the Lord you're all right, my lady."

"If anything had happened to you . . ."

She soothed them both, then quickly gave directions for the men in the wagon to be taken upstairs. Embarrassed now by their own fears about the old man, the two girls went along to help care for him.

Annabel could not go so easily. It seemed as though everyone needed to see their lord and lady. They received a rousing round of cheers which David brushed off with a smile.

"Good people," he said, his strong, assured voice carrying to the farthest reaches of the yard, "thank you for your concern, but it is very late and we are all tired. Let's to bed."

Even then they weren't anxious to let them go but finally a path was cleared. When they were at last alone in the great hall, Annabel turned to face her husband.

He did look weary but the light in his eyes made it clear he had no thought of sleep. As he took a step toward her, she said softly, "You've been missed, my lord."

He smiled in the darkness. "And you. Paris was . . . very cold."

A faint flutter of hope stirred within her. "How could it be? Spring has come."

"And the world is reborn, but some things have not changed." He was silent for a moment, reliving fragments of the last few weeks. Quietly, he said, "Napoleon is the same. When he finally agreed to see me, he made it clear that none of his intentions had changed. I tried to discourage him from leaving Elba, that is why I was in Paris during the winter. But once he made up his mind to go, I thought he might—just might—have decided to put his own lust for power aside and devote himself to helping France."

"But he has not?" Annabel asked.

David shook his head. Sadly, he said, "I think he is incapable of it. He has set himself on a course that will lead to his own doom. The only question is how many more will have to die before he is finally finished."

Please God, her husband would not be one of them. Softly, Annabel went to him. Heedless of the evidence of battle still clinging to him, she took him into her arms. For a moment, he was stiff with pride and anguish. Abruptly, he sighed and let his golden head drop to her shoulder.

"I made a mistake," he said against the silken smoothness of her hair. "Long ago I decided that order and stability were worth any price. They are not; freedom is far more important, especially the freedom to live in peace."

He raised his head and looked at her. "Napoleon will perish, I am certain of that. Louis will be back on the throne before the summer is out. I will have to make my peace with him."

Annabel smiled. She thought of the portly, sensible man she had talked with. He had feared that her husband might still support Napoleon but he had still troubled to send a message to him, hoping to avoid a split between them. Louis was far too intelligent and reasonable a man to seek conflict where none was needed. Especially not with one of the wealthiest and most powerful men in his kingdom.

"I believe," she said, "that you will find him agreeable."

David nodded slowly. He was coming to trust his wife's judgments about people. She had a gift for it that he did not. But then, she had many other gifts as well. Wisdom, courage, beauty of the spirit as well as the body. He was a fortunate man.

"Can you be happy here, Annabel?" he asked.

She looked at him, startled. "Why would I not be?"

"I snatched you from the world you had chosen, tricked you into marrying me—"

"Tricked? But it was my choice."

"Not really, when the alternative was to be parted from your child. It was true that I wanted Louis here where he belongs, but I wanted you as well. That's why I sent Nicole to play on your mother's love, telling you Louis would never be fully accepted and so on.''

Annabel's eyes widened. ''You sent her?''

''I'm afraid so.'' He had the grace to look regretful, if only a little. The effect was somewhat spoiled when he added, ''It worked quite well.''

''Aye, it did that. It put me in the palm of your hand, you great, arrogant man.'' She pushed away and glared at him. ''I should have known you'd do anything to get your own way. Well, let me tell you, things are going to be different around here from now on. I'm not some little twit to go falling into your arms whenever you like.''

''Of course not,'' he said solemnly. His eyes danced. ''However, feel free to fall into them whenever *you* like.''

''Oh, you . . .'' Annabel stopped. She stared at the tall, powerful man before her. A man who had conquered his own fears and his own mistakes to emerge stronger and nobler than ever before. Her husband.

''Tis funny,'' she murmured, ''but I can almost feel myself fallin' now.''

He laughed and caught her easily. Together, they climbed the steps to the vast, quiet room above. Beyond the high stone windows, beneath the spring moon, Montfort stood— proud, strong, eternal.

on a watchful gleam. "Have you eaten?"